HEXED

HEXED

THE SISTERS OF WITCHDOWN

MICHAEL ALAN NELSON

an imprint of Prometheus Books
Amherst, NY

Cover illustration by Larry Rostant © Boom Entertainment, Inc.
Cover design by Jacqueline Nasso Cooke

Inquiries should be addressed to
Pyr
59 John Glenn Drive
Amherst, New York 14228
VOICE: 716–691–0133 • FAX: 716–691–0137
WWW.PYRSF.COM

19 18 17 16 15   5 4 3 2 1

Library of Congress Cataloging-in-Publication Data

Nelson, Michael Alan.
  Hexed : the sisters of Witchdown / by Michael Alan Nelson.
    pages cm
  ISBN 978-1-63388-056-6 (paperback) — ISBN 978-1-63388-057-3 (e-book)
  I. Title.

PZ7.1.N45Hex 2015
[Fic]—dc23

2014049178

Printed in the United States of America

PROLOGUE

Gina jumped when the phone rang. The cordless receiver was on her vanity, almost lost among the dozens of lotions and makeup cases scattered across its surface. She wanted to get up off the floor and answer, but she couldn't make herself move. She just pulled her knees tight to her chest and watched the phone's orange light blink with every ring.

It was David. It had to be. He would have found out by now and would be trying to call her. She wanted to talk to him more than anything, but there was no way she was going to pick up the phone. It was sitting right beneath the large mirror, and there was nothing in the world that could make Gina stand in front of a mirror.

Not after tonight.

The ringing suddenly stopped. Everything dissolved into a muffled silence, as if someone had put a pillow over the world. She couldn't even hear the soft rustle of her bedroom curtains swaying in the autumn breeze. The only thing she could hear was the sound of her own heart pounding inside her chest.

She jumped again when she felt the sudden jolt of her cell phone vibrating in her jeans pocket. She pulled it out and nearly dropped it in her hurry to answer.

"H-h-hello?"

"Gina? Gina, what the hell is going on? Olivia called and said you freaked!"

"David . . . I'm so scared." Gina's voice started to crack. She had been able to keep herself from crying ever since she left the old Worcester House, but once she heard David's voice, her resolve vanished.

"Okay, calm down, sweetie, and just tell me what happened."

Gina wiped her eyes with the back of her hand. "It's real, David. All of it. I thought it would be fun, you know, just scaring each other, but . . ."

David was quiet for a moment before he spoke. "But . . . what?"

"I saw her. It was my turn alone in the room and . . ."

"Gina, you're imagining things. Or one of the girls was playing a trick on you."

"It wasn't a trick!" She didn't like yelling at David. His ex-girl-friend had always yelled at him, and she didn't want to be anything like her. So Gina took a deep breath and calmly said, "All the other girls were in the study with the book. I was the only one in the bedroom. She was there. I saw her. And when I saw her, I ran."

"It could have been your own reflection."

"No, David, I—"

"Gina, listen to me." His voice changed. He spoke more slowly, his tone deeper and more like an adult's. He talked like this whenever he wanted to take charge of a conversation. Even his teachers would sit quietly and listen when David used "the Voice." It was one of the things that Gina most admired about him. But she didn't admire it so much now that he was using it on her.

"There are no such things as ghosts. Or witches, or ghouls, or things that go bump in the night. They don't exist. Whatever you saw wasn't real. Either you imagined it or your brain misinterpreted something completely rational. Your mind will definitely play tricks on you if you're scared. And the Worcester House is a scary place at night. Okay?"

Everything he said made perfect sense. The sensible part of Gina's mind understood that. But Gina knew that it wasn't her imagination getting the better of her. She didn't just see the woman in the mirror. The woman in the mirror saw *her*.

"Where are you now?"

"Home. I ran straight here."

David gave a soft chuckle before he said, "Do you want me to sneak over?"

"Yes, but you can't. It's too late and my dad will be home any—"

As if on cue, Gina heard the front door open. "Gina? Are you here, kiddo?" her dad called from downstairs.

"David, I have to go. Dad's home."

"All right, babe. But listen, there's no need to be scared. I would never let anything hurt my girl. Promise."

Gina couldn't help but smile.

"I'll see you at school," David said. "Love you."

"I love you, too." Gina put her phone back in her pocket and forced herself to stand.

The door to her bedroom opened, and her father stepped in. He was an impressively large man. He had to duck his head to get under the door frame, and his massive arms were about to split the sleeves of his police uniform. When he saw Gina, he asked, "Gina? You've got every light on in the house. And aren't you supposed to be staying at Carly's tonight?"

Gina desperately tried to think of something to say but couldn't. Instead, she ran forward and threw her arms around him.

"Hey, hey . . . what's going on?" He looked down at her and lifted her chin. "You've been crying. Did something happen?"

If she told him that she and her friends had sneaked into the abandoned Worcester House, she'd be grounded for life. But Gina knew he wouldn't stop hounding her until he knew what was bothering her so badly. The cop in him could never let anything go unsolved.

"We . . . we were watching horror movies, and I . . . I got scared and came home." She wasn't lying about being scared, only the reason for it. But her dad could always tell when she was lying just by looking into her eyes, so she buried her face in his chest and squeezed harder.

Her dad patted her back. "Aren't you a little old to be getting that scared from movies?"

"I just wanted to come home where it's safe." Her dad may have been a cop and bigger than anyone she knew, but she felt safer around David. David had a way of making Gina feel safe without making her feel like a scared kid. But right now, she was happy to just have someone home.

"Gina . . ."

Gina looked up, expecting to see her dad smiling down at her. Instead, he was looking off in the corner. His brows were furrowed, and his mouth pinched to one side of his face. "Is there someone else in the room with you?"

Gina went cold. Her dad gently moved her behind him with one hand while putting his other hand on his gun. "Gina, if you have a boy in here, you best tell me now."

"N-n-no . . . there's no one. Why, what did you see? Dad, what did you see?"

Her dad moved across the room toward her closet in the corner. "I thought I saw . . . something. Just stay there." He opened the closet door with a sudden pull that made Gina take a step back. But there were only clothes inside.

"Hmmm . . . I could have sworn I saw something."

Gina could feel the cold grip of fear squeezing her again. But her dad was here. And he was a cop. A large one, at that. So she was safe. But if she truly believed that, why was she still so scared?

Movement caught the corner of her eye. She turned involuntarily and found herself staring straight at her vanity mirror. She could see her own reflection, the tangle of her frazzled hair, the tear-smeared eyeliner down her cheeks. For a moment, Gina was appalled at her appearance. But her disgust turned to horror when she saw the other figure reflected in the mirror.

It was the woman.

Gina wanted to scream, to run, but she couldn't move. The woman in the mirror held her gaze with wild, unblinking eyes.

Through her terror, Gina tried to make sense of what was happening. From the reflection, the woman should have been standing right in front of her, but there was no one there. The woman existed only in the mirror.

She was impossibly thin and so pale that Gina could see tiny black veins spidering underneath her skin. The woman's hair was gray and gnarled like a dirty mop left to dry in the sun, and her tattered dress looked even more ancient than she did. But the most unsettling thing of all was her smile. She had a mouth filled with bone-white needles.

Gina could see her dad still nosing around her closet out of the corner of her eye. She tried calling out to him but could only manage a tiny squeak. The woman grew larger in the reflection, as if she were stepping closer to the mirror.

". . . Dad?"

"Sorry, kiddo," he said from the closet. "I guess I forget to leave my police instincts back at the office. I didn't mean to scare you."

Her dad popped his head out of the closet. "It's okay, you can relax. There's no one here." He took a step toward her but stopped. From where he was standing, he couldn't see into the mirror, but the look on her face must have frozen him in his tracks. "Gina, honey, what's wrong?" Just at the edge of her vision, she could see her dad moving toward her. But even though he was only a few feet away, somehow she knew he wouldn't make it in time.

Gina tried to look away from the woman, but she still couldn't pull her gaze from her terrible eyes. Something deep inside her warned her to run, to get away as fast as she could. If she didn't get away right now, she knew that she never would.

Gina gritted her teeth. Then, with everything she had, she pivoted on the balls of her feet and dove straight toward her dad.

That's when the woman reached out of the mirror and grabbed her.

CHAPTER 1

Lucifer knew she was being followed. She started to walk across the street then stopped halfway and pretended to tie her shoe. A green minivan came to a screeching halt just in front of her, sending plumes of gray smoke rolling past. Lucifer crinkled her nose at the smell of burning rubber and stood up. She gave the woman driving the minivan an apologetic smile before crossing to the sidewalk.

Everyone on the sidewalk was watching her now. And that was the point. If someone was following her, they wouldn't want to risk being discovered by making eye contact with her. So Lucifer was looking for the person who *wasn't* watching her. But of all the faces staring at her, only two weren't paying her any attention: a cop writing a parking ticket down the street and a window washer cleaning the seventh floor of an office building half a block away.

She moved off the street, and everyone went back about their own business. If someone was following her, there was nothing she could do about it now. Besides, she had more important matters to deal with.

Lucifer opened a heavy metal door at the front of a bland brick building and stepped through. Inside, the walls of the small waiting room were a drab shade of blue. A few plastic chairs sat in front of a faded coffee table littered with old magazines. A man with a patchy beard who sat on one of the chairs pulled his nose out from a tattered copy of *National Geographic* to look at her. The way his eyes scanned her from head to toe annoyed her, but Lucifer ignored him and stepped up to the counter on the far side of the room.

The young woman behind the counter was giving Lucifer a curious stare. Her face was round, and she had a small dot on the side of her nose where, Lucifer suspected, a nose ring would be if she were allowed to wear one here. The woman brushed a lock of purple hair from her eyes and said, "Can I help you?"

"Yeah, I have a question."

The woman frowned. "Unless you have a referral, the doctor can't see you. And if you're not eighteen, you have to be accompanied by a parent or guardian." She leaned over the counter and arched an eyebrow. "Do you have ID?"

Lucifer shook her head. "No, I don't."

"Then I can't help you, sorry."

"Can't or won't? I just want to ask a question."

The woman with the purple hair gave a heavy sigh and crossed her arms. "What's your question?"

"Can you remove tattoos?"

The woman stood back and tilted her head. "Oh. You have a tattoo? Well, that's something we can do, but like I said, you need a referral and a parent or guardian."

"Are you sure? I need it removed *now*. I can pay. Cash. I just need to get rid of it." Lucifer realized she was gripping the edge of the counter and let go. "Please, isn't there some way?"

The woman's expression softened. "I'm really sorry. But we could get in a lot of trouble. Even places like this have to follow some rules. And if you're under eighteen, this is one of those rules. I'm really sorry."

"Can you do it?" Lucifer asked.

The woman shook her head. "I'm not a doctor. I'm only eighteen. This is my dad's clinic, so I help him out when I can. I've just started studying to be an emergency medical technician. So, I can help you with a sprained ankle, but no can do on the tattoo." The woman gave Lucifer a genuine frown of sympathy. "What kind of ink do you have?"

Lucifer gave the man in the plastic chair a quick glance. The woman looked at him then turned toward Lucifer. "Why don't you come in the back. We've got a private booth we can use."

Lucifer nodded and followed the woman toward the back. She was happy to have a little privacy, though it wasn't out of modesty. The fewer people that knew about her mark, the safer she would be.

The woman ushered her inside a small, well-lit room about the size of a walk-in closet. She closed the door and motioned toward a red leather table pressed against the wall. "Have a seat. What's your name?"

"Lucifer."

The woman sat down on a rolling stool and folded her arms. "That's an . . . interesting name."

"That's what everyone tells me."

"Did your parents not like you or something?"

I never knew my parents. "Luci Jenifer Inacio Das Neves. Lucifer for short."

The woman extended her hand and said, "I'm Trish. Nice to meet you." Lucifer took her hand and gave it a quick shake. "So," Trish said. "You want to show me this tattoo?"

Lucifer unzipped her black hoodie and tossed it on the table next to her. She grabbed the strap of her light tank top and pulled it down to reveal her right shoulder blade. Lucifer couldn't see the mark, but she didn't have to. She knew exactly what it looked like. The mark was a solid black symbol, roughly seven inches tall. It was shaped like a Gothic lowercase letter "h" that covered most of her shoulder blade. The sensation of its presence was subtle, barely perceptible, but Lucifer could always feel it. It felt like some stunted, malformed wing that withered and died before it was fully grown.

Trish traced the mark with her finger. "You're not eighteen, are you? Because whoever did this could lose their license for giving a minor a tattoo."

"Can you get rid of it?"

"Like I said, without a parent we can't . . ." Trish stopped talking. After a few seconds, she said, "Seriously, Lucifer. Who gave this to you? I've never seen ink like this before." Lucifer could feel Trish's breath on her skin as she leaned in for a closer inspection. "If I didn't know any better, I'd say this was a birthmark."

It wasn't the first time she had heard that. She had gone to a tattoo parlor earlier that week hoping they might be able to remove it. The artist she showed it to had the same reaction as Trish. He had even tried to stop her from leaving unless she told him who gave it to her. Of course, that's when Lucifer taught him that a guy with that much metal dangling from his face should think twice before bullying someone.

"Most people go with Eastern symbols of some kind. Why'd you choose an 'h'?"

Lucifer remained silent. *I didn't choose it. It was a gift, but not a gift for me.*

"I'll be honest, I don't know if we *can* remove that. That's like no tattoo I've ever seen before. If you wanted to get rid of it, you'd need a skin graft."

Lucifer pulled her shoulder strap back up and slipped her hoodie back on. "So, then you can't get rid of it. Well, I thought I should at least ask. Sorry to waste your time."

"I can recommend a hospital that might be able to help. A second opinion never hurt."

Lucifer knew that if she went to a hospital, being under eighteen with no guardian would be the least of her problems. There would be too many questions she'd have to answer. "Thanks, but that's okay. I guess I'll just have to get used to it."

"Hey, we've all been there. I got a tattoo on my eighteenth birthday and ended up covering it up three months later. I tell you what . . ." Trish reached into the back pocket of her black jeans and pulled out a business card. "When you do turn eighteen, let me know and I can take you to my tattoo guy. He's really good, and I can convince him to give you a discount. He can cover it with something you like."

Lucifer took the card. It was a sweet gesture, but just covering the mark wouldn't change anything. She'd still be hexed. The only way she'd ever truly be free would be to have it completely removed. Sadly, there didn't appear to be any way to remove it unless she flayed the skin from her shoulder. But Lucifer knew deep down even that wouldn't work. There was only one person in the world who could take it away, and she never would. It was *her* gift, after all.

Lucifer stepped out of the small room then turned back to Trish. "Do you have a back door?"

Trish frowned and gave her a questioning scowl. "Yeah . . . Lucifer, are you in trouble? Should I call the police?"

Lucifer stared at the heavy front door for a moment. Even though she wasn't able to see him, she knew someone was out there, waiting for her. "No. I'm fine. It's just . . . an ex-boyfriend. He can't seem to let go, you know?"

Trish gave her a knowing smile. "Oh, I know. C'mon. Follow me."

It was a lie. The idea of having a boyfriend was as foreign to Lucifer as having a horn sprouting from her forehead. But even though she knew Trish was just trying to help, Lucifer knew that "help" meant calling the cops. And the last thing Lucifer needed was a chat with the police.

Trish led her through the back of the parlor and past a small break room to another heavy door. She twisted the dead bolt and opened it. "Here you go. Take care."

"Thanks." Lucifer gave her a small smile, pulled her hood over her head, and disappeared into the alley.

CHAPTER 2

The sun was starting to set by the time Lucifer reached her apartment complex. It wasn't in the best neighborhood, but she didn't want to take any chances with a nosy landlord. And this was the only place a teenager could live on her own without arousing suspicion. As long as she paid her rent every month, no one ever asked any questions.

She took the stairs to the second floor, listening to the familiar creak of the steps beneath her feet. She moved past three older men having an argument about some sports game they had watched the night before. They were waving their hands about as they talked, not even giving Lucifer so much as a second glance.

As she was pulling her keys out of her pocket, she heard a CLACK! CLACK! CLACK! followed by giggling. Lucifer turned to see the Reneau twins playing at the far end of the hall. They were wearing brown paper shopping bags with holes cut in the sides for their arms and using wooden spoons as swords. Their mother, dressed in a tattered bathrobe and oversized slippers, came out of a nearby apartment. She saw Lucifer, gave her an apologetic smile then ushered the kids back into their apartment.

Lucifer opened her own door and walked inside. Her apartment was small. The only pieces of furniture she had in the main room were a leaking beanbag chair and a small desk lamp on a milk crate. The rest of the room was littered with stuffed toys, trinkets, and piles of books, several of them hundreds of years old.

Even though the place was cramped, Lucifer didn't mind. It was infinitely better than living on the streets in the Brazilian favela where she spent her childhood. Here she had electricity, hot running water, and shelter from the rain. But most importantly, there weren't any death squads hunting her. Or worse.

Though she could easily afford a better place, she knew a girl her age living that well would attract someone's attention. Money always attracted attention, and the last thing Lucifer ever wanted was people noticing her.

She walked over to her little kitchenette and pulled an apple out of the small refrigerator sitting in the corner. It had been hours since she had eaten anything, and she could hear her stomach growling over the muffled voices of the men arguing in the hallway. Lucifer made her way to the beanbag and plopped down to finish her apple. She leaned her head back and stared into her small bedroom a few feet away. On the far side of the room, a tall, thin object stood draped beneath a faded blue bedsheet, the tattered edges of the sheet lightly flowing in the soft breeze coming from the tiny square-shaped hole in the wall masquerading as a window. If it wasn't for the horrific thing hidden under the sheet, it would almost look pretty.

She turned her head away from the object under the sheet and took another bite from the apple. The day was too much of a disappointment, and she didn't want to dwell on it anymore. No one knew how to remove her tattoo. But part of Lucifer had already known that, though it didn't make it any less unbearable. For now, Lucifer was content to just listen to the world around her and forget the day's failures.

As she wiped a drop of sticky juice from her chin, the men arguing in the hallway suddenly went quiet. All Lucifer could hear were the groaning creaks of someone walking up the stairs. But the creaking sounds were louder, more strained. Someone heavy was coming up the stairs. Someone so imposing the arguing men decided it best to finish their argument another time.

Lucifer put her ear to her door and listened. Whoever was coming up the stairs was moving at a quick, steady pace. Which meant they weren't heavy from fat, but from muscle. The creaking stopped as the person reached the top of the stairs. When Lucifer heard the heavy footsteps start down the hall toward her apartment, she stepped back from the door and turned off the light. She thought she had lost whoever was following her at the clinic, but they must have been expecting her to duck out the back and followed her home.

For a moment, she thought she was overreacting until the footsteps came to a stop in front of her door.

KNOCK! KNOCK! KNOCK!

"Police. Open up," said a man with a deep, angry voice.

Lucifer looked back at the open window. It was more than big enough for her to slip through, and it wouldn't be too hard for her to scale the side of the building. But if she ran, she'd have to leave everything behind. And if this really was a cop, chances were good that all of her belongings would be confiscated. That could be a serious problem.

KNOCK! KNOCK! KNOCK!

"C'mon, I know you're in there. Open the door."

Lucifer stood stone-still. After a few moments, she saw the door handle start to move and jiggle as the person on the outside started to pick the lock. She could do it in a matter of seconds, so she knew it wouldn't take him very long to get the door open.

She had played with the idea of developing her own security system to keep local burglars and curious neighbors away. But anything above a dead bolt would tell them there was something in here worth protecting. The best deterrent she had was that, to average eyes, she had nothing of value. Yet, to those who walked in the same circles as Lucifer, she was sitting on a gold mine.

Lucifer ducked behind the front door, squeezing her wiry shoulders into the corner and hiding in the shadows. The doorknob continued to wiggle and click as the man struggled to unlock the door. It was painful to watch. Whoever it was obviously didn't have a lot of experience breaking into places. It was taking so long that Lucifer was almost tempted to reach over and unlock the door for him, but if he couldn't get it open, maybe he would just give up and go away.

MICHAEL ALAN NELSON   19

The handle clicked, and a thin line of light sliced across the room as the door opened. Lucifer pulled herself into the corner as tightly as she could. The man stood in the open doorway, his massive shadow stretching across the floor. He stepped into the apartment and slowly closed the door behind him. Even in the darkness, Lucifer could tell that he was one of the largest men she had ever seen. He was close to seven feet tall, and his muscles were almost comically huge. And he was most definitely a cop. The thick navy fabric of his South Haven police uniform stretched to near bursting across the bulk of his chest. His hand rested on the handle of the pistol holstered at his side, and his baton looked like a toy pencil as it clacked against the back of his heavy thigh when he moved.

Lucifer ran through the mental list of reasons the police might be after her. By the time she got to reason number 15, she decided it didn't matter. She had to get out of there, even if that meant leaving everything behind. She'd stolen it all once before; she could steal it all again.

"Lucifer, I know you're here. I'm not here to hurt you. I just want to talk."

She wanted to laugh. Lucifer knew that "I just want to talk" was code for "Stand still so I can kill you without having to work up a sweat." It was such a dead giveaway that Lucifer wondered why anyone would ever bother saying it. *Abestado.*

Fortunately, she knew how to take care of herself, even against bigger guys like him (though she had to admit she'd never seen anyone *that* big before). Most thugs would use their size to intimidate people, so they never really had to learn how to do anything other than growl and sneer. The threat of violence was enough. But this guy was a cop. Which meant that not only was he gargantuan, he was trained in hand-to-hand combat. That made Lucifer nervous.

Surprise was her only advantage. As quickly as she could, she shot forward and kicked him in the back of the knee, putting all of her weight into it. His knee buckled and he toppled backward, turning as he fell. Lucifer then made for the door but felt a hand as large as a dinner plate wrap around her arm. On instinct, she brought her free fist up under the arm that was holding her and hit the man in the armpit. Normally, his grip should have slackened, but he had so much muscle that her punch was ineffective. Without missing a beat, she took another swing at his head then buried her heel in his solar plexus. He let out a sudden, deep gasp that sent spittle flying in her face. But still he held on.

"Will . . . you . . . stop!" the cop wheezed. He twisted her arm, trying to force her to the ground, but Lucifer used the momentum to swing her body behind him and pull his own arm across his throat. She wrapped her legs around his massive torso and locked her arms under his elbow, pressing his forearm into his windpipe. He gasped, trying to say something but couldn't get enough air.

Lucifer knew that she couldn't hold on to him for much longer. He was too strong. Even with the right leverage, a girl as small as she was could only do so much to a guy as big as him. The cop suddenly jumped to his feet and grabbed Lucifer's wrist with his free hand and used her own arm as a fulcrum to pull her grip free. He turned faster than a man his size should have been able to and shoved her back, sending Lucifer tumbling across the floor. She came to a stop in a crouch. The cop was blocking her way to the door, but she could easily make the window before he could get to her. And he was too big to follow her.

"Would you calm down! I'm not going to hurt you."

"Oh, you've got that right."

Lucifer pretended to make for the door, forcing the cop to move to block her. He was quick, but with all his weight it would take him longer to change his direction. She pushed off the ball of her foot, ricocheting back toward the window. The cop almost lost his balance trying to follow her movement.

"No! Wait, please!"

The curtain slapped her in the face when she dove through the open window, stinging her cheeks. Lucifer grabbed the edge of the windowsill to keep herself from falling to the alley below. She was about to climb down when she heard the cop say, "Lucifer, I need your help!"

She hung for a moment, motionless. She watched a balding cat jump out a nearby Dumpster with some sort of prize hanging from its mouth and wondered if it was an omen. If it was, did it mean that she was the cat or the dead thing hanging from its mouth?

Lucifer put that thought from her mind and looked down to the concrete below. All she had to do was climb down and she'd be gone. Disappeared. So then why wasn't she moving? There had been something in the cop's voice that she recognized: desperation. Unfortunately, it was a tone that she was all too familiar with. So she took a deep breath, gave the alley cat a withering scowl, then pulled herself up to peek through the window.

The cop was sitting on the floor with his legs splayed to his sides. He was hunched forward with his head in his hands, his police cap on the floor next to him. He was so lost in his despair that he didn't notice Lucifer staring at him. He looked completely and utterly defeated.

Lucifer had a horrible feeling that she was going to regret what she was about to do. It was a feeling she'd had numerous times in the past, and every single time she *had* regretted it. Yet, for some reason, she always ignored the feeling, regardless of how much trouble she knew she was going to get into. Why should this time be any different?

She rested her chin on the edge of the windowsill and watched him for a moment. *Last chance. All you have to do is drop down and run.* But then she chided herself for even thinking it.

"What kind of help do you need?"

CHAPTER 3

The cop's name was Buck Pierce. He sat on Lucifer's beanbag as if he had just laid a sad, deflated egg. He held his police hat in his hands, fiddling the brim with a thumb nearly as thick as Lucifer's wrist. He opened his mouth to speak but then stopped as if he was unsure of what he wanted to say.

Lucifer sat on the floor across from him, waiting. She watched him glance around at the various trinkets and books littering her tiny apartment, his thick brows scrunched in thought. "Where are your parents?" he asked.

"Mom's in Heaven, dad's in Hell. I'm assuming, anyway."

He brought his gaze back to her. "I'm sorry to hear that. So, you live here alone?" he asked, giving her an accusatory look.

Lucifer leaned back and folded her arms. "I do."

"You know you have to live with a legal guardian until you're eighteen. What about grandparents? Older brother or sister?"

"Look, Buck—"

"Officer Pierce."

Lucifer curled the corner of her mouth in a twisted smile. "I have a rule. If I can put you in a headlock, I get to call you by your first name." She paused to let the concept sink in, then said, "I've been on my own since I was little girl. I don't have any family or friends. All I have is . . ." *Her*, she almost said. Lucifer unconsciously looked to the object under the bedsheet then back to Buck. "Me."

Buck pinched the bridge of his nose and gave her a small nod. "I know how tough life can be for a kid on the streets. I see it every day. It's not safe out there for a girl your age. For a girl . . ."

Buck grimaced and turned away. He covered his face with one massive hand and held up the other, silently asking for a moment to compose himself. It was a strange sight, seeing a man cry, though Lucifer knew he wasn't crying for her.

He turned back, snorting like a bull and said, "Sorry, it's just that I have a daughter your age and she's . . ." Buck took a deep breath. "She's missing. And I need your help finding her."

Lucifer sat still for a moment before saying, "Uh, why come to me? Shouldn't you, you know . . ." Lucifer gestured toward his uniform.

"Go to the police? I've been a cop for twenty-five years and I've seen plenty of crazy things, but this . . . I can't. They wouldn't believe me. Not even my partner. That's why I came to you. A friend said you'd be able to help me."

A cold wave passed over Lucifer. She stood slowly and let a hint of anger seep into her voice. "*What* friend?"

"She asked me not to tell you."

"Did she. Let me guess. Eight feet tall, sallow skin, having a bad hair century?"

"What?" Buck scowled in confusion. "No, 5'4", pale Caucasian, white hair cut to her jawline. Who are you talking about?"

Lucifer let out a sigh of relief. "No one." She glanced back at the object beneath the bedsheet. "No one at all." Lucifer was glad it wasn't who she thought it was but uneasy with the idea that someone else was keeping an eye on her. Lucifer did not like being on people's radar. Especially people she didn't know. "So, how does this friend of yours know about me and what exactly did she say?"

"That you were familiar with situations like this. That you were a . . ." He cleared his throat. "That you're a witch."

Lucifer couldn't stop laughing. "A witch? Seriously? Wow, is your friend off the mark. I'm not a witch. Not even close."

"Then what are you?" he asked.

Lucifer gave him a broad smile. "I'm a *thief*."

"A thief."

"Don't worry. I don't rob banks or pick pockets. I specialize in stealing . . . *other* things."

Buck tilted his head like a dog trying to understand its master. "What kind of things?"

Lucifer wasn't sure how much detail she wanted to go into. He was a cop, after all, and stealing was stealing. She was taking a big chance just by talking with him. "Let's just say that there are bad things in the world. And there are bad people who want to use those bad things for bad purposes. So I steal those things before they can."

She could see Buck trying to work it out in his head, but it would be impossible for someone unfamiliar with her world to truly understand. "I don't know how your friend knows about me, but you can tell her that she has no idea what she's taking about. And why would she even think a witch could help you find a runaway—"

"She didn't run away. She was *taken*. Right in front of me." Buck's eyes went out of focus as he spoke, as if he were trying to remember a nightmare against his will. "I just got home from my shift, and Gina was upstairs in her room. She was supposed to be staying with friends, but something scared her and she came home. She said it was a movie, but that was a lie. I knew it when she said it, but she wasn't lying about being scared. I'd never seen her that frightened. At first, I thought she had a boy hiding in her closet. That she was scared I had caught her. But it wasn't."

His eyes came back in focus, and he looked at Lucifer. There was a wildness to his expression, a desperation. His voice fell almost to a whisper. "It happened so fast. Gina was there, standing in front of her mirror, and then . . . then she wasn't. Something reached out from the mirror and snatched her like she was nothing but a rag doll." He shook as his hands clenched into fists. "Lucifer, something took her and I don't know how to get her back."

Lucifer walked over and put her hands around one of his fists. "It's okay, calm down."

"How can I be calm? Do you understand what I'm telling you? Someone or . . . *something* pulled my little girl *into* a mirror! How is something like that even possible?"

He was standing now, hovering over Lucifer with his chest heaving. He was clearly not a man used to being helpless, especially when it came to his daughter. Lucifer walked over to a pile of books and began scanning the titles. "What did the mirror look like?"

"The vanity? You mean the thing that grabbed her?"

"That too, but first things first. The vanity."

Buck held his hands palms up, shrugging his shoulders. "I don't know, it looked like a teenaged girl's vanity. What does that have to do with anything?"

Lucifer found the book she wanted then walked over to the object across the room and yanked the bedsheet away. Underneath was a tall, full-length standing mirror set in a dark mahogany frame. Strange and exotic symbols were carved along its edge, and there were smooth areas of black beneath the dark red stain where countless hands had handled the mirror over the centuries. So many times Lucifer had wanted to throw it away, but for some reason, she could never bring herself to do it.

"Did it have any of these symbols carved into it?"

Buck took a step backward, his eyes wide. "What is that?"

"What's it look like? It's a mirror, now focus. Did Gina's vanity have any of these symbols or not?"

"No."

"Are you sure?"

Buck took a tentative step forward to get a better look at the mirror. "Yeah, I'm sure. No symbols. Just pictures of friends, notes, that sort of thing. Nothing like that."

Buck reached out to touch the glass. Lucifer grabbed him so fast that the slap of her palm on his wrist sounded like a gunshot. "Don't touch." Quickly, she tossed the bedsheet back over the mirror.

"No symbols, that's good. And bad," she said. Lucifer began thumbing through the pages of the book. "If her vanity had any of these symbols, I'd know exactly where your daughter is. But since it doesn't, she's not there. That's a good thing."

"What's the bad?"

"All the other places she could be."

Buck desperately grabbed Lucifer by the shoulders. "What places? Tell me so I can go find her! Where's my daughter?"

Lucifer looked up from the book and very calmly said, "Officer Pierce, don't make me put you in another headlock."

He let go of her shoulders as if he had touched a hot stove. "Oh . . . I apologize. I just . . . I just need to find her."

Lucifer held the open book out for Buck to look at. The pages were brittle and yellowed with age, but the words and illustrations were still plain to see. "The thing that took her. Was this it?"

Buck took the book and squinted. On the page was an old woodcut image of a two-headed creature with tentacles for arms and one very fat, very short leg. "No. It looked like a woman. Very tall. Old with frazzled hair. Brunette, or was when she was younger. Black dress, tattered from age and her smile . . . Good God, her smile . . ."

Under normal circumstances, Lucifer would have been impressed. Most people can only remember a vague detail here and there. But since he was a cop, he was used to committing details to memory. Unfortunately, what he was describing was worse than the creature in the book.

Lucifer walked over to a small shelf on the far wall and grabbed a leather-bound notebook. Behind her, she could hear Buck flipping pages. "Are these things real?" he asked.

"No," she lied. "Here, take a look at this. Did the thing you saw look anything like this?" She pointed to a pencil sketch in the notebook. Though the sketch wouldn't win any art awards, it captured the image well enough.

"Yes! She looked like that! *Just* like that!"

Lucifer's heart sank. Even though she didn't know his daughter, she was suddenly very afraid for her. Lucifer knew that, wherever she was, she was in a great deal of danger.

"What is it?" Buck asked, his voice cracking with stress. Lucifer looked up at him and hoped he couldn't see how suddenly frightened she was.

"*That* is a witch."

CHAPTER 4

L ucifer stood in the shadows and watched the bizarre sight. The bleachers of the Jefferson High School gymnasium were littered with dozens of students, scattered about like flies on a piece of rotten fruit. Among them was a small gaggle of girls dressed in their school colors of blue and orange sitting in a huddle toward the edge of the court. They hovered over loose papers and textbooks, pretending to study as they watched several boys playing basketball.

They were girls her age, talking, laughing, and occasionally scowling toward a fellow student or teacher that crossed their line of sight. From the outside, it was easy for Lucifer to tell which one was the leader, which one wanted to be, and which one was grateful just to be part of the group. Of course, seeing people for who they were had always been easy for her. It was one of the few benefits of always being on the outside looking in.

For just a brief moment, Lucifer wondered what it would be like to be among them. To be smiling and laughing, flirting with boys and worrying about homework instead of thieving her way through a litany of horrors the rest of the world knew nothing about. But she quickly dismissed the thought as she subconsciously scratched at the mark on her shoulder. She couldn't picture herself as an ordinary teenager any more than she could picture herself an astronaut. No matter how much she wanted to.

Lucifer made her way toward the top row where she could get a good view of everything without attracting too much attention to herself. She sat on the cold, polished wood and leaned back. The sounds of bouncing balls, squeaking shoes, and chattering giggles ricocheted around the cavernous gym, turning to soup in her ears. It must have been deafening when filled with people. How discouraging it must be for a visiting team to be bombarded by the cheering, the screaming, the chorus of hundreds all shouting at them, letting them know that they were outsiders, unwanted, villains. She may not have been able to imagine the crushing cacophony of a full gym, but the feeling was something Lucifer could imagine quite easily. For her, every day was an away game.

One of the boys slapped the ball away from another player, sending it skittering across the floor toward the group of girls. Lucifer pulled the hood of her sweatshirt over her head to help funnel their conversation to her ears, but they were too far away for her to hear anything other than a word or two.

She reached into her trick bag and pulled out the yearbook that Buck had given her. He had insisted on coming with her when she talked with Gina's friends, and it had taken considerable effort on Lucifer's part to convince him to let her investigate alone. Lucifer didn't think that a stranger asking questions with a desperate cop the size of a bull huffing and puffing over her shoulder was likely to get many helpful answers. So he gave her the yearbook so she would have an easier time identifying Gina's friends.

She leafed through the pages, scanning the photos Buck had circled in red. Lucifer didn't recognize any of them from the girls in the gym. But as she flipped through the yearbook, Lucifer noticed that Gina was in almost every one of the circled pictures with her friends. She was beautiful despite having been cursed with Buck's broad brow. Or maybe because of it. What was obvious was that Gina had a smile that seemed to infect everyone around her. They all wanted to be near her. It was a concept Lucifer was having difficulty imagining. What would it be like to be surrounded by people who all wanted to be close to you?

Lucifer pushed the question from her mind. It wasn't going to do her any good to start the day being jealous of a girl who was just kidnapped by a witch.

Sadly, none of the people in the photos were at the gym. But just as Lucifer was about to put the yearbook away, she recognized one of the boys playing basketball. Lucifer found one of his circled pictures in the book. It was Gina's boyfriend, David.

David was tall with a swimmer's build and a shock of black hair that sprouted from the top of his head in short, wavy curls. It seemed that every time Lucifer turned a page, there was a photograph of him: giving a speech in front of an assembly, laughing with friends in the hallway, driving the basket in a championship game. *So this is what it looks like to be popular*, she thought.

She looked up from the yearbook and watched him drive the basket for an easy layup. He was in blue shorts and a sweaty gray tank top that clung to his smooth chest. Though he was obviously very photogenic, it was the way he moved that impressed Lucifer. While the other boys muscled their way around each other, David glided across the court with the natural grace of a dancer. It was easy to tell why he would be featured so prominently on the pages of the yearbook.

But something about him was rubbing her the wrong way. It took a moment for her to realize what it was. It was his smile. It beamed. And when one of his friends cracked a joke, David's laughter rang through the gym like a chorus of bells. He seemed happy. And that bothered her. His girlfriend had been ripped into another dimension by a witch and was suffering who-knows-what while he was here playing with his friends as if it were just another typical Saturday morning. But she knew that wasn't fair to him. Buck had told David that Gina was home, sick in bed. He had no idea what had really happened.

Lucifer walked down the bleachers toward the court. As she came closer, the group of girls stopped giggling and turned to watch her. She could feel their stares on her, like mascara-caked heat lamps boring into her skin. But it wasn't the disapproving way they stared at her that made her feel uncomfortable; it was that they were staring at her at all. Lucifer wasn't used to being noticed. She was a thief. And for a thief, being noticed was never a good thing.

She walked onto the court and headed straight for David, completely ignoring their game. "What the hell!" one of the boys said.

Lucifer craned her neck to look up at David and said, "David, can I talk to you for a sec? It's about Gina."

David's face went pale. "Is she okay? Her dad said she had the flu. Is it something else? What is it, what's wrong?"

As far as Lucifer could tell, he seemed genuinely worried. "She's fine. But can we talk over here? Privately."

Before David could say anything, one of the other boys said, "Hey, get off the court!"

"It's all right, Ethan," said David.

"No, it's not all right." Ethan hovered over Lucifer, the basketball tucked high under his arm. He was an inch taller than David with perfect skin and a face that Lucifer expected most people would consider pretty rather than handsome. But those pretty features were twisted as he scowled down at her. "You don't just walk out onto the court in the middle of a game." Then he leaned closer and said, "You could get hurt."

David came forward. "Calm down. I'll only be a minute."

"Don't tell me to calm down. We're in the middle of a game. This bitch can wait until we're done."

David and the other boys blanched. "Damn," one of the boys said. "Someone just grew a pair."

"Hey, easy, Ethan!" David said. "What's gotten into you?"

Lucifer had been called much worse and didn't particularly care, but she was more concerned about why he was so angry with her for interrupting the game. She didn't have much experience dealing with people in social situations, especially people her own age. She must have missed some kind of social cue, but she had no idea what it could have been.

Unfortunately, there were more important things to worry about.

Lucifer wasn't sure what kind of witch had taken Gina, but she knew she had only a tiny window in which to get her back safely. Like everyone else in the world, time wasn't a friend to her.

"Your name's Ethan, right?" Lucifer asked. "I'll tell you what. Since you want to play so badly, how about you play me." Lucifer reached into her trick bag and pulled out a five-dollar bill. "I'll bet you five dollars I can score on you in less than five seconds."

Ethan pulled his head back in disbelief, then he and the others burst out laughing. David stood quietly, his brow tilted in mild confusion over his pale-blue eyes.

Ethan smirked at her. "You're kidding, right?"

"Five seconds." Lucifer took the ball from under his arm and said, "Somebody count it down."

A boy with shoulder-length blond hair said, "I'll do it. Ethan, if you get owned by a girl half your size, I'll tell Coach to move you down to JV."

"Shut up, Greg." Ethan frowned. "You an all-star or something?" he asked Lucifer.

Lucifer shrugged her shoulders. "Never played a day in my life. Now c'mon. Let's see who's the bitch."

Greg laughed and said, "Okay, here we go! Ready? Five—"

As soon as Greg started counting down, Lucifer raised the ball straight over her head. Ethan reached out to snatch the ball from Lucifer's hands, his arms uncoiling as quick as vipers. When he grabbed the ball, Lucifer let go and twisted her hips as hard as she could, bringing her shin up between his legs.

There was the dull, wet sound of bone on flesh. The impact lifted Ethan clear off the ground, and he cried out with a sharp, brittle yelp. He seemed to hang in the air for a moment, confused and disoriented before falling to the ground in a fetal heap. The basketball fell and hit him in the head before rolling off the court, its bouncing pitter-patter the only sound in the suddenly silent gym.

The other boys erupted in laughter. Lucifer grabbed the five-dollar bill and tossed it down at Ethan who lay on the ground clutching his privates and struggling to breathe. "You win." She turned to David and grabbed his arm. "You, over here."

When they were on the far side of the court, David pulled his arm out of Lucifer's grip. "Was that really necessary?" he asked with a small twinge of anger in his voice.

"Necessary? No. Fun? Absolutely. Your friend is a jerk."

"He's actually a pretty sweet guy." David's expression twisted sideways again, his confused frown becoming even more striking than his eyes. "I've never seen him act like that before. I'm not sure what his problem is."

Lucifer looked back over her shoulder to see the other boys helping Ethan slowly back to his feet. "What can I say? I bring out the best in people."

"Yeah, who are you? What's this about Gina?"

"My name's Lucifer and I need to know what you and Gina talked about the night she . . . got sick."

"Your name's Lucifer?"

Every. Single. Time.

"Yes, David. Now focus. What did you talk about?"

David took a step back. "What business is that of yours?"

Lucifer pinched the bridge of her nose. *It's my business because your girlfriend was kidnapped by a witch.* She looked up and gave David an empty smile. "It's not, David. But do you mind telling me anyway?"

"Gina has the flu. What could our phone call have to do with that?"

Buck had told Lucifer that he actually liked David. Well, liked him as much as a father could like a boy who was dating his only daughter, anyway. He liked him because David was not only a star athlete; he was also one of the brightest kids in the school. So Lucifer wanted to see just how bright he really was.

"Did she sound sick the last time you talked to her?" Lucifer asked.

"No, not really."

"Have you talked with her since she got sick?"

"Her dad said she was too sick to talk."

"What about texts? E-mails?"

Lucifer could see David working something out inside his head. "I sent her a few, but she never replied."

"No contact at all since the night you talked."

". . . No."

"Why did you call her that night?"

"Olivia called and told me Gina freaked out, that she was scared and . . . wait. How do you know I called her?"

"I checked the caller ID on the phone in her room. Did she tell you why she was scared?"

A dark shadow fell over David's face. He scowled down at Lucifer and said, "Seriously, who are you? What are you doing looking at her phone?"

"Her dad let me look at it."

That caught him off guard. Lucifer glanced back across the gym to see everyone staring. Even though everyone was too far away to hear them, Lucifer lowered her voice and leaned close. "David, I need to know what scared her that night."

When David spoke, his voice was barely above a whisper. "Why?"

"So I can help her."

David shook his head as if trying to get water out of his ears. "Her dad said she was sick. What does a prank have to do with her having the flu?"

"So there was a prank."

"She and her friends went to the Worcester House that night to scare each other. Olivia called to tell me Gina got scared and that she went home. So I called to make sure she was okay."

"Worcester House. What's that?"

David gestured with a nod of his head. "It's an old abandoned house on the north side of town. It's supposed to be haunted. Kids sneak in there all the time trying to scare each other."

Lucifer smiled. "How do I get there?"

CHAPTER 5

The Worcester House was an ancient, dilapidated two-story house on the far edge of the city. Its walls were made from a cobbled collection of crumbling brick and brittle wood that had faded and cracked from decades of neglect. Its tall, arched windows had been shattered to dust long ago, and jagged boards rose up from the front porch like the rotten teeth of some great beast with a ravenous underbite.

"So. You going in or not?" asked David.

Lucifer stood with her arms folded across her chest, staring at the house. "Not yet."

David chuckled. "I told you it was a scary place."

Lucifer wanted to tell him that, as far as scary places go, the Worcester House was about as terrifying as an ice cream stand. But she had learned to trust her thieving instincts and always wanted to know as much as she could about a building before entering: who's inside, how many exits and entrances, roof access, basement access, etc. But if she tried to explain that to David, he would only ask more questions.

"I appreciate the ride, David. But I can handle it from here."

"If you're here about Gina, I'm staying. I want to know what this has to do with her having the flu."

His tone of voice made it clear that he was asking a question, but Lucifer ignored it. "Aren't your friends angry you bailed on them?" she asked.

David shrugged his shoulders. "They'll get over it. The season doesn't start for a few weeks yet. They can do without me for one Saturday." After a few moments, he said, "Gina isn't sick, is she?"

Lucifer gave him a pained expression. "No," she said. "She's missing."

All the blood drained from David's face, making the blue of his eyes stark and wild against his suddenly pale skin. "What do you mean *missing*?"

"She was taken the night she came here. Just a few minutes after you got off the phone with her."

"I don't understand. Taken? What does that mean?"

"She was kidnapped," Lucifer said.

A shadow fell across David's face. "We have to call the police."

"Her dad's a cop, remember?"

David ran his hands through his hair and started pacing next to his car. "Then we have to tell the school."

"David, calm down—"

"Who took her? Why?" His questions came at her like gunshots.

"That's what I'm trying to find out," she said.

"So you think she's here."

"I think there's a clue here that may tell me who *did* take her."

David brushed past her and walked toward the house, determination in every step. "Then what the hell are we waiting for?"

Instead of following, Lucifer leaned back against the front of his car and continued to scan the house, taking in the details. David stepped onto the porch, marching around the jagged planks and up to the front door. He stopped and looked back. "You coming or not?"

"No."

"Then why are you even here if you're not going to look for her? In fact, why aren't the police here? A cop's daughter was kidnapped, for crying out loud. Why aren't there . . . SWAT teams breaking down doors or something? Why isn't her dad here looking for clues? Why did he lie to me and tell me she was sick? It doesn't make any sense!" David's chest was heaving, his mouth twisted in rage. "*Where's my girlfriend?!*"

Lucifer patted the hood of the car next to her. "Have a seat."

"I don't want—"

"Gina's dad hired me to find her and that's what I'm going to do. Now please . . ." *pat pat pat* ". . . come over here and tell me what you know about this place."

David's breathing had slowed, but she could still tell he was amped up. He navigated his way off of the porch and back to Lucifer. With a frustrated sigh, he sat next to her, the car dipping under his added weight. "Let me get this straight," he said. "Gina gets kidnapped, but instead of calling the police, her dad, who just happens to be a cop . . . a very *big* cop, calls some teenaged girl named Lucifer to find her."

"Well, he didn't call me so much as break into my apartment and try to wrestle me into submission. But yeah, that's about it." David opened his mouth to speak, but she cut him off. "David, whatever it was that scared Gina that night snatched her right out from under her dad's nose. He saw it happen. But he couldn't explain it, couldn't understand it."

"How do you not understand your daughter being kidnapped?" David asked. He shook his head and said, "This is a prank. Gina's playing a joke on her dad for being so uptight. That has to be it."

"If she was pranking her dad, wouldn't she let you know?" Lucifer looked back to the house. "Her dad came to me because Gina was taken by something *supernatural*."

David pushed himself off the car and stared at Lucifer for a moment. Then he started looking around, craning his neck in all directions.

"What are you doing?" she asked.

"I'm looking for the hidden cameras."

"Well, if you find any, let me know." Lucifer continued studying the house. Something about it was nagging at her. She had seen plenty of old houses before, but for some reason, this one just wasn't quite right.

"So you're some kind of paranormal PI then?" he smirked.

Lucifer ignored the disdain in his voice. "A thief, actually. But since I run in these mystical circles, I have a better chance of finding her than the police."

David folded his arms across his chest. "You're serious, aren't you?"

"Yep, I really am a thief."

"I meant about—"

"I know what you meant. You don't have to believe me, and I don't have any particular desire to try and convince you. I'm just trying to find Gina."

"By standing out here and staring off into space," he said. Lucifer could understand the reason behind his terseness, but it still bothered her. She was trying to help, and he seemed to be coming at her as if it were somehow her fault.

"How long has this house been here?" she asked.

"I'm not sure. Since the twenties, I think. It was abandoned back in the seventies after the man who owned it killed himself and his family inside." He gave her a sideways smile. "Supposedly. The city tried tearing it down once, but some historical society was able to save it. Everyone says it's haunted." David looked at her. "You think she was kidnapped by a ghost?"

Lucifer kept her gaze on the house as she said, "No." She looked back to David when he pulled his cell phone from his pocket and started tapping the screen. "What are you doing?"

"I'm calling Gina's dad. If she was really kidnapped, I want to hear it from him. No offense." David held the phone to his ear, waiting for Buck to pick up the other end. After a moment, he said, "Mr. Pierce, this is David. Gina's boyfriend. Would you please call me right away? Thank you." He shoved his phone back in his pocket before leaning back against the car with a heavy sigh. "This is just absurd."

"Well, while you're waiting for him to call back, maybe you could help me. Do you notice anything odd or out of place?"

Exasperated, David looked to the house. "No. It just looks like an old house to me." He paused then said, "Do you?"

Lucifer frowned. "All the windows are broken," she said. "Probably have been for who knows how long." She leaned close to him and pointed toward the second story of the house. "All but that one."

David stared at the unbroken window. "A window is odd to you?"

"How many kids have thrown rocks at this place over the years? Hundreds? If this house was abandoned forty years ago, there shouldn't be a single window intact. Yet, there is."

"I suppose that is a little odd. Could be just a coincidence."

Lucifer arched her eyebrow as she stared at him. She pushed off of the car and bent over to examine the rocks at her feet. Once she found one to her liking, she picked it up and hurled it at the window. The rock whistled through the air until it hit the window with a crash, shattering the glass into a hundred pieces. Sharp, tiny shards rang out like dull chimes as they fell to the ground like deadly rain. Lucifer repositioned her trick bag over her shoulder and started walking toward the house. "Go home, David."

"Not a chance." His voice was lower now, his tone measured but firm. "I'm not going anywhere until I know what's going on with Gina. And I mean *really* going on with her, not this nonsense about some boogeyman. Consider me your shadow."

She looked back at him, wanting to give him a scowl. But when she saw the undercurrent of worry beneath his determined expression, she could only sigh. He cared about Gina. Lucifer wondered what it would be like to have someone worry about her like that. But just as quickly as the thought came to her, she pushed it from her mind. It was foolish to think about such things. People close to her always got hurt. Always. Besides, what in this world or any other would she do with a boyfriend, anyway? The idea was ridiculous.

"All right," she said. "But if I tell you to do something, you have to do it."

"Oh, do I?" He tried to smile at her, but his broad grin lay across his face in a half-hearted tilt.

"Yes, you do," she said with a healthy amount of venom in her voice. David blanched. Even Lucifer was surprised by her own anger, but she wasn't mad at him because he wanted to come along. She was mad at herself because she knew she was going to let him.

The outside of the Worcester House was a model of perfection compared to the mess inside. Trash was everywhere. Bottles, bags, papers, even a couple of shopping carts. The heavy odor of damp mildew and rot hit Lucifer in the face like a punch. The floor was a mish-mash of puke-green and amber tiles that had faded into a cadaverous gray. The original wallpaper hung from the walls like strips of dead skin, the exposed wood and plaster underneath covered with decades of graffiti. What little furniture still remained inside the house had been nailed to the walls and ceiling by some enterprising vandals in an attempt to give the place a surreal atmosphere. Lucifer had to admit to herself that it had the desired effect.

"So," David said as Lucifer inspected one of the walls, "you're named Lucifer. As in the devil."

Lucifer took a deep breath. "No, as in my two grandmothers. My full name is Luci Jenifer Inacio Das Neves. 'Lucifer' for short." She rubbed a bit of the hanging wallpaper between her fingers. "Tell me about this prank you mentioned. The one that scared Gina."

David stepped up next to her, squinting at the wall. "It was some Bloody Mary kind of thing. You know, stand in front of a mirror and say 'Bloody Mary' three times."

"Bloody Mary?" Lucifer gave him an incredulous stare.

"Yeah, only it wasn't that. It was some other name. Gina's friend

Olivia had a book she said was filled with spells or other such nonsense. They got the name out of there."

Lucifer should have figured as much. Mirrors were often used as gateways to other places, but it was very difficult to use them unless you knew what you were doing. And the only way to know what you were doing was to have the right book. Fortunately, those kinds of books were few and far between, but occasionally they fell into the wrong hands.

"Do you know what the name of the book was?"

"No. But Olivia should still have it."

"Good. So where's this mirror then?" she asked.

"Upstairs somewhere."

Lucifer started up the creaky stairs. The wood of the railing was soft and damp against her fingers. It was obvious that the roof did little to keep out the elements.

As David followed her up the stairs, he asked, "Aren't you worried people will think you're evil with a name like that?"

"My grandmothers were wonderful, highly respected women, and I'm proud to be named after them. If anyone has a problem with that, that's their shortcoming. Not mine."

"How about I just call you Luci."

Lucifer stopped at the top of the stairs and turned to face him. "How about I punch you in the neck."

David put his hands on his hips. "You're rather violent, you know that?"

"Yes, because it seems to be the only way I can get people to listen to me."

"Well, I don't see what's wrong with Luci."

She wanted to hit him, but what welled up from inside her wasn't anger. It was sadness. Lucifer was her name, it was who she was, *why* she was, and yet people always wanted her to be something else.

"David," she said, "I was named after my grandmothers because they both died saving my life when I was born. I'm alive because of them. *Both* of them. And I'm not going to disrespect their memory just to make other people more comfortable. My name is Lucifer. Not Luci. Not Jenifer. Lucifer. Accept it or go away."

David must have seen the hurt on her face because his expression softened. "Of course. I'm sorry . . . Lucifer. I didn't know."

She could tell he wanted to ask more questions, but thankfully he stayed silent. "It's all right. C'mon," she said and continued up the stairs.

The top floor of the house was less cluttered with garbage and debris than downstairs. Shafts of sunlight broke through the deteriorating roof in several places, illuminating an open area in the center of a large room where tattered pillows and an assortment of mismatched cushions were arranged in a circle.

"The girls would hang out here while one of them would go in the other room by herself."

"Where the mirror is?"

"Yeah."

Lucifer made her way to the other side of the room toward an open doorway. The door that used to cover the doorway was now resting on a couple of milk crates, serving as a makeshift table. Melted wax from at least a dozen candles caked most of its surface, several cigarette butts sticking up from the mess like insects trapped in amber.

When Lucifer stepped into the room, she felt a noticeable drop in temperature. There wasn't any direct sunlight coming in, so it made sense. Still . . .

The rock that Lucifer had thrown through the window was lying in the center of the room, small bits of glass trailing between it and the window. Other than the rock and the broken glass, this room was completely bare except for an old vanity and mirror in the center of the room. The white paint of the vanity had peeled and cracked to reveal the wood underneath.

Surprisingly, the room itself appeared to have weathered the years far better than the rest of the house.

"So, how long have you been doing this kind of thing?" David asked.

"Longer than I haven't."

"What made you decide to become a thief then?"

Lucifer gave him a sideways glance. "The brochure said I'd get to do a lot of traveling." She stepped over to the vanity. She could see bits of yellow and blue paint underneath the peeling white paint, but she couldn't find any symbols etched or drawn anywhere. "Come here and give me a hand with this."

David walked over and grabbed one end of the vanity while Lucifer held onto the other end. "No, seriously," David said. "Thief is a rather odd occupation."

Lucifer grunted as she slid her side of the vanity away from the wall. "It's more . . . hhnff . . . popular than you think."

"Yeah, but you're a girl."

Lucifer gingerly ran her hand behind the mirror as she examined the back of the vanity. "Your powers of observation are truly a wonder to behold."

"I didn't mean it like that. I just meant that you're a bit young to be a professional thief. How old are you anyway?"

Lucifer stopped to think for moment before she said, "I don't know."

"How can you not know?" David leaned against the vanity and said, "Oh god, are you going to tell me you're a vampire?"

She looked up from her inspection and stared at him. She shook her head and said, "Abestado," before opening the drawers in the vanity to look inside.

"Abestado? What's that?"

"It means 'idiot' in Portuguese." She pulled one of the drawers completely out of the vanity and tipped it over to see the underside. Still no symbols.

"Well, I just thought that if you didn't know your age it might be because you're too old to remember. You know. Like a vampire."

"There are a million ordinary reasons why someone might not know how old they are, but your first instinct is to go with vampire?"

"You were the one that brought up the supernatural." He was smirking, and the corner of his mouth was doing that curling thing again. She thought his mouth would be almost handsome if such stupid things would stop coming out of it. "So how come you don't know how old you are?" he asked.

"I don't remember my birthday."

"Everybody remembers their birthday."

"I'm not everybody." She said it a bit harsher than she meant to. "Pull those drawers out for me, please."

"How come?"

"I want to see if there are any symbols underneath."

He handed one of the drawers to her as he said, "I meant how come you don't remember your birthday?"

"You ask an awful lot of questions, you know that?" He just shrugged his shoulders and smiled. Lucifer sighed and said, "I grew up in Recife, Brazil, in a favela. It's . . . well, I guess it's what you'd call a shantytown. Only poorer than anything you could imagine. My parents died when I was young, and without my grandmothers . . . I had to live on the streets. And street kids don't have much use for birthdays. After a while, I just kind of forgot. But if I had to guess, I'd say sixteen or seventeen."

David watched her, his face expressionless. Lucifer didn't wait for him to respond and examined the last of the drawers. No symbols anywhere. And that was a serious problem. If there were no symbols on the vanity, that meant the gateway was somehow opened from the other side. But exactly who, or what, had the power to do that?

Lucifer couldn't help but feel as if the ground was opening beneath her and trying to swallow her whole.

"So, no symbols? No bubbling cauldrons? No dark, ominous words scrawled on the walls in blood?" David waved his hands about like a Vegas magician.

"No." Lucifer put her hands on her hips as she gazed around the room, hoping some clue would reveal itself. But other than a general feeling of "wrongness" about the room, she couldn't see anything.

David's sarcastic tone disappeared. "You sound disappointed."

Worried, more like. "It's not that. I was just hoping there would be . . . *something.*"

"Not to be rude, but maybe you're not that good of a detective."

"I told you, I'm not a detective. I'm a thief." She took another glance around the room but saw nothing of significance. "All right, where's this Olivia girl? The one with the book. I need to talk with her as soon as possible."

"Home, probably. I can drop you off."

Once Lucifer stepped out of the room, the feeling of unease lifted, as if a cold, wet towel had been lifted from her shoulders. She looked over at David and watched him reach back and squeeze his neck muscles, trying to loosen them. He felt it, too, though he was obviously unaware that it had anything to do with the room. Lucifer thought it best to leave it that way.

Outside, she and David got into his car. David slid behind the wheel but stopped just before turning the key. "Lucifer," he said. "I need you to be honest with me. Is Gina in trouble? I don't mean in trouble with her dad, like she's grounded or anything. I mean . . ."

Lucifer tried her best to smile. "I'm sorry, David. I wish I could say this was all just some hoax. But it's not."

His skin went pale again. "So she's really in danger."

She reached over and patted his arm. Lucifer was surprised at the firmness of his triceps. "Not enough for you to lose any sleep over."

"You promise?" he asked.

Lucifer glanced up at the second floor of the Worcester House to see that the window she shattered with a rock was now back in place and completely unbroken.

"I promise."

CHAPTER 6

It was Olivia's mother who answered the door. Her hair was shaped and curled within an inch of its life, and her bright blue dress was so tight Lucifer could have sworn someone had just stood over her with a bucket of paint and dumped it over her head. But the thing that immediately struck Lucifer was the overwhelming smell of perfume.

"May I help you?" she asked with a smile as fake as the flesh spilling from the top of her dress.

"Hi. I'm here to get a book from Olivia. For school."

"A book. From Olivia." The incredulous look on the woman's face left no doubt in Lucifer's mind that this was probably the first time she had heard the words "Olivia" and "book" in the same sentence for quite some time.

The woman turned and shouted, "Olivia! Olivia!" After getting no response, she turned back to Lucifer, her frown creating deep cracks in the thick makeup she wore around her eyes. "Come on in. She's upstairs in her room. And you tell her I said she has to be home by eleven tonight. I'm serious! When I call, she better be here to answer the phone or she'll be wearing an off-the-rack dress to the Homecoming Dance, I swear! You tell her that!" she said, putting her finger in Lucifer's face.

"Yes, ma'am."

"Good." The woman grabbed her purse off the back of a suede couch, adjusted one of her heels, and then whisked out the door.

Lucifer took a moment to get her bearings. The house looked relatively new and was clearly decorated by someone with more money than taste. She scanned the abstract paintings on the walls, the trinkets on display here and there, but didn't notice anything of mystical value. Not that she expected there to be, but on more than one occasion, Lucifer had found potentially dangerous objects in the homes of people who hadn't the first clue of what they had.

She made her way upstairs past a dozen framed family pictures. Some were of individual people, but most were Olivia and her mom on various vacations: at the beach, on the ski slopes, posed in front of the Eiffel Tower. And in each photo, Olivia looked about as excited as someone visiting the dentist. For everything she had, she seemed to be committed to misery.

When Lucifer reached the top of the stairs, she heard voices coming from behind a closed door at the end of the hall. The voices stopped when she knocked. Without waiting for an answer, Lucifer stepped into the room.

The room looked just like Lucifer expected a typical girl's room to look like. It was bright but cluttered with posters of boys and pictures of friends, though everything was a bit . . . *pinker* than she was expecting.

Olivia and another girl were sitting on a large bed, a cache of outfits strewn between them. Olivia was covered in as much makeup as her mother. It was heavy, bright, and thicker where she wanted to hide her blemishes, blemishes no doubt caused by her heavy use of makeup. Lucifer could see her harsh blue eyes staring at her through a shock of stick-straight blonde hair.

Lucifer recognized the other girl from Gina's yearbook but couldn't recall her name. She was much more attractive than Olivia but seemed to work at trying not to overshadow her friend. Her brown curly hair was pulled back in a haphazard way, and her fashionable clothes were at least a size too big. But whoever she was, she smiled at Lucifer until she noticed Olivia scowling. Then her smile dissolved, silently waiting for permission to return.

"Who the hell are you?" Olivia asked.

"Lucifer. David just dropped me off. He called and told you I was coming."

"For the book, yeah." Olivia made a show of examining Lucifer from head to toe.

"Is your name really Lucifer?" the other girl asked, leaning forward, a small smile of wonder across her face.

As a thief, Lucifer had to learn how to blend in, how not to stand out in a crowd. The way she dressed, the way she wore her hair, the way she carried herself, all of it was designed to make her completely forgettable. So it was odd having someone stare at her with such pleasant fascination. Even so, Lucifer couldn't help but smile back. "Yes, that really is my name."

"You're a friend of Gina's?" Olivia asked. "I've never seen you at school."

Lucifer didn't have the time or the desire to explain why she had never set foot in a classroom, but she knew that the truth always led to more questions. So she said, "I don't go to your school. I'm . . . homeschooled."

Both girls sat up straight and exchanged uncomfortable looks. "Don't worry," Lucifer said. "I'm not going to brainwash you into joining a cult or anything like that. I just need the book and I can get out of your hair."

Olivia got off of the bed and walked over to a desk just large enough to hold the massive computer monitor resting on it. She opened a drawer and pulled out a large book, bound in dark aged leather. When Lucifer saw it, her heart went cold. Even from across the room, she could tell that it was bad business. Mostly because it was bound in human skin. But that was a detail she thought best to keep to herself.

"So . . . where exactly did you get that?" Lucifer asked.

"Isis picked it up at the library. She found it in the rare books section."

"Did she." Lucifer seriously doubted an ancient book bound in human skin came from a public library. Even if a library did have such a book, it would never let it be checked out, especially by someone obviously looking for some cheap scares.

Olivia walked over and held out the book toward her. But just as Lucifer was about to take it, Olivia pulled it back. "Are you going to tell me why David was lying to me?"

"Lying? About what?"

Olivia tucked the book under her arm. "Please. I know when a boy is lying to me. Gina isn't sick. That girl is never too sick to text or e-mail. She's grounded, isn't she?"

"In a manner of speaking."

Olivia turned to the other girl and said, "Did I call it or what, Kenna? She wigged and told her dad we were at the Worcester House."

The other girl, Kenna, looked horrified. "Do you think he'll call my parents?"

Olivia shrugged her shoulders and said, "Probably." She then turned back to Lucifer, handing her the book. "Let me guess. Gina's dad is now part of this homeschooling cult of yours and you guys are going to have some kind of old-fashioned book burning."

"My parents are dead and Gina's dad could care less about calling yours," Lucifer said without even looking up. "But burning this book might not be such a bad idea."

Lucifer took the book and began to examine the cover. The leather was old, scarred, and there was no printing anywhere, not even on the spine. The only marking she could find was a handwritten name toward the bottom of the front cover: *Helen Peltier*.

The name was written in smooth, clean lines. Whoever had written the name—Helen herself?—had taken great care to do so. It was something Lucifer would definitely have to look into.

Lucifer walked over to the bed and sat down. Kenna shifted her weight away from her. "That book creeps me right the hell out," she said.

Lucifer placed the book down and said, "Me too." Then reached into her trick bag, pulling out a pair of novelty sunglasses. The sunglasses were bright green, and each lens was in the shape of a giant butterfly.

"Nice glasses," Olivia said through a contemptible snort.

Lucifer put them on and gave Olivia a friendly smile before looking back at the book. "Ridiculous, right? But they do the job."

Kenna leaned a little closer. "What job is that?"

"They let me see things that aren't visible to the naked eye."

"Like a microscope?"

"No." Lucifer put on the glasses and examined the cover of the book again. "More like polarized sunglasses that let me see under the surface of a lake."

With the glasses on, Lucifer could make out dark, striated shapes on the cover, as if the veins in the skin used to make the cover had been rearranged to form symbols. But one symbol stood out among the rest. It was a circle with two jagged hooks spiraling away from its center. She hadn't even opened the book yet and already things weren't going well. Lucifer was going to have to take this home and study it thoroughly, but first, she had to deal with a much more pressing problem.

Lucifer took off the glasses and closed the book. "Did either of you open this book? Look inside?"

Olivia stepped over toward the bed and sat down next to Kenna. "Just the night we were in the Worcester House. Why?"

"You too, Kenna?" Lucifer asked.

Kenna nodded yes. Lucifer put the glasses and the book into her trick bag and pulled out her cell phone. With a couple quick swipes of her finger across the screen, she opened up a simple app and began scrolling through a gallery of symbols, picts, and simple images until she found the one from the cover of the book. She tapped it, and a symbol filled the screen. This one was a series of elegant lines all converging to a single point.

Lucifer held her phone up for Kenna. "Kenna, what do you see?"

"Oh, how pretty. It's like those old Spirographs my dad used to have. Did you draw that yourself?"

"No, but I did make the app." Lucifer held the phone out toward Olivia. "Olivia?"

Olivia frowned as she folded her arms across her chest. "What?"

"On my phone. What do you see on the screen?"

Olivia rolled her eyes before leaning forward to get a good view of the phone's screen. She squinted her eyes before settling back. "I see your greasy fingerprints smudged everywhere. Seriously, do you ever clean that thing?"

"Take a look again. Do you see anything else? Anything at all?"

Olivia squinted at the screen again. "No."

Kenna pointed to the screen. "It's right there! You can't see that? The lines go from here—"

"Please, don't trace the symbol, Kenna. That would . . . complicate things."

"But how come she can't see it?"

"Because there's nothing there," Olivia insisted.

"Is it like some color-blind kind of thing?" Kenna asked.

"I'm not color-blind!" Olivia shouted. But then she looked at Lucifer from the corner of her eye. "Am I color-blind?"

Lucifer quickly put her phone away and turned to squarely face Olivia. "The good news is that no, you're not color-blind."

Olivia turned to Kenna. "I told you I wasn't color-blind. I've had LASIK surgery."

"That doesn't have anything to do with—" Lucifer started to say before Kenna interrupted her.

"Wait, you said, 'Good news.' That kind of means there's bad news, doesn't it?"

"Bad news?" Olivia squeaked. "What do you mean *bad news*?"

Lucifer grabbed both of Olivia's hands. The gesture was meant to calm her, but it seemed to only make Olivia even more anxious. "Okay, you know how sometimes things sound a lot worse than they really are? This is one of those things, so I need you to not panic, okay?"

"Panic? Why would I panic? What things are you talking about? I don't know any of those things. What sounds worse than it really is?" Olivia was squeezing Lucifer's hands hard enough that her fingers were going numb. "Why couldn't I see it?"

"All right, this? This right here? This is the panicking thing that I didn't want you to do. You have to calm down," though as soon as the words left her mouth, Lucifer was fully aware that the horse had already left the barn on that one.

"Oh god, it's eye cancer, isn't it?" Olivia whimpered. "I have eye cancer!"

Sometimes it was better to just yank the Band-Aid off as quickly as you could. "No, you don't have eye cancer, Olivia . . .

"You're possessed."

CHAPTER 7

Olivia shared a glance with Kenna before looking back at Lucifer. "Possessed? Okaaay . . ." Olivia let the word hang in the air, not even attempting to mask her contempt. "You should probably go now."

Lucifer understood her skepticism, but there was something about Olivia's dismissive attitude that really rubbed her the wrong way. Part of her wanted to leave and just let Olivia deal with this herself, but that would be completely unfair. Olivia didn't grow up in a world of demons and magic and monsters, human or otherwise. She didn't know any better. As far as Olivia knew, Lucifer was just some crazy zealot come to preach the evils of her lavish lifestyle. Still, educating her might be a bit of fun.

Lucifer rummaged through her trick bag until she found a silver Zippo lighter engraved with the image of broad, feathery wings. She reached toward Olivia, but she jumped from the bed when Lucifer got close. "What are you doing?" she asked, holding her arms up in a decent facsimile of a defensive position. "Get out of my house! I have a purple belt in tae kwon do, so you better run if you know what's good for you!"

Lucifer held her hands up in submission. "Well, lucky for me I have a black belt in running for my life. I just want to show you something. But to do it, I need a hair from your head."

"Is this part of your crazy cult thing? You use your phone to trick me, then try to fix me with your creepy homeschooled . . . voodoo or whatnot?"

Lucifer held out her hand. "Olivia, please. Just one hair. I swear, if I can't convince you, I'll leave and you'll never see me again. I promise."

Olivia stared at Lucifer's outstretched hand, thinking. Eventually, she said, "Fine," and plucked a strand of perfect gold from her head. "Take it. Little Miss Cray-Cray."

Lucifer took the hair, ignoring the insult. "Kenna, come closer so you can see, too." Lucifer opened the lighter and flicked it to life. She slowly lowered Olivia's hair over the flame until it began to curl and smolder in the heat.

"Oh, yes," Olivia said, her voice flat and mocking. "Burning hair. I've never seen *that* before—"

The hair suddenly split open at the end, peeling back on itself like the skin of a tiny banana. Thick black smoke rose from the withering hair and formed tiny wisps of fangs and claws born on sharp, angular wings before dissipating into the air with a foul and acrid stench.

Both Olivia and Kenna stood in stunned silence until Kenna excitedly shouted, "Do it again!"

"NOOO!" Olivia shot Kenna a look of utter shock and disgust before recoiling into the corner of her room, hugging herself.

"What the hell was that?"

"Calm down, Olivia—"

"Don't tell me to calm down! What did you do? How did you do that?!"

"Kenna, why don't you grab that chair and put it in the center of the room for me, please," Lucifer said as she pointed to the small wooden chair in front of Olivia's desk. Lucifer walked over to Olivia and gently put her hands on her shoulders. "Olivia, look at me. Look at me." Olivia's wide blue eyes slowly rolled back to Lucifer. "It's okay. You're going to be okay. There's nothing to be afraid of. Now why don't you come over here and sit down in the chair."

Olivia pushed Lucifer out of the way and began violently tearing at her hair, yanking out thick blonde hunks with every pull. "Get it out of me! Get it *OUT*!" Lucifer grabbed her wrists and spun behind her, pinning her arms to her side in a bear hug. "Kenna, the chair!"

Instead of getting the chair, Kenna was slowly backing toward the door. "Is . . . is that the demon?"

"No, this is just your friend panicking like I asked her not to. Now please, grab the chair and put it in the center of the room before I have to do something drastic!"

"Drastic like what?"

"Kenna!"

"Okay, okay!"

Kenna rushed over and grabbed the chair. She slid it to the center of the room and then took a few tentative steps back as Lucifer led Olivia to the chair and sat her down.

"Is her head going to start spinning around?" Kenna asked.

Olivia shot her friend a terrified glance before Lucifer said, "No, that's not how it works." *Usually*, she thought. Lucifer grabbed Olivia's shaking hands. "I know you're scared and that's okay. I was scared the first time it happened to me until I realized how easy it is to fix."

"You've been possessed before?"

Lucifer smiled. "Not me personally, but someone I knew. And by something much nastier."

"What . . . what is it?"

"A filcher demon." Before Olivia could begin another frantic freak-out, Lucifer put her hand up to stop her and continued. "It sounds bad, I know, but trust me. As possessions go, this is weak sauce. You only looked in the book a few days ago, and it takes weeks if not months for a filcher demon to eventually get control of you. The longer you wait, the more difficult it is to get it out of you, but anything less than a month or two is cake."

Kenna stood next to Olivia, wringing her hands. "Am I possessed, too?"

"No. You saw the symbol on my phone. And filcher demons are Fibonacci-blind."

"Fibo . . . what?"

Lucifer opened the drawers in Olivia's bureau and started going through their contents. "Fibonacci. There's something called the Fibonacci sequence. 0, 1, 1, 2, 3, 5, 8 . . . it's a ratio thing. It shows up everywhere in nature, but filcher demons have a hard time seeing *unnatural* things with that sequence. Like the symbol I showed you." She pulled out a handful of scarves and some long socks then turned back to Olivia. "How you doing, Olivia?"

"I'm freaking the Mack Truck out and you guys are talking about math!" Olivia's hair was stuck to the side of her face by sweat and tears as dark streaks of mascara streamed down her puffy cheeks. A tiny ball of guilt sat in the pit of Lucifer's stomach. She wanted to get back at Olivia for her condescension, but she didn't want her to be *this* scared.

Lucifer gently pulled Olivia's arms behind the back of the chair and started tying her wrists together with one of the scarves.

"What are you doing?"

"This is just so you won't hurt yourself. Kenna, use the socks to tie her ankles to the chair legs. Tight."

"Hurt myself? Why . . . why would I hurt myself?"

Finished, Lucifer stepped in front of Olivia and put a comforting hand on her arm. "This is just a precaution. Sometimes the extraction can be . . . violent." Lucifer didn't think it was possible, but Olivia's eyes opened even wider.

Lucifer opened her trick bag and pulled out a small glass jar filled with a rusty powder. "Kenna, sit here on the bed behind her. Whatever you do, don't get in front of her. Understand?"

Kenna nodded.

"What's that?" Olivia asked, nodding toward the jar in Lucifer's hand.

"It's just paprika. See? Nothing to worry about," Lucifer said.

Olivia jerked back wildly, the wooden chair creaking under the sudden strain as it teetered on two legs. Lucifer reached out and caught Olivia before she fell over, but the poor girl was still struggling to get away.

Kenna jumped up from the bed and screamed, "Oh god, her head is going to start spinning!"

"Her head is not going to start spinning, now will you get a grip!" Lucifer turned back to Olivia. "Olivia, calm down. I said it's just—"

"I'm allergic to paprika! I'll go into anaphylactic shock!" Olivia shouted.

Lucifer wasn't expecting that. It wasn't really that big of a deal since almost any spice would do. Paprika was just what she happened to have in her trick bag. But the paprika seemed to frighten Olivia even more than being possessed.

Quickly, Lucifer stashed the bottle back into her trick bag. "Okay, sorry. I didn't know. It's gone now. You're fine."

Olivia was sucking in huge mouthfuls of air. "I . . . I can't . . . breathe."

"You can breathe. None of it got out of the bottle."

"Are . . . are you sure?"

"I'm positive." Lucifer stepped in front of Olivia. "Are you allergic to pepper?"

"Pepper? No. No, just paprika." Poor Olivia was breathing heavily, but Lucifer suspected that was from having had a complete freakout rather than an allergic reaction.

Lucifer turned to Kenna. "Go to the kitchen and get me some pepper."

"Yeah, okay," Kenna said. "Are you sure her head isn't going to spin? 'Cause . . . that'd be kinda cool to see."

"Jesus, Kenna!" Olivia shouted.

Lucifer waved Kenna toward the door. "Go, Kenna. Hurry up." Lucifer squatted down in front of Olivia, looking her square in the eyes. "Look at me, Olivia. Look. That's good . . . on the way up to your room, I saw a picture of you on a mountain, holding a pair of skis. How good are you?"

"What does that have to do with—"

"How good?"

"I . . . pretty good. I started skiing the black trails last year."

Lucifer smiled and spoke softly, calmly. "The first time you skied a black trail, I bet you were pretty scared. Right?"

"A little." There was still a waver in Olivia's voice, but her breathing was becoming less labored.

"But when you reached the bottom of that black trail, how did it feel?"

A small, fragile smile spread across Olivia's face. "Good. Like I could do anything."

"That's right. Very few people can ski the black trails. I know I couldn't. But you did. You were scared, but you did it. Because you *can* do anything. And this isn't any different."

Kenna burst into the room holding out a jar of black pepper. "Got it! Did I miss anything?"

Lucifer motioned her to sit on the bed. "Not a thing." She went through her trick bag again but frowned when she didn't find what she was looking for. "Olivia, do you have any stuffed animals?"

"Uh . . . yeah. In the corner on the other side of my bed. Why?"

"I need to steal one." Lucifer walked around the bed and saw about a dozen dolls and stuffed animals neatly arranged in the corner of the room. She bent down and picked up a small, pink bunny with floppy, pointed ears. "Perfect."

Without another word, Lucifer grabbed an eyeliner pencil from Olivia's vanity and used it to draw a small, delicate pattern of curved lines on the foot of the stuffed bunny. When she was satisfied with the design, she placed it on the floor several feet in front of Olivia.

"Now, this is the easy part," Lucifer said as she pulled her phone from her pocket. "The only thing you have to do, Olivia, is sneeze."

"Sneeze?" Olivia's voice was almost a whisper. "That's it?"

"That's it." Lucifer tapped the screen of her phone a few times until she found an image of a sunflower. She held it up to Olivia and said, "Tell me what you see?"

"I see a . . . it's . . . a . . ." Olivia's face went slack, her eyes still fixated on the screen of Lucifer's phone.

"Kenna," Lucifer said softly. "Open the jar of pepper and put some under Olivia's nose. But no sudden movements, okay?"

"What's happening?"

"A sunflower is a perfect example of the Fibonacci sequence in nature. But the photograph itself isn't natural. So the filcher demon inside her is . . . *confused* for the moment. It's lost its grip on her. But any sudden movements will distract it. So move slowly."

Kenna came around Olivia's side and very gingerly placed a pinch of pepper on top of Olivia's upper lip.

"That's enough," Lucifer said. "Now get back, please."

As Kenna made her way back to the bed, she asked, "What happens now?"

"When she sneezes, the filcher demon should be expelled."

"Uh, is it safe to be standing in front of her?"

Lucifer kept her eyes on Olivia's slackened face. "No. When the demon comes out, it's going to try and kill me."

"What?!" Kenna shouted. Olivia blinked and her eyes fluttered, but Lucifer moved the phone to keep the photo of the sunflower in her vision. Lucifer gave Kenna a quick, withering scowl.

Kenna dropped her voice to a loud whisper. "Sorry. Sorry. But I mean, what? I thought you said this was weak sauce."

"It is. Relatively speaking."

Olivia's nose twitched, and her chest rose with a quick intake of air. Lucifer jumped and rolled to the side just as Olivia sneezed. Olivia's arms and legs stiffened so violently that the chair disintegrated beneath her, the sound of the sneeze as loud and deep as mortar blast. Lucifer could feel the concussion of air burst through the room, knocking picture frames from the walls and tipping over a nearby lamp and table.

When Lucifer looked up, she saw a thin humanoid figure about three feet tall hunched on the ground in front of Olivia. Its arms and legs were impossibly long, bending at unnatural angles, and its bald, jagged head was covered in thick amber scales. The filcher demon turned its lidless black eyes back toward Olivia and sneered. Olivia sat on the floor in a heap of splintered wood and rags, a howl of terror caught in her throat.

Lucifer jumped up and stood in front of the demon. The filcher demon rose up on its haunches and let out a piercing screech that felt like ice picks in her ears. It took a step toward her, but then stopped. The demon looked back over its crooked shoulder to see its legs dissipating into a red mist. It looked back at Lucifer, who stood calmly, writing letters in the air with her finger. "L. Eight. R. Buh-bye!"

The demon turned back toward the pink bunny rabbit as the dematerialized parts of its body were being sucked in by the toy's eyes, the symbol on the rabbit's foot glowing with a bright, blue light. The demon sank its mottled claws into the carpet in a desperate attempt to free itself from the forces that pulled at it, but more and more of its body dissolved until there was nothing left but a sickly haze. There was a sudden burst of light and clap of thunder as the last wisps of the demon were rapidly sucked into the stuffed animal.

Lucifer bent over and picked up the bunny. The symbol was now burned into its foot like a cattle brand, and a small trace of smoke rose from it, giving off a faint hint of cinnamon. She looked back over her shoulder and said, "You girls okay?"

Both Olivia and Kenna were silent. Olivia still sat on the floor, her mouth agape, while Kenna stood on one leg and hugging herself in the middle of the bed like some 50s housewife who'd just seen a mouse in her kitchen.

Lucifer grabbed Olivia's wrist and helped her stand. She tapped a few icons on her phone and pulled up the first symbol. "What do you see?"

Olivia wiped her eyes with the back of her hand. "Some . . . curly thing."

"Good as new." Lucifer smiled. She waggled the stuffed bunny and said, "What did I tell you? The bunny trail of demon possessions. Now, your friend Isis. The one who found the book. Where does she live?"

Kenna said, "Just down the street, but she's not there. She's with Brooklyn at the mall. Looking for dresses."

"Was Brooklyn with you that night, too?" Both Olivia and Kenna nodded. "Anyone else?"

"No. That was it." Olivia looked down at the ruined chair at her feet. "I'm never reading another book as long as I live."

"No, no," Lucifer said. "You can read whatever you want now. This kind of possession is a lot like chicken pox. You get it once and then you're done." Lucifer put the stuffed bunny in her trick bag then slung the bag over her shoulder. She gave both Olivia and Kenna a pointed look. "But don't try and summon anything again."

"We didn't know this stuff was real," Kenna said.

"Now you do." Lucifer turned to leave, but stopped and looked back. "But keep that to yourselves."

Lucifer was at the bottom of the stairs when she heard Olivia say, "Gina's in trouble, isn't she?" She turned to see Olivia and Kenna at the top of the stairs, looking down at her. Olivia's mouth was turned down at the edges, her eyes filled with genuine worry.

After what Olivia had just been through, Lucifer didn't feel right lying to her, even if it was meant to protect her. "Yeah. I'm afraid so. But not for much longer if I can help it." Lucifer patted her trick bag with one hand. "Thanks for the book." She turned and headed out the front door.

As she moved along the walkway toward the sidewalk, Lucifer struggled to ignore the feeling of guilt welling inside of her. This morning, the most pressing concern in both Olivia's and Kenna's lives was deciding which dress to wear to the dance. Now they knew that demons and magic were real. Lucifer had taken their innocence. Even though she did it to save their lives didn't make it any easier to live with. And poor Olivia and Kenna were horrified enough by the filcher demon. How would they react if they knew that filcher demons were just the tip of a very large, very dark and ugly iceberg floating beneath the surface of the mundane?

Lucifer watched a middle-aged man in a frumpy brown suit trundle down the sidewalk toward her and was overcome with jealousy. What was his biggest worry in life? Changing the oil in his car every three thousand miles? Getting his kids into the right schools? Paying his mortgage?

As the man approached her, Lucifer toyed with the idea of telling him just how lucky he was. But when he was about to pass, she just smiled at him instead. Her smile tilted into a confused frown when she saw him pull something from his pocket.

Then her face turned to fire.

CHAPTER 8

The pain was excruciating. It was as if her face had been slammed into a blast furnace. Lucifer's eyes were swollen shut, and the inside of her mouth tasted of molten lead. Every time she struggled to take a breath, her lungs turned to fire. Her chest convulsed in terrible spasms with every violent cough, shredding the back of her throat.

Though she couldn't see, she could feel the man standing over her, desperately trying to yank her trick bag off her shoulder. Lucifer flailed at the shoulder strap, trying to wrap it around her wrist, but her arms wouldn't obey her. She rolled on top of the bag, using her weight to keep him from taking it away. He pulled hard at the strap, lifting her from the ground with a strained grunt. Just as suddenly, he dropped her back to the ground, knocking what little breath she had left from her lungs.

The man grabbed Lucifer's shoulder and rolled her over. But instead of trying to take the bag, Lucifer felt him rummage inside. She didn't care. The pain, the desperate need for air was so great now that all Lucifer wanted was to get away, to crawl somewhere safe like a dying animal.

There was a sudden jerk as the man pulled something from her bag. She heard his shoes slide across the pavement as he turned and ran away. Lucifer listened to the man's quickly retreating footsteps clacking down the sidewalk until there was nothing left but her own phlegmatic gasps and the mocking chorus of songbirds in the trees overhead.

When her eyes were finally able to open, she was face-to-face with Buck. He loomed over her, filling Olivia's front room with his massive frame. He smiled and gave her a fresh handful of ice cubes wrapped inside a kitchen towel.

"How's the breathing?"

Lucifer's voice came out harsh and broken. "Better." She pulled the ice away from her eyes and gave him a pointed stare. "He took the book."

Buck didn't say anything, just gave her a small nod before sitting down in the lounge chair across from her. Olivia walked in with a glass of water and handed it to her.

"I'm so, so sorry. Kenna and I didn't know what was happening until we heard you coughing out the window. We were going to call the police, but we didn't know if it was the . . . we didn't know what happened to you, so we called Gina's dad."

Lucifer took a sip. Even the water burned as it went down. "Thanks." She noticed Kenna sitting on the far end of the couch, looking more frightened than she had during their earlier impromptu exorcism. Lucifer understood. The most frightening monsters weren't the ones with fangs and claws that hid under your bed, they were the ones who walked among us.

Buck said, "Girls, you want to give us a moment, please?"

Kenna nodded and rose from the couch while Olivia said, "Yeah, sure. Lucifer, can I get you anything else? More water?"

"No, I'm fine. Thanks, though."

"No problem." Olivia started to follow Kenna out of the room, but stopped and looked back. "Mr. Pierce. I'm really sorry about Gina. We didn't know. We . . . we just didn't know." She turned and left.

Buck leaned forward, his thick leather belt creaking as he did so. "I see you told them what really happened. Are you sure that was a good idea?"

Lucifer peered at him from under the ice-filled towel. "I'm not so sure getting out of bed this morning was a good idea."

"I'm surprised they believed you."

"Well, it wasn't that hard to convince them. Sneezing up a filcher demon tends to persuade even the most hardened skeptic."

"What?"

There was no point in worrying Buck any further by telling him about Olivia's possession, so Lucifer gave him a dismissive wave with her free hand and said, "Bad joke, sorry."

"Lucifer. Are you okay? Did he . . . *hurt* you?"

"A face full of pepper spray isn't exactly a day at the spa."

"I meant—"

"I know what you meant. No, he didn't." Lucifer repositioned the ice over her eyes. "He was after the book."

"Lucifer, this is very important. Can you tell me what he looked like?" Buck's voice was strained, and the veins in his thick neck bulged like tree roots trapped under his skin.

"White guy. Tall, thin."

He pulled a small black notebook from his pocket and scribbled on its pages. "Hair color?"

"Dark with bits of gray, but most was missing on top. Cheap suit. Brown, about two sizes too big."

"What else? Can you remember anything else? Anything at all?"

"Buck—"

"Was he wearing a tie? A hat? Any scars or tattoos? You have to help me, Lucifer!"

"Buck!" Lucifer forced her eyes open as wide as her swollen lids would allow. "He doesn't have your daughter."

"You don't know that!"

"Yes, I do. Gina was pulled into *another dimension*. But this guy comes at me with pepper spray? Doesn't exactly scream 'mystical mastermind' now, does it?"

Buck sat back, his nostrils flaring. "It was mace, not pepper spray."

"Are you sure it wasn't napalm?" Lucifer touched the swollen tissue around her eyes. It was still sensitive, but the pain was tolerable. "I'm sorry, Buck. I wish I could tell you more, but I couldn't see much with my eyes, you know, melting inside my skull."

Buck pressed the palm of his hand against his temple and sighed. His eyes were bloodshot with dark circles hanging beneath them. It was obvious that he hadn't slept much since Gina was taken. "I'm going to find him, Lucifer. And when I do—"

"You'll come get me."

"Excuse me?"

"Do you want to find Gina?"

"Of course I do!"

"Then you come get me. This is my world, Buck. I know what I'm doing. And I know the right questions to ask. You don't."

Buck stood up, his broad chest swelling with every deep breath he took. "You said it yourself. This guy isn't a mystical mastermind. That makes him part of *my* world. And I've been a cop longer than you've been alive. I know how to question a perp. He might not know where Gina is, but he damn well knows someone who does!"

Lucifer sat back and shook her head. "You don't get it, do you? That guy knew about the book."

"So? What's your point?"

"My point is that someone knows I'm looking for Gina and doesn't want me to find her."

"Yeah, the witch that took her."

Lucifer wiped away a stream of cold water dripping from her cheek. "Yes, but why? She pulled Gina into another dimension. The witch wouldn't have any worries about you following after her. Why would she? You don't know anything about dimensions, and even if you did, you don't have the first clue about how to travel among them, let alone find the correct one and then get you and Gina back safely."

"No, I don't. But *you* do."

Lucifer slowly nodded. "Yeah. Which means that the guy not only knew about the book, he knew about *me*. And I work very hard so that *no one* knows about me. Buck, my survival depends on it. I'm a thief who's stolen some very powerful things from some very powerful . . . people. If the wrong person finds me, I'm dead."

Buck's mouth pursed in thought. "If he wanted you dead, it wouldn't have been a can of mace he pulled on you. So maybe he doesn't know about you. Maybe he just knows someone with knowledge of *your* world is looking into Gina's disappearance."

"Maybe." Lucifer carefully placed the towel down next to her and watched Buck a moment before speaking. "Buck . . . how, exactly, did you find me?"

Buck frowned. "I told you. A friend of mine said you could help me."

"What. Friend?"

"Lucifer, we've had this conversation. She asked I not tell you and I'm not going to break that promise. It's not her, if that's what you're thinking—"

"Is her name Helen Peltier?"

"No. Who's Helen Peltier?"

Lucifer strained her ears but couldn't hear anything off in his voice. He was telling the truth. Or he was at least lying well enough that she couldn't tell the difference. "The name was written on the cover of the book."

"Is that the name of the witch?" he asked.

"I don't know. It could be, but I doubt it—"

"Dispatch, this is Officer Pierce." He was suddenly speaking into the handheld microphone hanging from his shoulder. "Give me what ten-fourteen you have on a Helen Peltier. Start with the web to get a DOB then cross-reference with NCIC."

"You think she might have an outstanding ticket or something? Parked her broom in a handicapped spot?"

"I think that if she's in the system, we can get an address. Or at least a phone number." Buck tucked his notepad back into his pocket then stopped. He looked at Lucifer and asked, "They don't really fly brooms, do they?"

Lucifer just glowered at him.

"I didn't think so."

Lucifer stood up. Her back was getting stiff from having been slammed against the pavement. It was going to be tough for her to move tomorrow.

"Lucifer, you should really rest for a while. At least until I can get some info on this Helen Peltier."

Lucifer slung her trick bag over her shoulder. "If you do find any info, send it to me. You've got my number. Same thing with the guy who mugged me. You find him, you let me know. I'm serious, Buck. It's very difficult to question a dead body."

Buck shirked back, clearly offended. "What kind of person do you think I am?"

"The kind of person who would have no trouble going to jail for putting the hurt on a suspect if it meant finding his daughter. Besides, if anyone has the right to hurt this guy, it's me. I don't want you bogarting my payback."

When Buck spoke, he didn't bother disguising the worry in his voice. "Are we going to be able to find Gina without the book?"

"I don't know," she said, "but I do know that we can't leave it out in the wild. It's dangerous in the wrong hands. And if you do find it before I do, whatever you do, don't open it." She grabbed the glass and downed the rest of the water in one big gulp.

"Where are you going?" Buck asked.

Lucifer was halfway out the front door when she said, "To the mall."

CHAPTER 9

T he mall was cold and crowded. Small groups of people lumbered down the halls like blood clots being flushed through bright, fluorescent veins. Some groups would duck into every store they passed while others moved from display window to display window without ever committing to anything more than a casual glance at the merchandise.

Lucifer listened to the sounds of laughter, shouts, and the occasional baby's cry bouncing off the walls. She saw several children taking turns on a coin-operated rocking horse until a woman huddled them together to give them each a fistful of candy. The woman glanced up and saw Lucifer, gave her a weak smile, then quickly ushered the children in the opposite direction.

Everyone who walked past Lucifer looked at her, letting their stares linger for a second or two longer than was comfortable before stepping aside to give her a wider berth. Though the swelling in her face had gone away, her eyes were still bloodshot and her skin red and irritated. She thought about putting her hood up over her head to hide her face, but she knew that would only make her look even more suspicious. She wasn't used to being noticed. Lucifer prided herself on her ability to move through the world without attracting attention. It's part of what made her such a great thief. But she didn't have the several hours to wait for her face to heal. Lucifer needed to find Brooklyn and Isis, not just to make sure they hadn't been possessed, but to find out just where the book came from. She highly doubted it came from a library.

As Lucifer looked in her trick bag for Gina's yearbook, she took quick stock of the items inside. Thankfully, nothing was damaged during the attack. The only thing the man stole from the bag was the book. But that was small consolation. He had taken something from *her*. And not just the book. He had taken her sense of security.

It wasn't the first time Lucifer had ever been attacked. Such things were, sadly, a part of life for a street kid in Recife, not to mention a thief in an underworld of the mystical and magical. But this . . . this was just an old guy with a can of mace. Lucifer had survived death squads and roving street gangs, stood against hordes of unnatural horrors, and had come face-to-face with things that have driven men mad just to look upon. But some bald asshat in a cheap suit had come along and made her feel *helpless*.

And that *really* pissed her off.

Lucifer realized that her anger must have been showing on her face. Coupled with the aftereffects of the mace, it was no wonder people were giving her strange looks. As if she didn't feel out of place enough as it was.

All the people Lucifer's age didn't seem to be doing a great deal of shopping. Instead, they wandered the halls, laughing at each other's jokes, flirting with other groups of kids that happened by, just enjoying being together. This was the life of the average American teenager. No fear, no concern of where their next meal was coming from, no burden of inconvenient knowledge that underneath their world of friends and boys and music was a seething nation of darkness that wanted nothing but to swallow whole everything they knew and held dear. It was as if Lucifer was at a zoo, watching some exotic animal exhibit, though Lucifer couldn't help but feel that *she* was the one caged behind six inches of plexiglass.

She took a deep, calming breath and flipped through the pages of the yearbook, looking for circled pictures of Brooklyn and Isis. Both girls were photogenic and, judging by the number of times their photos appeared, nearly as popular as David. Lucifer stopped turning the pages when she came across a picture of David in a suit and tie, speaking in front of a small group of students. He photographed equally well, but Lucifer thought he was even more hand-some in person.

Lucifer slammed the yearbook shut and shoved it back in her trick bag. *Focus, girl.* She scanned the various groups of girls mean-dering through the mall until she found the ones she was looking for. Brooklyn and Isis were with several other girls and one boy on the level below her. They were coming out of a shoe store, all following behind Brooklyn like ducklings.

As she rode the escalator down to the lower level, Lucifer watched Brooklyn and the others stop in front of a kiosk to try on some hats. They all took turns showcasing their favorite finds with grand poses and gestures while the poor young woman working the kiosk did her best to smile.

Brooklyn slowly pulled a red bowler from off her head when she saw Lucifer approaching. The others stopped their conversations and stared as well. Brooklyn smiled, her teeth bright and perfect. "You must be the devil girl who tied Olivia to a chair," she said.

Lucifer glanced around to see who was listening in, but everyone other than Brooklyn's friends were too busy going about their own lives to pay any attention. "So, she called you. What all did she say?"

"Enough to make me think she got into her mother's medicine cabinet. That girl was talking cray-cray. Did you really try to kill her with paprika?"

"I thought it'd be cleaner than a butcher knife," Lucifer said as she pulled out her phone and tapped the screen. "Tell me, what do you see?"

Brooklyn didn't bother looking at the screen but continued to stare at Lucifer. "If I say I don't see anything, that means I'm *possessed*, right?" She made air quotes when she said the word.

"What you say doesn't matter. What you *see* does," Lucifer said, giving some air quotes of her own.

Brooklyn held Lucifer's gaze for a moment before glancing down at the screen. "I see spirals."

"Good."

"Good? So . . . that's it? You're not going to try and tie me to a chair?"

Lucifer winked at her. "Not unless you want me to." She walked over to Isis, who was standing at the back of the group of friends. Unlike Brooklyn, Isis didn't appear to find any of this amusing. "Isis, what do you see?"

"I see the scaly bitch who's about to get my fist down her throat for kicking my boyfriend."

"You want to go that route, fine," Lucifer said, "but mall security would most likely call the cops and have us arrested. Now, I'd be fine in jail, but you look a bit . . . fragile. So why don't we skip all that and you just tell me what you see."

Isis peered at the screen, but her eyes went wide. "I . . . I don't see anything."

"No?" Lucifer looked at her phone, feigning confusion. "Oh, sorry. I must have pressed the wrong button." She tapped her phone's screen and held it up. "Okay, now tell me what you see," she said, trying her best not to let her smirk show.

"I see spirals, too," Isis said flatly.

"Why are you asking her?" Brooklyn asked.

"Because she looked inside the book, too."

"Is *that* what this is about? That stupid book?" Brooklyn tossed the red hat back on the rack. "God, no one cares! Our parents were cool with us sneaking into the Worcester House because they knew we weren't drinking or getting high. We were just having fun trying to scare each other. But Gina's dad has to go sniffing around for something to get *us* in trouble with the 'rents so he doesn't look like such a fascist troglodyte."

Brooklyn walked up to Lucifer and folded her arms across her chest. "Let me guess. You're one of his undercover cop buddies. One of those old people who only looks sixteen, right?"

"I can assure you," Lucifer said. "I'm not a cop. I just want to know about the book. Where did you get it?"

Brooklyn was athletic and at least six inches taller than Lucifer. She leaned over, forcing Lucifer to strain her neck. "The library. You know. Where the *books* come from."

"There's no way that book came from a library."

"Are you calling me a liar?" Brooklyn's half-smile dissolved into a sneer.

Lucifer shrugged her shoulders. "Well, I don't know of many libraries that let people check out books bound in human skin."

Brooklyn pulled back. "Shut up. It was not."

"It was." Lucifer leaned in close to Brooklyn and whispered, "And not from the nice pieces, either."

Brooklyn started rapidly shaking her hands as if she were trying to dry them. "I'm going to retch. That is so foul."

"You didn't know?"

"Are you retarded? Of course I didn't know!" Brooklyn looked at Isis and said, "How could you let me touch that?"

The rest of Brooklyn's friends were giggling to themselves as Brooklyn made a show of how disgusted she was having touched the book. Isis ignored her and said, "We *did* get it from the library. We just didn't check it out. We didn't want anyone to know we were reading that kind of stuff so we . . . we stole it."

"But it was *at* the library? Do you remember which section?" Lucifer asked.

Isis shook her head, her blonde hair whipping back and forth over her tiny shoulders. "I don't know. Somewhere in the back with all the books that nobody ever reads."

"Then what were you doing back there?"

"What's it to you?" Isis snapped.

"I know what she was doing back there," the only boy in the group said.

"Shut up, Greg. It wasn't like that. We were just talking."

"Well, you were using your mouths, anyway."

Isis punched Greg in the arm. Then the two of them began hurling ugly insults at one another, trying to one up each other with just how disgusting and crude they could be. Lucifer wondered if they were really friends or not, but the way the others playfully joined in suggested that this was fairly common behavior.

Lucifer tried to break into the chaotic conversation to ask more questions, but the group talked around her as if she wasn't even there. It was like a game of verbal keep-away. They tossed clusters of words back and forth, keeping them just out of Lucifer's reach. She knew that she could get their attention if she really wanted to, but she doubted they had any more useful information for her.

Brooklyn led the boisterous gaggle of friends back into the general din of the mall, leaving Lucifer standing back at the kiosk like one of the colorful hats. She had been just interesting enough to notice for a moment, but once that interest faded, she was tossed aside and easily forgotten.

Lucifer stood at the calm center of the human cacophony swirling around her. For a moment, she pretended to be a part of it all, just another piece in the grand machine of ordinary life. But the illusion only lasted for a moment. She reached back and felt the imperceptible weight of the mark on her shoulder, the hex that stuck to her skin like the lifeless wing of a melted sparrow. As much as Lucifer hoped and dreamed otherwise, she knew she belonged to another world. She belonged to *another*. And there was no escape from it. At least, not for her.

But maybe, just maybe, there would be for Gina.

Lucifer readjusted her trick bag to a more comfortable position then left to find someplace a bit more quiet.

CHAPTER 10

The Yarsborough County library was at the corner of one of the city's busiest intersections, directly across from the modest Brisendine Art Gallery and a coffee shop bursting at the seams with the young and beautiful waiting for their morning dose of steaming energy potions. The library sprawled across most of the block with thick green vines winding along its marble walls.

Lucifer smiled when she saw the two granite griffins on top of the towering columns that flanked the library's doorway. She loved libraries. They were temples of knowledge, and this building looked every bit the part. Even inside, the silence was reverential. The shelves were dark and weathered from decades of use, and the natural light shining through the vast windows gave the appearance that the books were glowing.

She made her way past the front desk. A young librarian looked up from carefully inventorying returned books and gave Lucifer a quick smile. Lucifer took care to notice the woman's name tag and the titles of her personal recommendations displayed on the desk in front of her. She then walked to the far side of the first floor, where a row of computer screens sat on top of long tables in perfect alignment like tiny square soldiers awaiting orders. Since most people had laptops or tablets of their own, the library's public computers often sat empty and unused.

Lucifer picked the one most out of view of the people browsing behind her and started logging in. After a few minutes, she was able figure out the young librarian's username and password. It wasn't very hard. Most librarians used the title of their favorite books as passwords, and since Ms. Mendez was kind enough to give Lucifer a list to choose from, it was just a matter of trial and error before she figured it out. But hacking into the system as a librarian wasn't about hiding her tracks. It was about gaining access to restricted records.

The book was incredibly old, which meant it would have most likely come from the library's collection of rare books. And since libraries usually only let professors or academics have access to those books, the list of rare books out on loan should be short. If Lucifer had the titles of those books, it should only be a process of elimination to discover which one was the book Gina and her friends had used at the Worcester House.

But after an hour, she wasn't any closer to finding the book than when she walked in. None of the library's rare books were out. All were accounted for. And there was no indication that the records had been maliciously altered.

Lucifer entertained the idea that magic was somehow involved, that there might be a ghost in the machine hiding the information behind its pale and tattered rags. But if there was anything magical going on, Lucifer would know. Magic and technology didn't mix terribly well, so whenever someone tried, there were always telltale signs. But there was nothing. According to the records, the book just simply didn't exist. None of this made sense.

Isis said that this was where she found the book. But rare books were often tucked away in a room where the public didn't have access to them. Lucifer supposed someone might have accidentally shelved the book where anyone could just take it. That might explain why there was no record of it missing. Even though that was a possibility, it seemed highly unlikely. Was Isis lying? Now that was certainly a possibility, but Lucifer didn't think so. But if she wasn't lying, then what was that book even doing here?

"Hey you."

Lucifer turned to see David smiling down at her, his perfect teeth glinting in the surreal sunlight beaming through the windows. But there was no joy in his expression, only the calm confidence of a mark standing over a Three-Card Monte game convinced he knew which card was the ace. He sat down next to her and placed his elbow on the table, resting his chin in the palm of his upturned hand. "I just had the most interesting phone conversation with Olivia."

Lucifer rubbed her eyes, trying to ease the tension from having stared at a computer screen for so long. "What part of 'keep it to yourself' does that girl not understand? What exactly did she tell you?"

David's mouth curled in slight confusion. "Well, let's see. She said you tied her to a chair and tried to poison her. Right before she . . . hmmm, how did she say it? Puked up a leprechaun with scoliosis."

"Don't be silly. Leprechauns aren't real."

"You don't say." After a moment, David asked, "Is it true you were attacked?"

Lucifer nodded and gestured toward her face. "I normally don't look quite this hideous." David only stared at her. Lucifer could feel her face getting even redder. "I'm a bit busy right now—"

"Gina's dad finally called me," David said with an expression more worried than angry. "He wouldn't tell me anything, just that Gina's sick and she'll be fine in a few days. But I could tell he was lying to me. I don't believe any of this supernatural garbage you talked about, but I know that Gina really is missing. And I want to help find her."

She stared at him in silence. Gina was his girlfriend and he had a right to know, but Lucifer absolutely hated this. There were few things worse than being the teller of this unfortunate truth: magic was real. Whether he wanted to believe it or not, it was real and it was often dark and ugly and people were always better off not knowing it existed. And short of a lobotomy, there was no way to ever un-know. But Lucifer knew from the pained look on David's face that being kept in the dark was even worse.

"All right. I'll let you help."

"*Let* me?"

"Yes, let you. You want to help? Take me to the section where all the kids make out."

David didn't move. "Lucifer, are you trying to tell me you want to kiss me?"

Lucifer could feel her face flush. Suddenly, all she could do was stare at David's mouth and the way the corner of his lip curled into a tiny wisp of a smile. She lifted her gaze and looked at his eyes, but that just made it even worse. Why did he have to be so damn pretty? It was distracting. "Most every library has a section where kids go to be alone together. And Isis said she found the book in a section where she was kissing somebody."

David laughed. "Ethan. That's the only reason that guy would ever be in a library."

"Oh, basketball guy."

"He's Isis's guy friend," David said.

"You mean 'boyfriend'?"

"I don't know if I'd consider Ethan her boyfriend. They're not really dating, just sort of going through the motions. You know?"

"Not really."

David shrugged his shoulders. "Neither do I, but I think it's because Isis and I used to go out."

When Lucifer didn't say anything, David continued. "We dated for a little while, but we weren't really right for each other, so we broke up. And then one night, Olivia threw a party when her mom was out of town. Half the school was there. Anyway, Isis saw me there with Gina and got a bit jealous. So she kissed Ethan, hoping it would get to me. But it didn't. And since she'd never admit that that's why she kissed him, she's been kind of stuck with him ever since."

The way David described it made it sound so mundane, but to Lucifer it was like listening to a fairy tale. Kissing, parties, jealousy

. . . Lucifer had seen things and been to places that few people alive even knew existed, but David's world seemed more strange and alien to her than any of them. David's boring memory fascinated her. But Lucifer had to push that fascination to the back of her mind. There wasn't any room in her life for such things, and there was no point in wishing for something that could never be.

"That sounds . . . complicated."

"Welcome to high school."

Desperate to change the subject, Lucifer quickly logged off then slipped her trick bag over her shoulder. "I'm following you."

"This way," David said.

He led her through a maze of shelves that snaked around a small cluster of tables and chairs being used by a number of people who Lucifer assumed must be students at the university. Most of the library was well lit with plenty of room to browse the shelves without bumping into other people, but the deeper into the library they went, the darker and tighter the rows became. They came to an intersection with Applied Sciences heading off into one direction and General Reference in the other.

David said, "Over here," then reached down and grabbed her hand. Her hand almost disappeared inside his, his fingers completely wrapping around her palm. The pleasantness of it surprised her. It felt as if a soft wave of electric current was running up the length of her arm. He gently pulled her between the stacks where the height of the shelves kept out the fluorescent light from overhead.

As they stepped into the shadows, Lucifer saw a couple leaning against the shelves, lost in a kiss. David looked down at Lucifer and said, "I think this is the place." The couple looked up, surprised to discover they weren't alone.

"Oh, hey," said the boy. His hair was long and wavy, and he had a bit of blond scruff jutting from the end of his pointy chin.

The girl he was kissing wiped the side of her mouth with the back of her hand and gave David a broad, toothy grin. "Hi, David." Her gaze was locked on David, as if Lucifer wasn't even there. Lucifer couldn't help but wonder if she appeared just as idiotic as this girl did whenever she looked at David.

The boy gave Lucifer a quick glance before nodding at David with a knowing smile. "What's up, bro?"

David shrugged. "Doing some research for Ackerman's class. My paper is due in a couple of weeks and I haven't even started yet."

When the girl finally pulled her gaze away from David to look at Lucifer, her goofy smile instantly vanished. Lucifer didn't realize she was still clutching David's hand until the girl looked down at them. Lucifer quickly let go. "So, David," the girl said, looking back up at Lucifer. "How's Gina?"

"Good, for the most part. But she's home with the flu."

The boy put his arm around the girl's shoulders. "Hope she feels better." Then he shot a quick glance at Lucifer before saying, "Good luck with your paper."

"If you need a study partner, just let me know," the girl said through the blinding perfection of her smile. The boy scowled at her as he ushered her away. As they ducked around the far bookshelf, Lucifer heard the girl say, "What? I've got Ackerman third period."

David leaned back against the bookshelf and sighed. "Ah, the curse of being attractive. But I'm sure you already know what that's like."

Sadly, Lucifer knew all too well what it was like to be cursed. But attractive? She became acutely aware of how red and irritated her face was and pulled her hood up over her head. "Keep a lookout for me, okay?"

Lucifer reached into her trick bag and pulled out a pair of surgical gloves. After snapping them on her hands, she pulled out a thin bundle of waxed brown parchment paper tied closed with a brittle piece of twine. She set the parchment on the floor and carefully untied the twine, revealing the object inside. It was a shiny black feather roughly twelve inches in length with a red quill that grew deeper in color the farther along it came to the end.

"What's that?" David asked.

"Supernatural garbage."

"Ha ha. But seriously."

Lucifer looked up and said, "You're not doing a very good job of being a lookout."

"Don't worry. It's just us back here." He squatted down next to her. "Why the gloves? Afraid some crazy magic might hex you?"

David blanched from Lucifer's scowl. Her entire life had been turned upside down because she *had* been hexed by crazy magic, and it was certainly nothing to scoff at. "David, you know that curse you have? The curse of being pretty? You're about to have it lifted."

He raised his hands up in submission. "Easy, now. I didn't mean anything by it. It's just this all seems a bit . . . silly to me."

"Then I'm really sorry, David."

"Why would you be sorry?"

"Because it's all about to become very un-silly to you." Lucifer held the feather out at arm's length, giving David a good view of it. "This is a feather from a Strix. And, thankfully, there haven't been any around in well over a thousand years. But to keep it from disintegrating I have to take precautions. Like wearing rubber gloves." Of course, that was only partly true. The real reason Lucifer wore gloves was because Strix were foul, disgusting birds, and the idea of touching one of its feathers grossed her out. But David didn't need to know that.

"So what do you do with it?" he asked.

"This."

Lucifer let go of the feather and watched it slowly drift toward the floor. Just before it touched the ground, it raised up in the air as if caught on a current of air and hovered between them.

David reached out and moved his hand through the empty space above the feather. "How are you doing that? There aren't any strings!"

Lucifer gently pulled a wide-eyed David against the bookshelves as the feather danced in tiny circles as it floated past. "The Strix were owls known for their love of eating human flesh. Their feathers are magically drawn to dead things, particularly dead . . . human . . . things. I stole this one from some grave robbers who were using it to pillage undiscovered burial sites. Stupid *chacais*."

"You think there's a dead body here?" The look of wonder on David's face was replaced by one of disgust.

"No, the book was bound in human skin. You don't find books like that in public libraries. But Isis insists this is where she found it. If she really did, the feather should show me exactly which shelf it came from."

The Strix feather bobbed in the air for a moment before turning the point of its quill toward a shadowy corner of a nearby bookshelf and darting through the air. It hit the edge of the shelf with a soft *TINK!* and quivered like an arrow in a bull's-eye.

The shelf was filled with books on subjects that Lucifer doubted anyone had ever bothered reading. Economics, statistics, and a few on governmental tax codes during specific presidential administrations. She could feel herself getting drowsy just reading the titles.

However, the space above the feather was empty.

"I guess Isis was telling the truth," Lucifer said. "It was here. But what was it doing in a section about economics?"

"That was bad . . . *ass!*"

Lucifer looked back at David. "Really? You think?"

"Hell yes!" He walked over and examined the feather stuck in the wood of the shelf. "Magic is real!"

Lucifer gently pulled out the feather and wrapped it back up in its packaging. "Let's keep that to ourselves, okay? It's bad enough

Olivia's telling everyone about our little exorcism party. I don't need you adding fuel to that fire."

"Don't worry. I can keep a secret." David ran his hand through his hair. "But I'm still having a hard time wrapping my head around this."

"Yeah, floating feathers can take a little getting used to." She softened her sarcasm with a grin.

"So, were you born a witch or did you have to study to become one?"

"What is it with people thinking I'm a witch? I'm not a witch."

"You can do magic. How does that not make you a witch?"

"I can hammer a nail into a board, too. Doesn't make me a carpenter. And I can't *do* magic. Only use it. If you had dropped the Strix feather, it would have done the same thing. And it wouldn't make you a witch any more than it would me."

Lucifer took several of the books off the shelf to see if there were any magical markings etched into the wood, but other than some rather crude scratchings of various body parts, there was nothing. "The book was definitely here, but it's not in the library's system. And if it were, why was it shelved here? This just isn't making sense." She turned to David, only to find him staring at her like a mangled knot he was trying to untie. "What?" she asked.

"Who are you? Really?"

"Oh David, we don't have time to get into that."

He took a small step forward, gently pressing her back against the bookshelf. Lucifer strained her neck to look up at him as he stared down at her, his brow knit in confusion. "You're a teenage thief, you can perform exorcisms, make feathers fly like arrows, even shrug off being attacked by a man with a can of mace. I've never met anyone like you. You're . . . you're fascinating."

"Fascinating, like rainbows are fascinating? Or like . . . bug guts are fascinating?"

"Rainbows. Definitely rainbows."

Lucifer didn't know what to do. She spent her life moving through the shadows, trying to remain unseen. She had no idea how to deal with this kind of scrutiny. And the way his blue eyes looked almost black in the low light made her palms slick with sweat.

"David . . . there's something happening in my pants." She reached into her pocket and pulled out her vibrating cell phone. "Yeah?"

As soon as she heard Buck's voice on the other end, the spell David had over her disappeared. She easily moved past David, focused on what Buck was telling her. "Do you have an address?" Lucifer asked.

"*Why? There's nothing you can do,*" Buck said.

"Do you remember what I told you at Olivia's? I said it was very difficult. I didn't say it was impossible."

Buck was silent for a moment before saying, "*God, Lucifer. I'll do anything to get Gina back, but . . . but this?*"

"Don't worry. You're not doing anything. I am. Now give me the address."

Lucifer reached into her trick bag and pulled out a pen. She pressed her phone to her ear with her shoulder and grabbed David's hand. As Buck gave her the address, she scribbled it on David's broad palm. "Got it. I'll let you know what I find out."

"*Lucifer, be careful. This is getting . . . darker than I expected.*"

"It always does."

Lucifer put her phone back in her pocket and leaned back against the shelf with a heavy sigh. David stared at the address scrawled across his palm, then said, "That was Officer Pierce, wasn't it? Is this the address of the guy who attacked you?"

"No. Helen Peltier. The woman whose name was written on the book."

"Then why are you sulking? Let's go talk to her!"

"That's the address to Crestview Cemetery, David. Ms. Peltier's dead."

David's excitement evaporated. He fell back against the bookshelf next to Lucifer and stared off into the shadows. "What do we do now?"

"Something I really don't want to." Lucifer looked up at David, trying to ignore the sick feeling in her stomach.

"We're going to need a couple of shovels."

CHAPTER 11

T he gibbous moon fell behind a thick column of black clouds. Faint shadows of gravestones swelled and grew until they bled into the surrounding darkness. The only thing Lucifer could clearly see was the silhouette of a twisted, leafless tree rising from the center of the tiny graveyard, back-lit by the fake sunrise of distant city lights reflecting off the clouds above.

Crestview was an old cemetery lost on the side of a forgotten road that wound its way through the countryside west of the city. Each gravestone sat at an imperfect angle, leaning in exhaustion after decades of neglect. From what Lucifer could see, it had been quite a long time since anyone had been buried here.

She cringed when she heard the car trunk slam shut and the shovels clink as David tossed them over his shoulder. "Stealth, David. All the kids are trying it these days."

David sauntered over to her, the crunch of gravel beneath his feet screaming in the still darkness. "Sorry. But c'mon. There's no one here. The nearest house is at least a mile away, and we haven't seen a single car since we got off the highway. Who's going to hear us?"

Lucifer could hear the highway traffic in the distance, softly thrumming like an approaching swarm of insects. She took one of the shovels from David and said, "I don't like advertising what I'm doing, even if there is no one around to see. And it's always a good idea to keep quiet when sneaking around cemeteries at night. Besides, we're about to do something very offensive. Let's not be obnoxious about it, okay?"

David squared his shoulders and nodded. "You're right. I apologize. It's just that this reminds me of sneaking out to tee-pee people's houses."

"Tee-pee? What's that?"

"Toilet paper. You throw rolls of toilet paper over the house, into the trees, that kind of thing. It's a pain to clean up."

Lucifer studied his face for a moment. "That is simply the stupidest thing I've—"

"Ever heard. Yeah, I know," David said rather bashfully. "Definitely seems even more so now. Please don't judge me."

"Why in the world would you ever . . . you know, never mind. Just try and keep it down to a mild roar. This way." She wanted to be annoyed with him, but she was too busy being annoyed with herself for letting him come along. This wasn't something civilians should be doing and she knew it, even if it was his girlfriend that was missing. But here he was, following along like a tall, handsome puppy eager to play. And as much as she didn't want to, she had to admit that she liked that. Which annoyed her most of all.

When Lucifer stopped to examine a gravestone at the edge of the cemetery, David said, "What was the woman's name again?"

"Helen Peltier."

"Do you want me to start looking at the other end of the cemetery and then we meet in the middle?"

Lucifer moved to the next grave, feeling the cold stone with her fingertips. "No. Cemeteries like this have a basic design to them. The oldest graves tend to be in the center while the newest are out at the edges."

"When did Helen die?"

"1957. And it's Ms. Peltier."

"Okay. Does it really matter if I call her Helen?" David asked.

"It does to me." Lucifer stood and pointed toward a cluster of several towering stones farther into the cemetery. "I'd say she's several rows in that direction. C'mon."

Lucifer led the way through the rows of graves. The grass was tall and brittle, but the earth beneath was soft and spongy. Dew-covered spiderwebs hung between a few of the gravestones, the tiny drops of moisture occasionally glinting in the fading moonlight. "Lucifer," David said. "How many times have you done this?"

She stopped to examine a short stone carved into a Celtic cross, but the name and dates were too weathered to read. "Too many. It's pretty common for people to be buried with artifacts. It's actually the safest place for them. But every once in a while, someone will go looking for them and I have to beat them to the punch."

When they reached the cluster of large gravestones, Lucifer felt the ground grow firm and the grass more pliable. Lucifer handed her shovel to David and set to examining the nearest of the stones. There were five of them, nearly identical. Each was a rectangular slab of black granite that tapered into a pyramid at the top with smooth and unbroken lines. And while the other markers in the cemetery littered the ground like long-forgotten toys, these five stood perfectly upright.

She reached for the nearest marker and ran her fingers over the name. *Donald Peltier, 1884–1948.* The next gravestone was for Mary Peltier and the next for Elizabeth Peltier. Each of the five gravestones belonged to someone with the last name Peltier. But none of the gravestones belonged to Helen Peltier.

"I found her," David said.

Lucifer saw David standing over a tiny and sad rectangular plaque overgrown with weeds just beyond the firm grass beneath the Peltier gravestones. David squatted down and read. "Helen Peltier, born 1895, died 1957." He stood and casually leaned on the shovels. "Guess her family didn't like her that much."

Lucifer scanned the tall, perfect monuments, taking in the dates of the deceased. Then she smiled. "No, I think they loved her very much. At least she loved them. They all died before she did, so there was probably no one left to bury her. With no family left, they just put her in her family plot with a simple marker and called it a day."

Since Helen's name was on the book, it was a safe bet to assume that she had some knowledge of the arcane. That explained why the Peltier family plot didn't seem to deteriorate as much as the surrounding graves. Ms. Peltier worked some magic to keep her family's eternal resting place respectable. She loved them. And knowing that made this even harder for Lucifer.

"So what now?" David asked.

"We dig."

Lucifer took a shovel from David and slammed it into the earth. After the third shovel-full, David said, "Lucifer, I'm not comfortable with this."

She stopped. "You have no idea how glad I am to hear that, David. I'm not comfortable with this either. But if I want to find Gina, this is what I have to do. If you want to wait in the car, I understand."

He stood quietly, staring at Ms. Peltier's little marker. "I'll do anything to find Gina. Even this. I just thought she'd be buried in a tomb or something. I didn't think we'd have to actually dig her up. Can't you cast a spell or something to just make her pop out of the ground?"

"No. And even if I could, I wouldn't. Exhuming corpses shouldn't be an easy thing to do," she said as she went back to digging. Soon, David joined her, and they spent the next hour in silence.

As much as she hated to admit it to herself, Lucifer was glad that David was with her. And not just because he made the digging go so much more quickly. She liked looking up and seeing him there, the way his shoulders flexed beneath his sweatshirt when he tossed dirt out of the hole, his solid silhouette towering over her. She moved in a world that was too often ugly and terrifying. It was nice to have something beautiful around.

Thunk!

Lucifer's shovel hit something solid. "Here, take this," she said as she handed her shovel to David. The smell of soil and decay was thick in the air. When she knelt down, the damp soil soaked into the knees of her jeans and sent a chill up her spine. She cupped her hands and began pulling at the dirt. Roots, rocks, and a few squirmy things thankfully unseen in the darkness came away by the scoopful until a small area was cleared and Lucifer could see the dull shine of Helen Peltier's coffin.

Lucifer grabbed a small flashlight from her trick bag and handed it to David. She pointed, saying, "Shine the light on the ground there." She knelt back down and carefully scooped more dirt.

"I've never seen a dead body before," David said.

"And you're not going to see this one. Once I have the viewing door uncovered, I want you to crawl out and wait for me." David opened his mouth to protest, but Lucifer interrupted him. "Please, David."

David sighed and clicked on the flashlight. "All right, Lucifer."

The remaining dirt was dense and came away in chunks. The more she scooped away, the more she could tell the coffin had been deformed by the pressure of the earth on top of it. Once she had it completely exposed, she would need the shovel to pry it open.

"Stop looking at me," she said.

"What?"

Lucifer moved another scoopful of dirt. "You keep shining the light in my face and not the ground. You were looking at me."

"Sorry." He moved the light back to the coffin. "Lucifer, what kind of artifact do you think Ms. Peltier has?"

"None that I'm aware of."

"Then what exactly *does* she have?"

"An answer."

After another minute, Lucifer had the top of the coffin completely uncovered. She took the flashlight from David. "Thanks. Now up you go. This will only take a minute." Once David was out of the hole, Lucifer took a shovel and pressed the tip of the blade into the crease of the coffin's head door. She put all her weight on the shovel handle and held it there until the lid slowly opened with a cacophonous creak. She was instantly hit with the familiar smell of mold and long-rotted flesh. With a final push, Lucifer opened the lid the rest of the way and looked at the woman buried inside.

Helen Peltier had been buried over fifty years ago and was now only skin and bones. Her hair rested around her head like a nest of wires, and her faded yellow dress was so brittle that it crumbled at the slightest touch. It was impossible to tell from the state of decay, but Lucifer judged from the structure of her skull that she was beautiful in life.

"How's it going down there?" David asked, but Lucifer ignored him. She put the flashlight between her teeth and reached into her trick bag. She pulled out a silver hand mirror. The handle was made of pearl that had started to fade to a dull yellow hue while the silver around the glass of the mirror was stained with age.

Lucifer inhaled deeply then held the mirror up to her mouth, breathing on it to get it as foggy as possible. Very carefully, she placed the foggy mirror over Helen Peltier's face. "Where is Gina Pierce?" she asked. She didn't see anything happen, but she could feel the mirror gently vibrate in her hand. The vibration lasted only a few seconds, but it was long enough for Lucifer to know that she got her answer.

"Thank you," she said. "Sorry to have disturbed you." After she closed the casket lid, Lucifer held the mirror up to the flashlight. When she saw the mirror, her heart went cold. There, written on the foggy glass was only a single word:

Witchdown.

"Lucifer? Lucifer, are you okay down there? You've been awfully quiet for a while."

It took her a moment to find her voice. When she did, she said, "Let's fill it up," and crawled out of the hole.

They shoveled in near silence. David tried prodding her with questions, but Lucifer didn't speak. She couldn't. The horror of it all squeezed her chest, making it hard to breathe.

When the hole was almost refilled, Lucifer said, "Do you have any paper in your car? Napkins, anything?"

"Are you going to tell me what happened down there?"

"David!"

"Jeez, yes! Okay?"

"Sorry. Could you . . ."

"Yeah. I'll be right back." He threw more than dropped his shovel and slinked off into the darkness.

By the time he came back, Lucifer had the hole filled and was tamping the dirt down with her feet. David handed her a bundle of napkins left over from some burger dinner he had left in his car. She took one and started rolling it into a loose tube. In just a couple of minutes, she had made a respectable origami rose and placed it on Ms. Peltier's marker.

"We can go now." Lucifer turned and walked toward the car.

She got into the passenger's seat and waited for David to put the shovels in the trunk. When he slid in behind the steering wheel, he put the keys into the ignition but stopped. The two of them sat in the dark, the muffled sound of their breathing roaring in the silence.

"You're scaring me, Lucifer. Please, tell me. You said you were looking for an answer. Did you find it?"

". . . Yes."

"And?"

Lucifer hugged herself to fight the chill that would not seem to leave her. She looked up at David, at his perfect mouth and worried eyes. "I'm so sorry, David," she said. "But you're never going to see Gina again."

CHAPTER 12

"**E**xplain."

"I don't know if I can, David." Lucifer wrapped her hands around the tiny cup of tea and took a sip. The tea was bitter, but its warmth fought against the chill that had taken residence inside her. When she saw the black crescents of grave dirt caked under her fingernails, Lucifer quickly hid her hands under the table. "It's complicated."

"Try."

Before Lucifer could begin, a waitress in an apron stained with grease, eggs, and chronic disappointment glided up to their booth. "Cheeseburger and fries?" David gave the waitress a small, apathetic nod, and she set the plate down in front of him. "Anything else for you?" she asked Lucifer.

"No, just the tea is fine. Thank you."

Outside, semitrucks wandered through the parking lot, their tires hissing through the drizzle of rain that started just after Lucifer and David had left the cemetery. Slow, aimless rivulets of water slid down the windows.

"We went to the cemetery for an answer," David said. "What was it? Where Gina is?"

Lucifer nodded as she folded a corner of her napkin and used it to dig under her nails. It helped some, but dirt still filled the lines and creases of her hands like tiny cracks in a winter pond, revealing the dark water swirling underneath the snow-covered ice.

Lucifer looked up. David's normally calm and focused eyes wandered erratically across her face as if he could will the truth from her features. "So you know where she is."

"Yes." Her voice was barely audible over the grumbling conversations of truckers squatting at the counter. She cupped her hands and blew a short blast of hot breath into them, hoping it would bring a bit more feeling back to her digits. But just thinking about where Gina was made all the heat in Lucifer's body drain away.

"*And?*"

"She's in Witchdown, David. Gina is in a place called Witchdown."

David stood and pulled a wad of cash from his pocket. He tossed the money next to his untouched food and said, "Let's go."

"Go where?"

"This Witchdown place. C'mon."

"Your Romeo plan is very noble. Truly it is, but it's not that simple."

"No, Lucifer, it really is that simple. We get in the car and we go. Or am I going by myself?"

"Where, exactly?" Lucifer asked. "Just where are you going to go, David? You think you can punch 'Witchdown' into your GPS and drive there?"

"I don't know, but it's better than sitting here and doing nothing!"

Two men in canvas jackets and dirty ball caps gave David a hard stare. Lucifer flashed them a quick smile, and the two men nodded before returning their focus back on their biscuits and gravy. "David," she said. "I know you're worried about Gina, but right now all you're doing is attracting attention. Attention we don't need considering we just *committed a felony*. So please, sit back down."

David balled his hands into fists. After a moment, he slid back behind the booth. "Okay, so Gina is in a place called Witchdown. What is it? Some kind of hippie commune?"

"I promise you, it's not."

David leaned forward, the steam from his food curling up and around his face. "Then what is it? Why can't we just go there? I know, you said it's complicated. So simplify it for me. I'm new to this whole magic thing."

"Simplify. All right." Lucifer took another sip of her tea. "Seven Sisters, all of them witches, came here to the New World three, four hundred years ago to escape a very specialized group of German Inquisitors who were hunting them. The Sisters formed a small village that became known as Witchdown. But the Inquisitors found them and tried to kill them. The only way the witches could survive was to pull their entire village into another dimension called the Shade. A dimension only the dead can travel." Lucifer sat back and folded her arms across her chest. "That's about as simple as I can make it."

Outside, a pickup truck trundled through the parking lot, the hiss of rainwater under its tires dulled by the thin windows of the diner. David sat in silence, unmoving. Two days ago, he had no idea magic was real. Now he was hearing about witches and inquisitors and dimensions. Lucifer knew it was a lot to process.

"How did you learn about these things?" The way he asked the question did little to hide his skepticism.

"Stealing things."

"Oh yeah. Because you're a thief."

Lucifer scratched the imperceptible outline of the mark on her shoulder. *Among other things.*

"So it was one of these witches that took Gina," David said. "One of the Seven Sisters."

"It looks that way, yeah."

"Well, that's not that bad, is it? I know a couple of witches. Wiccans. They seem pretty harmless."

"David, we're not talking about Gaia-worshipping, peace, love, and good happiness stuff here. Your friends can call themselves whatever they want, but they aren't real witches. The Seven Sisters are. They're witches with a capital 'W.'"

"What's the difference?"

"You have to do some pretty horrific things to become a real witch."

"Like what?" he asked. "Skin a black cat?"

"If only." Lucifer didn't want to scare him further, but she didn't want to lie to him either. He needed to understand exactly what they were dealing with. "The final ritual to becoming a witch is the worst. It's . . . unthinkable. To truly become a witch, you have to make a sacrifice. A sacrifice 'born of one's own flesh.'"

"Born of one's own flesh?"

"Their own child. It's why only women can be witches. And also, thankfully, why so few women are." It was also the reason Lucifer absolutely hated it when people accused her of being one.

"Who could do such a thing?" David asked.

"Very dangerous people."

"And you're sure there's no way to get to this Witchdown. No way at all?"

Lucifer shook her head. "David, the Shade is a place of death. Life isn't tolerated there. The creatures there hate the living, and I mean *hate*. It could be jealousy, fear, resentment, I don't really know. All I do know is that only the dead can get there."

All the blood drained from David's face. "So Gina's dead," he said, his voice shallow and small. His defeated expression hit Lucifer like a knife plunged in her chest. But it wasn't seeing the gravity of David's pain and loss at losing Gina that broke her heart: it was jealousy.

Lucifer pushed the uncomfortable realization to the back of her mind. She reached across the table and grabbed his hand. Its warmth seeped into her cold, stiff fingers, feeling better than even the cup of hot tea. "No, she's not," she said. "A Sister of Witchdown wouldn't go through all the trouble of reaching into our world and kidnapping her just to kill her. Gina has much more value alive."

Lucifer became acutely aware that she was holding his hand. It was only a short stretch of imagination to picture herself sitting across from David in a quiet restaurant. The bright cacophony of the diner dissolved into the distant murmurs of a hundred pleasant dinner conversations. She could picture a single candle between them, lighting David's face with a perfect glow. She would say something benign and unimportant, and he would laugh. Soft shadows would play across his face, his perfect mouth curled in a smile. And he would whisper her name. There would be no witches. There would be no deadly dimensions and no magic save for the spell of his presence. Most of all, there would be no Gina. Only Lucifer and David, the two of them doing what Lucifer imagined two people falling in love would do.

David pulled his hand away and pressed his fingers to his temples, shattering the illusion. The diner came back in a rush. The brusque and offensive clatter returned, the golden candlelight replaced with the cold fluorescents buzzing overhead. The specter of Gina rose between them like smoke from the extinguished flame of her imaginary candle.

"Let me get this straight," David said. "Gina is alive. But she's in Witchdown. Witchdown is in the Shade. And only the dead can travel to the Shade."

"That's right."

"That doesn't make sense. If Gina's alive, how can she be in Witchdown?"

"Because . . ." Lucifer paused, unsure of what to say. If Gina was still alive, which Lucifer firmly believed she was, the denizens of the Shade would be relentless in trying to kill her. A living soul would be a beacon. Every dark thing in the Shade would seek it out like moths drawn to a flame. Which meant the Sister who took Gina would have to be protecting her. Lucifer knew the Sisters of Witchdown were powerful, but were they strong enough to keep the entire Shade at bay? That was more power than Lucifer wanted to contemplate.

But David was right. If Gina was alive and in Witchdown, then there was a way the living could survive in the Shade. And to some extent, the Sisters themselves were even proof of that, though they weren't exactly what one would call living. They had to sacrifice their own flesh to escape into the Shade. But apparently they had finally figured out how a living body could survive there. It had only taken a couple of centuries to do it.

"Lucifer?"

"You're right, David. Gina's alive and in Witchdown. Which means there has to be a way to get to her. I just have no idea what it is."

"But there has to be someone who does, right? You know this world, Lucifer. Is there anyone out there who would know how a living person can go to the Shade?"

The answer to his question coiled around her chest like a black tentacle and squeezed the air from her lungs. "There is." The words came out in a whisper.

Lucifer drank the rest of her tea in a single swallow. "I'll be back. I have to use the restroom." Ignoring David's protests, Lucifer got up from the booth and made her way to ladies' room on the far side of the diner.

Inside, she locked the door and slumped to the floor. Rings of toilet paper lay curled on the floor like the ancient skins of some beast who shed them in a mad dash to flee the stench that had invaded its lair. Lucifer clasped her hands together to stop them from shaking. Gorge rose in her throat when she saw the dirt still caked under nails.

She stood, went to the sink and emptied the small dispenser of soap into her hands. Lucifer scrubbed until her fingers were as raw and pink as the acrid soap she was using. She hated disturbing Helen Peltier's eternal rest. But as much as she hated doing it, she hated what she was about to do even more.

The mark on her shoulder seemed to pull at her, weighing her down. Part of her wanted to smash the mirror above the sink and use the broken glass to flay the mark from her body. But there was no point. She'd known this day would come sooner or later.

Lucifer stared at her reflection through the mildew-stained glass.

More than anything she wished she saw someone else looking back at her. That her only concern was brushing her disheveled hair or fixing her makeup.

But most of all, she wished she could look at a mirror and see only painted glass.

By the time Lucifer got back to David, the waitress had already cleared the table. "Let's go," Lucifer said.

"You going to tell me where we're going next?" David asked.

Lucifer wasn't ready to have this conversation. She knew he would insist on going with her, and there was absolutely no way she would ever allow that to happen. No matter how much she wanted to be near him.

"You're taking me home."

"You said you know someone who can tell us how to get to Witchdown. So let's go talk to him and go get Gina back."

Lucifer put her hand on David's arm, giving it a gentle squeeze. "David, I know you're scared for her. I am, too. But in the past forty-eight hours I've eaten a can of pepper spray, dug up some poor woman's grave, pulled a filcher demon out of a girl who wouldn't spit on me if I was on fire, and had to go to a shopping mall. I'm exhausted. Take me home so I can get some rest and then we can talk in the morning. Please."

David nodded. "Sorry, I just . . ."

"I know. It's okay. C'mon. It's getting late."

They hardly spoke during the drive back to Lucifer's apartment. Instead, they listened to the constant pattering of rain against the windshield. When they finally arrived, Lucifer hesitated a moment, though she wasn't sure why. Was it because she was afraid of what she was about to do? Or did she want to enjoy the illicit thrill of being alone with a boy in a car for just a little longer?

David reached into the backseat for something before getting out of the car. Confused, Lucifer sat still until David came around and opened the door for her. He held an umbrella above his head with one hand and extended the other toward her. Lucifer took his hand and let him escort her to the front door of her apartment complex.

"Thank you," she said, watching steam rise from David's damp shirt in thin, white wisps. His body heat blazed next to her like a furnace.

"You'll call me tomorrow?" David asked.

"As soon as I wake up. Promise."

"You better." David smiled. He waited until she was inside the building before he gave her one final wave and returned to his car.

Lucifer rubbed her hands together as she made her way upstairs. Once inside her apartment, she removed her dirty, wet clothes and tossed them into a pile against her bedroom wall. She stepped into the shower, hoping there was still some hot water left. There wasn't much, but there was enough to take away the constant chill Lucifer had been fighting since the cemetery.

She rested her head against the wall and watched the filthy water drain away at her feet. Exhaustion overwhelmed her. She hadn't lied to David. She really did need sleep, but she needed an answer more. And there was only one person who could give it to her.

When Lucifer had finished soaking up about as much heat as the shower could give her, she dressed in dry clothes and combed the tangles from her hair. She ignored the siren call of her bed and turned to the sheet-covered object on the far side of the room.

She grabbed the sheet and yanked it away, revealing the ancient mirror hidden underneath. It was full-length and quite large enough for Lucifer to see her entire reflection from just a few feet away. She ran her hand over the various symbols and glyphs etched deep into the edges of the ancient wooden frame, feeling their familiar shapes beneath her fingertips. She stopped when she found the one that matched the mark on her shoulder. Lucifer took a deep breath before tracing the symbol with her index finger.

Lucifer heard a sound like the faint spasm of breaking ice at the upper limits of human perception. The glass vibrated, and the reflection rippled like waves in a pond. The waves rolled back on themselves and multiplied, growing smaller and finer until the entire surface was a kaleidoscope of color.

Lucifer stared at her reflection, broken into a thousand pieces. She reached out toward the glass and watched her hand disappear beneath its shimmering surface. Impossible cold bit into her skin, causing the breath to catch in her throat. She wanted nothing more than to turn around and crawl into her warm, inviting bed, but there was no point in delaying any further. The longer she put this off, the less likely she would be able to help Gina.

Lucifer gritted her teeth as she stepped through the mirror and into the Aether.

CHAPTER 13

L ucifer felt a slight shift in gravity. It pulled at her from off-center, as if the world she had stepped into was somehow crooked, off-balance. The effect was subtle, almost imperceptible. Up was still up and down was still down, but her inner ear struggled to compensate for the tilt, no matter how small it might be.

A wave of a nausea rolled through her. Lucifer grabbed the edge of the mirror to balance herself and waited for it to pass. Her lack of sleep wasn't helping with the queasiness either, but after several deep breaths, her stomach settled.

Lucifer took a moment to get her bearings. She was in a vast room filled with a variety of standing mirrors. There were dozens of them, perhaps hundreds. Most were ancient. Their glass was filmed by age and neglect while only a handful appeared freshly polished. The strange shadow sun of the Aether broke through the vaulted windows high above, its light reflecting off the mirrors in harsh, bright spikes. A grand chandelier of twisted iron and heavy chains hovered directly overhead, its candles melted into useless stalactites long ago.

Below her, a faded burgundy carpet stretched all the way to the bare marble walls. The smell of cedar hung in the air, its sweet scent masking the heavy stench of ash and scorched decay hiding underneath: a lingering remnant of the war that was waged outside these walls.

It was impossible to know just how large the structure was. How many rooms did it have? How many floors? Each time Lucifer came here it seemed different than the time before. Sometimes larger, sometimes smaller, but always reflecting the particular mood of its sole occupant.

Lucifer stepped through a small archway on the far side of the room and into a well-lit sitting room. The walls were covered with dozens of picture frames, all varying sizes and each one completely empty. Their arrangement was haphazard, as if the person who hung them had no sense of right angles. She reached out and straightened one. The paint of the frame was faded beyond any recognizable color, and it flaked away at her touch. When she stood back to admire her handiwork, she noticed that it only served to bring more attention to how crooked the other frames were. It was as if straightening one frame only made the others more skewed.

"There you are!"

Lucifer turned. A well-dressed man with a perfectly manicured three-day beard stood behind her, his hands on his hips. He made a show of looking her up and down, clearly unimpressed by what he saw. He said, "I've been wandering around here for hours looking for you. What kind of a place is this?"

Lucifer didn't move. She only stared at the man.

"You've heard the expression 'Time is money'?," he asked. "Well, mine is worth more than anyone else's. It's bad enough it took six months to figure out how to even get here, the least you could do is make yourself available when a client arrives. Now, let me tell you what I need and what I'm prepared to offer. First . . ."

Lucifer started to protest, but the man talked right over her. He droned on about portfolios and board meetings and hidden accounts. He stopped occasionally to ask if Lucifer followed what he was saying. She didn't, but it didn't matter because the man didn't bother to wait for her to answer. He just continued on, oblivious to Lucifer's disinterested scowls . . .

And to the creature that was emerging from the shadows behind him.

It was the Keeper of Secrets. She drifted out of the corner of the room, every stride as silent as a ghost's breath. The shadows parted around her like black water breaking before the bow of an impossible ship until she came to rest directly behind the man.

The Keeper of Secrets was easily seven feet tall, though the wild waves of ebony hair that swirled around her head made her closer to eight. Lucifer might almost say she was beautiful. Even hauntingly so. She was somehow disheveled yet tidy at the same time. Like Chaos made presentable. The gray, slightly greenish hue to her ageless skin and the violet flecks that swirled in her eyes hinted at the otherworldly power she possessed. But there was one thing even beyond her wicked beauty that was unmistakably clear: the Keeper of Secrets was utterly, completely, and categorically insane.

The man was unaware of the figure towering over him. "So, what I want," he said, "is the name of his top three investors and access to their shell company. And I'll cut you in for three percent after the merger. You'd be stupid not to take this deal." When Lucifer didn't respond, he continued. "You're the Keeper of Secrets. You know everything, right? So you know three percent is too good to pass up. But the longer you make me wait, the lower that number is going to go."

Lucifer was going to say that his particular brand of confidence was about to get him tossed into a well, but before she could speak, the Keeper of Secrets held up a slender finger to her lips, bidding silence. Lucifer felt gravity shift again when she saw the malevolent joy dancing in the woman's eyes.

"Hey," the man said, snapping his fingers in Lucifer's face. "I asked you a question. Are you going to say something or just scowl at me all day?"

The Keeper of Secrets placed her elegant hand on his shoulder then bent down and whispered in his ear. "She isn't scowling at *you*, darling," Her voice was soft, but a tremendous weight coiled beneath it, ready to strike.

When the man turned and saw her, all the color drained from his face. "I . . . I thought she was the Keeper of Secrets," he said, pointing at Lucifer with a shaky finger.

"Oh, no, darling. At least, not yet."

"Uh, not *ever*."

"Wait your turn, Lucifer." She straightened herself and smiled down at the man. "Hello, Karl. I am the Keeper of Secrets, but most people simply call me the Harlot. I'm so sorry to have kept you waiting. Follow me. I've prepared some tea." Without another word, the Harlot turned and walked away, the deep folds of her black dress billowing in a breeze only it could feel.

The man, Karl, stood unmoving as Lucifer stepped past him. She followed the Harlot to the far side of the sitting room where a tea set waited on a warped mahogany coffee table. The Harlot motioned to a faded red couch as she took her place in a high-backed velvet chair.

"He might be a while. You take some time getting used to," Lucifer said.

"He'll find his courage soon enough." The Harlot smiled as she picked up the teapot and began to pour. "And I'm sorry about your shoes."

"My shoes?"

At that moment, Karl came in. He stood next to Lucifer but didn't sit. "I don't like being made to wait." He looked down and scowled at Lucifer. "Or being made a fool of."

"You also don't like deep water, snails, or people with differing opinions," the Harlot said. "And no one likes being made a fool of, darling. You aren't special in that regard." She blew across her cup, cooling her tea. "Or in any other, if I must be honest."

"Excuse me? I cut million-dollar deals before this one even gets out of bed in the morning," he said, thumbing toward Lucifer.

"I doubt that," said Lucifer. "I don't sleep much."

"If I wanted comments from the slacker generation, I'd start a YouTube channel. Who the hell are you, anyway?"

The Harlot put the cup down and waved toward Lucifer. "How rude of me. Karl, may I introduce Lucifer. My heir."

"Lucifer? You're the devil?"

Lucifer leveled her best sneer at the Harlot. "You just *love* doing that, don't you?"

"Lucifer is a thief, not a devil. And she is rather proud of her name. It's a celebration of the two women who gave their lives to save hers." Then the Harlot leveled a sneer of her own. "What a shame she doesn't extend that courtesy to all the women who have saved her life."

Lucifer scratched at the mark on her shoulder and frowned.

"I don't care about her," Karl said. "I want to know if we're in business. My offer is three percent."

"Three percent!" The Harlot put her hand to her chest in a show of feigned delight. "Oh, Karl. You are confused about the nature of the services I provide. I sell secrets, but you do not dictate the price of those secrets. I do."

"Now hold on just a minute, harlot, whore, whatever you are—"

The Harlot was out of the chair faster than Lucifer's eyes could follow. She had knocked the coffee table aside and had Karl by the throat so quickly that the teapot had already shattered on the floor before Lucifer could put her arms up to protect herself.

"Lucifer is not the only one who is sensitive about her name," she said as Karl ineffectually clawed at her wrist, trying to free himself. "I am not a harlot. I am *the* Harlot. And if you refer to me as a whore again, I will sew your face into a coin purse." She leaned in, her nose almost touching his. "While you watch."

The Harlot tossed Karl to the ground like a discarded tissue. He landed with a heavy splat, right in the middle of the spreading puddle of water soaking into the carpet. Steam rose around him as he rubbed his throat and gasped for air.

Lucifer herself had been on the business end of the Harlot's wrath before and couldn't help but feel an odd twinge of sympathy for Karl. But she also knew that if the Harlot followed through on her threat, Karl was getting off easy. The Keeper of Secrets was quite capable of doing worse than creative haberdashery. Much, much worse.

"Your overbearing machismo has grown tiresome, Karl. So let us conduct our *business* and be done."

Karl stood, his clothes dripping. When he spoke, his fragile voice was barely more than a whisper. "How much?"

"This is a day of sad educations for you, Karl. You discover that your time has no more value than the time of others, that the only person impressed by your boardroom antics is yourself, and, what I'm sure will come as a rather confusing surprise to a parasitic leech such as yourself, that I have absolutely no use for money. I daresay, you are in a rather weak negotiating position."

Karl swallowed, grimacing in pain. "If you don't want money, then what do you want?"

The Harlot settled back into her chair, the black fog of her dress billowing over the arms in graceful waves. "I want your fondest childhood memory," she said.

"I don't understand. You want me to tell you what my favorite memory is?"

"No. Not tell me. *Give* me. Offer it to me as payment for the secrets you wish to know, and I will pluck it from your mind. But understand, Karl. It will never come back to you. It will cease to exist. Even if you were to write it down, it would be as if you were reading someone else's words. They will have no meaning for you. That memory will be lost. Forever."

Lucifer watched Karl's face twist in confusion, but she understood perfectly well. The Keeper of Secrets didn't want money. She wanted things that were precious to you. Sometimes it was as simple as a family heirloom. Other times she wanted your kidney or the last five minutes of your life. Whatever it was that she wanted, no matter how mundane, it was something you were going to miss. Whether you realized it or not.

"So, that's it? You'll tell me the secrets I want to know, and all I have to give you is my favorite memory?"

"Your favorite *childhood* memory, darling. You can keep that debaucherous evening in Lisbon."

Karl straightened himself and extended his hand. "You have a deal."

The Harlot rose from her chair and glided forward. She stared at his hand for a moment before speaking. "There is no going back, Karl. Are you sure this is what you want?" She asked with absolutely no malice in her voice.

"I can make new memories."

"Very well." But instead of shaking Karl's hand, the Harlot quickly wrapped her arms around him and kissed him. He struggled uselessly against her grip. The fabric of her dress danced around them, circling them in slow, undulating waves. Her wild hair snaked forward and inched across his face like the roots of a dying tree desperately searching for water. Karl couldn't move. Only his wide, unblinking eyes indicated that he was aware, alive.

The Harlot held him there, savoring the embrace until Karl's eyes began to flutter and close. Slowly, her hair fell back into the chaotic curls around her own head, and her dress succumbed once again to its peculiar laws of gravity. She lowered him to the ground and stepped away once he was able to stand on his own.

Karl shook his head and blinked his eyes. "What did you do to me?"

The Harlot smiled. "What I told you I was going to do. I took your favorite childhood memory." The Harlot swooned. "And oh, what a delicious memory it is!"

Karl slapped his face a couple of times like he was trying to keep himself awake. "All right, so you got what you want. My turn."

The Harlot walked toward a nearby fireplace that Lucifer couldn't remember being there, let alone having a fire burning inside. She pulled a yellowed parchment from the mantel and tossed it into the fire. Green flame immediately erupted from the parchment as it caught fire. Before it could be completely consumed, the Harlot pulled the parchment from the fire and extinguished the flame with a quick puff of air.

"Here," she said, handing the scorched paper to Karl. "I believe this will satisfy your curiosity."

As Karl studied the blackened images on the page, his eyes widened. "This is . . . thank you, Harlot. Thank you." Karl kept mumbling "thank you" over and over again as he stared at the paper, meandering his way back toward the hall of mirrors.

Once he was gone, Lucifer asked, "Well?"

"Well, what, darling?"

"What was the memory?"

The Harlot took Lucifer's arm and guided her down an adjacent hallway. "It was the one and only moment in his life when his father told him he was proud of him."

"Oh," Lucifer said. "That actually makes me kind of sad for him."

"Don't be. He was fifteen years old and had just beaten up a younger boy for having the misfortune of wearing pink to school. Neither Karl nor his father are terribly likable human beings."

"And now Karl's going to be a rich, unlikeable human being."

"Richer, actually. But his newfound fortune won't last long. Men like Karl are saddled with insecurity. They're always trying to live up to some cartoonish idea of masculinity in order to impress the people around them. Especially their fathers. But without this memory to temper that desire, his greed will run unchecked. By month's end, he will be ruined and throw himself out of an office window."

The Harlot looked down at Lucifer and gave her arm an affectionate pat. "Just like you're going to do."

CHAPTER 14

"**I**'m not going to kill myself!"

The Harlot looked down at Lucifer while escorting her past dozens of inhuman trophy skulls mounted to the walls. "Yes, Lucifer, you are," she said, more as a command than a basic statement of fact. "But that wasn't what I was referring to."

"Okay, don't do that," Lucifer said.

"Do what, darling?"

"You know damn well what!" Lucifer pulled her arm free. "Don't pull that fortune-teller crap with me! I hate when you do that. Things don't always happen the way you say they will."

"I didn't mean to upset you. But I will not insult you by lying. You *will* toss yourself from a building window. You *will* kill yourself. Your coming here has all but ensured it."

Lucifer imagined her own skull on the wall next to the others. Would the Harlot ever stop to admire it, or would it become just another forgotten decoration? "You would never let that happen," Lucifer said, more in an attempt to convince herself than the Harlot.

"You are my heir," the Harlot said with finality. "Not even death will free you from that obligation."

The Harlot led Lucifer through a vaulted archway adorned with intricate sculptures of fairies and imps carved into the ancient wood. The faeries rose along the left side of the arch while the imps clawed their way up the right until they clashed at the top of the arch in a writhing mass of twisted claws and paper-thin wings.

Past the archway was a cavernous dark that seemed to grow deeper the harder Lucifer tried to peer into it. It was impossible to see anything beyond just a few feet in front of her, but Lucifer could feel the vastness beyond, as if she were standing on the edge of a cliff on a moonless night. The Harlot pulled on a golden rope hanging down a nearby wall. Curtains the size of swimming pools parted to reveal a massive window that filled the room with the Aether's golden light.

They were in the Library of Secrets. Bookshelves hundreds of feet high stretched out into the darkness beyond what the light could penetrate. Several winged creatures dropped from their perch atop one of the great shelves and glided deeper into the dark recesses of the library.

The Harlot moved toward a wide circle of wooden pedestals in the center of a large reading area. Each pedestal displayed an open book of varying size, all bound in ancient leather, which, thankfully, wasn't human as far as Lucifer could tell. The biggest book was the size of a car door and bound with brass rivets, while the smallest could have fit in the palm of Lucifer's hand.

"You've been busy," the Harlot said, casually paging through one of the more reasonably sized volumes.

"Yeah, well, I'm trying to save a girl's life."

"I was speaking of that, darling," the Harlot said, pointing to the floor.

Lucifer looked down and saw what the Harlot was referring to. In the center of the circle, a series of inlaid tiles several shades darker than the surrounding marble floor formed a huge symbol that was almost impossible to make out. But Lucifer didn't need to climb to a higher vantage point to know what it was. It was the same symbol tattooed on her shoulder: the strange lowercase "h."

Lucifer scratched her shoulder. "Don't worry. No one knows how to remove it."

"Because it *can't* be removed. Did you honestly think, after all I went through to mark you as my heir, that I would allow it to be so easily undone?"

"I'll find a way to get rid of it." Lucifer didn't try to hide the venom in her voice. "Someday, I'll get rid of this tattoo and be done with you."

"No, Lucifer. You won't."

The Harlot turned and stared out the window. Beyond the soiled glass, the blasted wasteland of the Aether rolled out to the misshapen horizon. Wilted trees rose from the blackened soil, their branches splintered and twisted at unnatural angles. The red and orange hues smeared across the sky were clotted with gray and yellow clouds that hovered like bad moods waiting to vomit their anger onto the parched earth below.

"You once stood on the shores of the Abyss amidst the slaughter of deities and demigods," the Harlot said. "Yet you survived. Becoming my heir was a condition of that survival."

"Okay, two things," Lucifer spat. "First, I was in the middle of that mess because you put me there. You orchestrated the whole damn thing just so you could mark me, so don't make it sound like you did me a favor. And second, that was a condition I never agreed to. I never wanted to be your heir. I'd rather be eaten by rabid badgers than spend eternity here, going insane from all the secrets bouncing around inside my head. But you forced it on me. And now my life is one giant carnival of magic-covered suck." Lucifer gave the Harlot a thumbs-up. "Thanks for that."

"Are you quite finished?" the Harlot asked. "If I hadn't marked you as my heir, you would be dead. Or worse. So, you're welcome for that." The Harlot gently held Lucifer's chin in her fingers. "You are a gifted young woman, and it would have been a waste to simply let you die, your potential unfulfilled."

"So now I'm the 'chosen one.' Hurray for me."

The Harlot laughed. "Darling, you were the one foolish enough to steal from me. Had you not made me aware of your existence, you would have died in that favela and I would have found another to be my heir. You chose yourself."

"Is that really true?"

"More or less."

"Well, don't hold your breath waiting for a thank you. On second thought, go ahead. Hold your breath. Hold it as hard and as long as you can."

The Harlot turned back to the book, ignoring the insult.

Lucifer said, "So what you're saying is that if I hadn't robbed you, I wouldn't have this stupid 'h' on my back."

The Harlot turned and gave Lucifer an incredulous stare. "You are marked heir to the Keeper of Secrets. A station that predates English script by several thousand years. Why would you possibly think the symbol is an 'h'?"

"You know . . . for 'Harlot' or whatever."

The Harlot shook her head and turned back to the book.

"Why do they call you the Harlot, anyway?" Lucifer asked. "Or would that cost me my happiest childhood memory?"

"You have no happy childhood memories."

"If you don't want to tell me, fine. But you don't have to be a dick about it."

"Is that really the secret you came here to learn?" the Harlot asked.

"Of course not." Lucifer stood next to the Harlot to look at the book on the pedestal she was leafing through. The pages were completely blank. "I have to get to Witchdown," she said. "A girl, Gina, is there and I have to save her."

The Harlot produced a large quill from her sleeve and began to write in the book, her scratchings a collection of jagged lines that somehow formed words. "Why do you want to save this girl?"

"Uh, she was kidnapped by a witch. And I could be wrong, but I don't think it was just so the witch could have someone show her how to update her iPhone."

"But why you? Why are you so focused on saving this girl?" the Harlot asked.

"Her dad hired me. I'm getting paid."

"You are a skilled thief worth ten times your weight in gold. You don't need money. So I will ask again. Why?"

For a moment, Lucifer didn't speak. The only sound in the great library was the Harlot's quill scratching across the paper and its echoes disappearing in the dark.

"Her dad, Buck," Lucifer finally said. "You should have seen him, Harlot. Such a proud, powerful man. But he was broken. Desperate. When his daughter was taken, he was *destroyed*. Gina must be somebody special."

Lucifer looked up from her thoughts when she noticed the Harlot had stopped writing. The Harlot was staring off into the dark, her voice barely more than a whisper. "All daughters are special," the Harlot said.

"Not everyone thinks so," Lucifer said.

The Harlot turned, pulled from her reverie and said, "No. Not everyone does." She turned and brushed a strand of hair away from Lucifer's eyes and said, "But everyone should."

Lucifer wanted to push the Harlot away but just stood there instead.

"So you wish to get to the fabled town of Witchdown," the Harlot said, turning back to her book. "Witchdown is in the Shade."

"I know."

"Yes, you do. Thanks to poor Helen Peltier. I'm sure she didn't mind being woken from her eternal slumber and forced to crawl back into her corpse just to satisfy your curiosity."

"Please, don't, Harlot. I feel bad enough as it is."

The Harlot closed the book and hid the quill inside her sleeve again. "Good. Mrs. Peltier was a kind and gentle woman who sought to make the world a better place. You shouldn't have disturbed her with your petty resurrections. You should have come to me instead."

"And how much would that have cost me? Huh? Seriously, you'd think that being your heir would at least get me a discount!"

"Contrary to what you might think, I help you as much as I'm allowed."

"So you'll tell me how to get to the Shade?"

"That is a secret I cannot share for free. I'm sorry, Lucifer."

"But there's a way. You're telling me there's a way."

"There is, but only for those rare individuals born with the gift of magic. And even then, it is a deadly proposition. It's only been attempted a few times before and successful even fewer. Most recently, a sorceress of incredible power was able to travel there, though only for the briefest of moments and not without suffering . . . consequences."

"Will she help me?"

"If she were able, I believe that she would. But she is consumed with helping her nephew at the moment. That poor boy has even worse luck than you, darling."

"I find that hard to believe," Lucifer said. "But what about me? I'm a thief, not a sorceress. How can I get there?"

The Harlot shook her head. "The price for that secret is more than you would be willing to pay."

"Try me," Lucifer said.

"Emotions." The Harlot spat the word as if it were sour in her mouth. "If you wish to know the secret of traveling to Witchdown, you will give me your emotions. *All* of your emotions. You will give me your capacity for love, hate, sadness, joy, empathy, sympathy, pathos of every stripe. I will turn you into a husk devoid of any and all feelings. A homunculus incapable of experiencing anything endemic to the human condition. *That* is the price of this secret."

Lucifer scratched her head. "Okay, is that just a fancy way of saying I'd never be happy again?"

"No, darling. It is a very plain way of saying you would never even know if you were. Do we have a deal?"

"Of course not." There was a part of Lucifer that liked the idea of not feeling anything. A life without experiencing sadness or regret would be wonderful indeed. But no joy? No happiness? She couldn't agree to that, no matter how rare those moments were.

Lucifer had hoped that being the Harlot's heir might have some benefit when it came to learning secrets, but she should have known better. Hope was not a plan. "Then is there anything you can tell me? Anything at all? I have no idea how much time Gina has, or if she's even still alive."

The Harlot took a deep breath and placed her hand on the closed book. "I cannot tell you how to travel to the Shade without exacting a price. There's nothing to be done for that. What I can tell you is that there are others who may know."

"Others?"

"The Shade is a realm of death, yet Witchdown is an oasis in that desert of life. An oasis created by witches."

"Yeah, I already know that."

"Then why do you insist on playing the dimwitted child when the solution is obvious? If you seek secrets from the province of witches, ask a witch."

"But you're the only witch I know—" Lucifer snapped her mouth shut. She wished she could take the words back, but it was too late. She herself hated being called a witch because she knew very well the horror one had to embrace to become one. And though there was no doubt that the Harlot was a monster, she wasn't *that* kind of monster. At least, as far as Lucifer knew.

The Harlot faced her without turning around. She seemed to fold in on herself until she was looking directly at Lucifer, wisps of shadows bleeding off of her like black steam. The swirling darkness of her eyes stilled and swallowed the light around her.

"Harlot, I'm sorry, I just meant—"

"*SILENCE!*" The Harlot's incredible shout hit Lucifer like a wave from a blast furnace. The sound echoed through the library, kicking dust from the ancient shelves and creating a bilious fog that rolled into the dark beyond. "I. Am not. A *witch*," the Harlot said, her voice filling Lucifer's ears with a dull ache. "You wish to know the benefits of being my heir? Here. Allow me to introduce you to the last man to have insulted me so."

The Harlot grabbed the book she had been writing in and tossed it at Lucifer's feet. When Lucifer was finally able to look away from the Harlot's terrible gaze and at the book, she noticed that she had been wrong earlier. This one *was* bound in human skin.

"If you can't hold your tongue, I will hold it for you." The Keeper of Secrets stepped forward, the delicate sound of her footsteps whispering like distant thunder. "The Seven Sisters of Witchdown were vile, monstrous creatures powerful enough to find refuge in the Shade. If you want me to tell you how, you know my price. If you will not pay, then ask someone else. Now if you will excuse me, I currently find your presence distasteful and wish to be elsewhere." The Harlot breezed past her, the smell of cedar and ash clouding Lucifer's senses as she passed.

Before the Harlot disappeared under the great arch, Lucifer said, "I don't care if you can see the future, Harlot. Or how many secrets you know. Because, I can promise you. I'm not going to kill myself."

The Harlot stopped. Without looking back she said, "For Gina's sake, I hope you're wrong."

CHAPTER 15

L   ucifer   mirror and into the dark of her apart-
        ment   light from the flickering streetlamp
that illuminat   hrough the spaces between the window
blinds, leavin   kly light across the wall on the far side
of her bedro   ed a crumpled sheet from the floor and
tossed it ove   rror before collapsing on the mattress in
the corner o

   Sleep p   pale hands clawing from the depths of a
dark sea. L   re than anything to let it drag her under,
but she wa   h adrenaline from her encounter with the
Harlot. S   r that she was going to kill herself. That
she would   a window just like that man, Karl. The
horrible   self around inside her head like an impossible pu   ts pieces together. She didn't care that the
Harlot   of time and knew how events would come
to pass.   cidal. It wasn't going to happen.

   Lucifer   blanket over her head to shield her eyes
from the light leaking through the blinds. She hoped the darkness
would calm her mind, but it only seemed to focus her thoughts. She
always felt a powerful mix of rage and sadness whenever she spoke
with the Harlot. It was hard not to feel sorry for a woman who was
driven insane by the constant rush of information being magically
forced into her brain. But that woman had also condemned Lucifer
to the same fate by choosing her as her heir. The Keeper of Secrets
had manipulated the events of Lucifer's life to her liking, moving
and positioning outcomes to her will until Lucifer was caught in her
intricate web. Lucifer was given absolutely no choice in the matter.
And for that, she hated her.

She knew she should be poring through her books and her copious notes to find the information she needed, but Lucifer was simply too tired to move. When sleep finally came, it was full of nightmares. They were nothing new to Lucifer. In fact, she couldn't even remember a night she didn't have them. Most of her bad dreams just left her unrested and cranky the following morning, but a few had been so bad that she had woken up to find herself scribbling protective runes on the wall.

In this dream, Lucifer was back in the Aether with the Harlot, watching the Keeper of Secrets sit in her chair and sip her tea with a long, elegant hand. She was entertaining a client. Only instead of some lonely old man looking for lottery numbers, it was David. He calmly sat across from the Harlot, his letterman's jacket looking anachronistic against the neglected Victorian decor of the Harlot's sitting room. Lucifer tried to call to him, to tell him to get as far from her as he could, but her voice was nothing more than a whisper. When she tried to move, the floor fell away and she was falling through the orange hellscape of the Aether's sky. Karl was next to her, shouting obscenities over the roar of wind rushing past them. As they fell, Karl's angry face pulled and twisted against itself until it was David falling next to her, his perfect mouth tilted in that half-smile that made her knees go weak. David reached out and took her hand, but just as he started pulling her close, Lucifer looked down to see the blasted ground rushing up to meet them. She looked back up to David to warn him, but David's expression was blank, almost as if he suddenly didn't recognize her. He pulled his hand away, and Lucifer fell past him. She tumbled away, faster and farther while David hovered above her, calmly watching, getting smaller and smaller until he was nothing more than an indifferent dot in the ruined sky. She called out his name but was brought short when she slammed into the ground.

Lucifer woke with a start. She was sitting upright on her mattress and shivering. Her fingers ached where they were clutching at her sweat-soaked sheets. The harsh light from the lampposts had been replaced by the warm glow of the morning sun.

She made her way to her tiny kitchenette and concocted a poor facsimile of a cup of tea before getting to work. She scooped an arm full of books from a corner shelf and spread them out on the floor, each open to their table of contents. If she wanted to know how to get to the Shade, she needed to ask a witch. But before she could do that, she had to find one. And witches had never been terribly fond of advertising their presence. They much prefer their anonymity, which is why asking one for mystical directions was a great way to get your-self killed. Or worse.

But Lucifer would have to worry about that later. Right now she simply had to find one, and that wasn't going to be easy. There weren't very many witches to begin with, and the few there were were generally hermetic. They often went to great magical means to hide themselves from the world. Though there were ways to expose them, they tended to make them infinitely more unpleasant.

Three cups of tea later, Lucifer found what she was looking for. A witch by the name of Minnie Hester had come to prominence during the Great Depression. She was a huckster who took advantage of everyone's hard luck by posing as a fortune teller. That wasn't ter-ribly uncommon since most witches thrived on others' misfortunes. Mostly she just took what little money they had and then told them what they wanted to hear. A typical grift of the time, but she also used her sessions as a way to learn who was thinking of leaving town for greener pastures. When those people suddenly vanished from town, no one ever thought twice about it.

It wasn't until the great hurricane of '36 when the flooding unearthed the ritually mutilated bodies of all those people buried under her home that she became suspect. But no one had seen her since that horrific storm. She was presumed killed by the hurricane, though several locals swore they saw her standing on the rocks just

MICHAEL ALAN NELSON   123

offshore, naked, howling into the tempest that wiped their poor town of Cape Vale from the map.

The town wasn't too far away. Only a few hours by car. Lucifer felt both relieved and a bit disconcerted. She wouldn't have to travel out of the country to find a witch, but only because one lived nearby. And there was no guarantee Minnie Hester was even still there. It was true that witches had unnaturally long lives, but it was quite possible that Minnie was swept up in the waves along with the rest of Cape Vale. But at least it was a place to start.

Now all she needed was a plan. Because if she was going to ask Minnie how to get to Witchdown, Lucifer was going to need a plan if she wanted to survive the experience.

Lucifer pulled her phone from her trick bag and typed a quick text message to David.

Got a lead. Pick me up in 1 hr. Wear something nice.

She took a quick shower and then picked out her wardrobe. Lucifer much preferred wearing neutral colors that allowed her to blend in and go unnoticed: grays, greens, browns, and the occasional blacks. Unless you were on a night gig, wearing all black often made you as conspicuous as a dog walking on its hind legs. For the first part of her plan, Lucifer was going to need something a bit more typical for a girl her age. She ultimately decided on a pair of capri pants and a bright-orange blouse adorned with a pattern of yellow flowers. The clothes made her feel awkward, exposed, like she was wearing a giant neon sign that said, "Over here! Look at me!" But that was also the point.

Lucifer grabbed a couple of hair bands and pulled her hair into pigtails before slinging her trick bag over her shoulder and rushing downstairs. David was already waiting for her, patiently leaning against his car. David was wearing chinos and a madras button-up shirt that made his eyes shine like winter ice in morning sunlight.

"Lucifer, is that you?" David asked. "I almost didn't recognize you. You look so . . ."

"Ridiculous?"

"I was going to say 'cute.'" His hypnotic smile spread across his face but then dissolved into an embarrassed frown. "I mean, not that you weren't cute before, but, uh . . . I just . . . uh . . ." He trailed off, pinched the bridge of his nose and sighed before saying, "You look very nice, Lucifer."

"Thank you," Lucifer said, becoming suddenly aware that she was blushing.

"You said to wear something nice. I hope this is okay," he said, gesturing at his outfit.

Lucifer forced herself to focus on the task at hand and ignore the way his forearms peeked out from beneath his rolled shirt cuffs and the line of his collar bones visible under the light fabric. "It'll do," she said.

David opened the passenger door, and she got inside. When he slipped behind the wheel, he asked her, "So, you've got a lead on how to get to Witchdown?"

"I do."

"Okay. So then where are we going?"

Lucifer self-consciously twirled one of her pigtails around her finger. "On a date."

CHAPTER 16

They arrived at the Brisendine Art Gallery just before opening. The day was shaping up to be unseasonably warm, and the only evidence of the rain from the evening before were a few dark puddles still clinging to life in the shadows. The grounds of the gallery were impeccably designed. Greenery spiraled up the walls of the building in perfectly symmetrical columns, while the stone walkways meandered among odd sculptures of angled steel and flowered butterfly sanctuaries.

Lucifer and David sat on a small bench across from a water fountain. The water shot out of the base in thick lines that arced over a pool where a handful of sparrows splashed about in the shallow water. But Lucifer wasn't paying attention to the chaotic dance of the birds or the pristine beauty surrounding her. She was at work, and she had her eye on different things.

However, David was making it very difficult for her to concentrate.

His presence was really becoming a distraction, but it was a distraction Lucifer found herself wanting more and more. She could be herself around him. Yes, he was handsome and intelligent, but it was the way he was around her that she found so intoxicating. David knew she was a thief, he knew she moved in a world of magic, and most importantly he didn't flinch or scowl every time he said her name. When she was near him, she felt normal. He made her forget all about the Harlot and the horrible mark on her shoulder.

David said, "Gina and I came here once."

Lucifer's stomach twisted.

"It was our second date, I think. We didn't stay very long, though, since my buddy Crix was having a pool party the same day." He turned to Lucifer and smiled. "I'm looking forward to actually seeing some of the art this time."

Lucifer ignored the roiling inside her and said, "Are you an art fan?"

"Not really. I wrote a pretty in-depth paper on the Impressionists for an AP class, but I did it more for the college credit than any passion for art. What about you?"

"I love art. But I have absolutely no idea who any of the artists are or why one piece is better than another. I just like looking at pretty things."

"So do I," David said.

Lucifer wasn't sure if it was the way her hair was pulled up into pigtails or the way David was looking at her that made her blush. She would have given anything to be wearing her hoodie at the moment.

"So, what exactly are we doing here?" David asked.

"Working."

"Working," David said, nodding his head. "'Cause it feels a lot like sitting."

"Patience isn't a strong suit of yours, is it?"

He grimaced. "Sorry, it's just that I'm supposed to be helping save my girlfriend's life and instead I'm here on a date."

"David, by helping me you're helping her," Lucifer said. "And this *isn't* a date. It's only supposed to look like a date. You're my beard."

"Excuse me?"

"My beard. You know, like a costume."

"I know what 'beard' means." David bit his lip, suppressing a chuckle. "What if I want to be a sexy mustache instead?"

"Oooo, gross."

"Hey, my dad has a mustache."

"Then I feel sorry for your mom."

David frowned. "Yeah, I do too. It's one of those bushy, muskrat-looking things." David waggled his fingers under his nose in a way that made Lucifer cringe and giggle at the same time. "Why do you need a beard?"

"We're supposed to look like a typical couple on a date."

"I've figured that much, at least. But if we're not on a date, what exactly are we doing here?"

Lucifer smiled. "We're casing the joint. There's something inside I need, but before I can steal it, I need to know exactly what I'm getting into. Like I told you at the Worcester House, I don't like going into a place without knowing all the ins and outs."

"You're going to teach me how to be an art thief?" The excitement in David's voice sent the frolicking birds scattering into the air.

"No," Lucifer said as she reached up and playfully put her hand over David's mouth. She could feel his warm breath on the palm of her hand. "Keep your voice down. You want everyone to hear?"

David gently pulled her hand away, but instead of letting go, he held onto it, pressing it against his chest. The butterflies in Lucifer's stomach fluttered wildly enough to have set off a thousand hurricanes on the far side of the world. David said, "Sorry, sorry, but I've never cased a joint before."

"Oh, please don't say that. For some reason it sounds ridiculous when you say it."

"What? Case the joint?"

"Stop."

David curled his lip and spoke in a whiny gangster drawl that sent Lucifer into fits of laughter. "Listen here, see. We're casin' the joint, see. Any lip from you and I'll pump you full of lead, see."

"Enough!" She gave him a gentle, playful push. He laughed and let go of her hand, a gesture that surprisingly disappointed her. Lucifer composed herself all the while castigating herself for pushing him. If she hadn't pushed him, maybe he would still be holding her hand. And right now, holding his hand seemed like the most important thing in the world.

"I may not look like a thief," David said with a throaty whisper, "but I'll have you know that I can be dark and mysterious, too."

This time Lucifer didn't try to stifle her laughter. "Okay there, Vincenzo Peruggia. What are we looking for, then?"

David looked around for a moment before pointing to one of the security cameras over the front door. "We find out where all the cameras are—"

"Good god, man, stop pointing!" Lucifer quickly pulled his arm down. "Maybe you should just stick with being pretty," she said.

David pretended to flip his hair behind his shoulder and fluttered his eyelashes. "No one ever loves me for my mind."

"Oh, shut up," Lucifer said, punching him in the arm. "C'mon, I want to walk around the grounds a bit before they open up."

When they stood, David reached out and grabbed her hand. When he saw Lucifer's surprised expression, he said, "I'm your beard, right? Then I better look the part."

It was a fiction. It wasn't a real date, and Lucifer knew that he was only here to help Gina, but she wanted to pretend. She wanted to imagine herself spending the day at an art gallery with a nice boy. No Harlot, no mark on her shoulder, no living as a thief in the mystical underbelly of the world. Just a normal girl on a normal date with a normal boy. She was never going to know what it was like to live life as a normal girl, so there was no harm in pretending just for an afternoon. Was there?

They walked hand-in-hand along the winding pathway to the back of the gallery where a small labyrinth of hedges sat on a shallow rise. Birds flitted and chirped among the thick brambles while a small squirrel made its way across the dewy grass in stops and starts. But the thrill of holding David's hand turned Lucifer's surroundings into misty watercolored pastels floating at the edge of her perception. The moment was perfect, as if she were in a fairy tale. It was magical. Only real magic was never this beautiful.

She took a deep breath and tried to focus. She was here to learn as much as she could about the gallery, not get all flustered by her "date."

It's all part of the disguise, she told herself. It was time to pay attention and do what she came to do. *Stop letting the pretty boy distract you!*

But why the hell did he have to smell so good?

As they moved around the outside of the gallery, Lucifer made note of any security cameras. The cameras shouldn't be a problem, but Lucifer was concerned about visibility from the street. Fortunately, the southeast corner was hidden from both cross streets and would serve as the best place to start.

"Okay, I've seen what I need to see," Lucifer said. "They should be open now. Let's head inside."

"Anything in particular we should be looking for?"

"No, but I'll know it when I see it. Let's just go in and enjoy ourselves."

Lucifer had to admit that the inside of the gallery was quite impressive. She wasn't lying to David when she said she liked to look at beautiful things. And the pieces on display here could keep Lucifer enthralled for days. Sculptures, paintings, photographs, there were even several exhibits of modern art; her favorite piece was a series of identical black cats perfectly arranged in a series of concentric circles, all facing outward with one claw raised.

She loved the gallery. Not only was it beautiful, it was calming. The white walls, the birch wood floors, the ambient lighting, all worked to give the gallery a bright, warm, and minimalist atmosphere. Compared to the clutter and chaos of Lucifer's own life, it was heavenly.

David talked about various paintings and the artists who made them as they moved from exhibit to exhibit. Lucifer found that listening to him was the most enjoyable part of the experience. His voice, along with his knowledge and playful banter all combined like the ingredients of a spell designed to captivate her. She couldn't remember the last time she had this much fun without committing a felony or making a magical baddie squirm.

"What's this one here?" Lucifer asked. It was a painting of an empty stone bench in the middle of a wide clearing, surrounded on all sides by an ominous forest. Most of the vegetation was dark with bare and twisted branches, while bright shafts of light broke through, illuminating the bench.

"That's *The Empty Garden*. By De Guerra, I think."

"Isn't he the one who cut off his ear?"

"No, that was Van Gogh," David said. "Though, I think De Guerra may have cut himself shaving once."

Lucifer didn't react to the joke. Instead, she just stared at the painting, taking it in. She was fascinated by the way the rays of light illuminating the bench glowed next to the dark and gloom of the surrounding forest. How an artist could create something so bright using nothing but paint was a magic foreign to even her.

"Is this what you've been looking for?"

"I don't know, maybe," Lucifer said. "But I will say this. Some of the pieces here shouldn't be on display."

David shrugged. "I admit, some of the contemporary art is a bit weird," he said.

"No, nothing like that. I'm talking about that over there." Lucifer motioned toward a short, rectangular pedestal on the far side of the room. On the pedestal sat a delicate tangle of resin wires that wound itself into the shape of a twirling teardrop three feet high.

"Oh, I like that piece. It's oddly soothing," David said. "What's wrong with it?"

"Nothing. But the pedestal it's sitting on is the base of a Calling Column. A thing used to summon lesser demons. There should be a summoning disc attached to the top, but thankfully that's been removed. So it's pretty harmless. Still, whoever decided to use it either had no idea what it was and decided to use it because it was pretty or, worse, knew and didn't care. There are a couple of things here in the gallery like that. Nothing really dangerous, but in the wrong hands could be problematic."

"How can you tell it's a part of this calling thing and not just a normal pedestal?"

"The fluting. There are six separate grooves running parallel on each side of the pedestal. But if you look at the top of the first groove and follow it straight down, you end up at the bottom of the second groove. Go ahead. Try it."

David tilted his head in mild amusement before turning to look at the pedestal. Soon his amusement turned into confusion. "It has to be a trick of the light."

"The same thing would happen if you traced it with your finger. It would move across the side of the pedestal like a needle following the grooves of a vinyl record."

"Then we have to go try it!"

"Absolutely not." Lucifer grabbed David's arm and pulled him close. "The whole point of all of this is to *not* attract attention."

"You know, I come to the gallery and all I see are pictures and statues. But you, Lucifer . . ." David shook his head. "The most exciting this gallery gets for me is a place for a third date."

The only thing Lucifer could think of that would be more exciting than a third date would be a first date. But for David, going on dates, being with friends, studying for class was all part of his everyday existence. Boring. Routine. All the things that made his life amazing and wonderful, he found mundane. Lucifer would take all of that over Calling Columns any day.

Still, part of Lucifer couldn't help but be flattered. She would be lying if she said she didn't enjoy the attention David was giving her. She loved how excited the littlest hints of magic seemed to spark a genuine childlike fascination within him. But that was only because he hadn't seen what magic could really do. The horror it could unleash. Yes, his girlfriend had been kidnapped with magic, but he didn't see it, and David had no idea just what a Sister of Witchdown was capable of. If he did, Lucifer had no doubt his excitement would wither and die.

"To be honest, a Calling Column is about as exciting as duct tape. Also, it's not why we're here."

"Can you show me more?" he asked.

"Not. Why. We're. Here."

David sighed. "I know, I know. We're on the job."

Lucifer patted his arm. "C'mon. There's more I need to see."

The last few exhibits didn't offer anything Lucifer could use either. Lucifer certainly enjoyed the artwork, but she still wasn't able to find quite what she needed.

After moving through the final exhibit, they came to a large ante-chamber labeled the Swan Room where a small gathering of adults in suits and formal gowns drank from champagne flutes and nibbled on hors d'oeuvres.

"This way," said Lucifer.

They made their way to the open archway leading into the Swan Room, but a man in a sloppy black suit stepped in front of them and said, "I'm sorry, but this is a private function and closed to the public."

"We just want to look inside real quick," Lucifer said as she twirled one of her pigtails.

"I'm afraid that isn't possible," the man said without bothering to smile. And with that, the conversation was over.

Lucifer and David stepped away as a well-dressed couple saun-tered past. Lucifer wanted to get a better look at what was on display but had to make due with surreptitious glances around the growing crowd of people inside.

David put his hand on her shoulder and said, "While you're playing spy, I'm going to the restroom. I'll be right back. You'll still be here?"

"I'll think about it," she said.

"Just remember, I'm your ride home."

"You just remember, I'm a thief and I've already stolen your car keys."

David reflexively put his hand in his pocket to check, visibly relaxing when he felt the familiar tangle of keys.

"You are so easy," Lucifer smirked. "Hurry up. And don't go messing with that pedestal. Remember. Covert."

David winked and gave her a mock salute before turning and walking away.

Lucifer stood on her tiptoes but still couldn't get a good view of the pieces inside the Swan Room. She could always investigate the room during the heist, but the more time she spent looking for the right thing to steal, the more likely there would be complications. She wanted to get in, get the piece, and get out. In order to do that, she needed to know exactly what she was coming here for.

"It's much easier to admire the art if you're actually in the same room."

Lucifer dropped back down to her heels and turned to see a woman standing next to her. The woman was older, perhaps in her early fifties, with short white hair that stopped sharply at her jawline. The woman wore gray slacks with a man's black sport coat tailored to fit her small but athletic frame. It was a stark contrast to the other women Lucifer had seen wearing various styles of dresses.

The ice in the tumbler of brown liquid the woman was holding clinked when she gestured toward the crowd. "Are you familiar with Felino?" the woman asked.

Lucifer didn't want to waste any time getting caught in small talk. "I don't know much about art, really. I'm just here with . . . my date. I should probably go find him."

As Lucifer started to walk away, the woman said, "Are you sure you don't want to see the Felino Exhibit? She's quite talented."

Lucifer stopped. That was exactly what she wanted. "It's a private showing. The public isn't allowed," she said.

The woman took a sip of her drink. "Yes, the professional art community can be right snobs sometimes. C'mon, let's go crash their party."

"I, uh—" Lucifer tried to say something, but the woman put her arm around her shoulders and guided her to the entrance of the Swan Room. Lucifer definitely wanted to get inside and look around, but she also knew that her typical teenaged girl costume was going to look wildly out of place among the formal attire. That was if this woman could even get her in.

The man in the sloppy suit came forward when he saw Lucifer. He opened his mouth to speak, but closed it when he saw the woman with her. "Oh, Ms. Brisendine," he said, nodding his head. "Good afternoon."

The woman, Ms. Brisendine, politely smiled but said nothing as she ushered Lucifer past the man and into the Swan Room.

"Ms. Brisendine. This is your gallery, isn't it?" Lucifer asked.

The woman smiled down at Lucifer and said, "It is indeed. But please, call me Val. Only people who owe me money have to call me Ms. Brisendine. And you are?"

"Lucifer," she said and instantly scolded herself for telling her. She had several aliases that she used from time to time since "Lucifer" wasn't exactly a name people forgot. And if she was planning on robbing the gallery, it probably wasn't a very good idea to have given the owner her real name.

"Lucifer," Val said. "That's such a pretty name for a girl."

Lucifer was taken aback. No one had ever told her such a thing. It was always some comment about the devil or how much her parents must have hated her. But Val Brisendine thought her name was pretty? Now Lucifer felt guilty. She was still going to rob this woman, but she certainly was going to feel bad about it afterward.

By now, everyone else was staring at them, mostly with smiles but a few with bemusement. Lucifer's discomfort must have been visible on her face since Val said, "Don't let all the fancy dress fool you. Everyone here is harmless." Val stared at her over the lip of her tumbler, eyeing Lucifer with one eyebrow arched. "Well, almost everyone."

A man walked by holding a silver tray. Val swallowed the last of her drink and placed her empty glass on the tray. She said, "I'm afraid I have to go play host now. It was very nice meeting you, Lucifer. Feel free to enjoy the exhibit. And if there's anything you need, all you have to do is ask." Val then turned to an attractive couple politely waiting nearby and shook their hands, losing herself in conversation.

Lucifer looked back through the archway and saw David on the other side, staring at her. She held up a finger then scanned the exhibit as quickly as she could. The patrons seemed more interested in each other than the exhibit, which made it easier for Lucifer to move from painting to painting.

One of the paintings had a small plaque at the base of its frame that read *Night on 47th*. The painting was an impressionist take on a modern city street. Warm pastels imitating the unnatural lights that illuminated the city with smears of orange and red cast odd shadows against the black slabs meant to represent buildings. Only a few yellow windows occupied the dark rectangles, showing a city barely clinging to consciousness. It was quite beautiful.

And it was exactly what Lucifer needed.

A few minutes later, she met David just outside the Swan Room. "How did you manage to get in?"

"I met the owner. Or more like, she met me."

"What about this being a covert operation?"

"Operation is over. Let's go."

"So you found something?"

Lucifer looked back into the Swan Room where Val was holding court with a handsome man twenty years her junior. The woman caught Lucifer's gaze for a moment, giving her a quick nod before turning her attention back to the man.

"Yeah, I found something." Lucifer put her arm through David's and led him to the door. "And tonight, I'm stealing it."

CHAPTER 17

"Pull up here."

David did as he was told, but he said, "The gallery is three blocks up the street. I can get you closer."

"I don't want any security cameras picking up your car," Lucifer said. "Here is fine."

The city was dark except for the lampposts snaking along the sidewalk. The skyscrapers and office buildings in downtown proper just a few blocks away were lost in the early morning fog, their weak light swallowed by the mist. The moon was low on the horizon, just beginning its slow crawl across the sky.

Lucifer felt more relaxed now that she was in more suitable attire. She wore dark jeans, an olive T-shirt, gray sneakers, and her ever-present black hoodie. Her hair was loose again, and the headache she had from wearing pigtails had finally worn off, allowing her to think more clearly.

Though Lucifer was always focused when on a job, David's presence was distracting. A pleasant distraction, but still, his being there kept getting in the way of her thoughts. Instead of imagining the layout of the gallery or the details of her plan to sneak inside, her mind wandered to thoughts about David. The way he held her hand, his crooked smile, his calming yet engaging voice. She needed to be on top of her game, and he was making that difficult.

Lucifer could see David's scowl in the dim red light of his dashboard. He had been in a sour mood ever since she told him he wasn't coming with her. It was her own fault, she supposed, since she never expressly told him he wasn't.

David pulled his car to the side of the road and killed the engine.

The fog outside turned the city into puffs of black and amber cotton while a small cloud of condensation crept up the windshield in its slow, determined quest to hide the already blurry world from view.

"You don't have to stay here," Lucifer said.

"I might as well," said David. "The least I can do is drive the getaway car. I'm sorry. I mean the *most* I can do."

Lucifer chuckled. "Don't be a brat about it. I told you. This is serious stuff. I'm about to commit a felony that could land me in jail for decades."

"This is to help Gina, right? Then it's a risk I'm willing to take."

Lucifer pulled her hood up over her head and started tucking her hair safely inside. "It's not a risk I'm willing to take. And it's my decision. Not yours."

"Gina is my girlfriend."

"And I'm really happy for you," Lucifer said, though the words came out harsher than she had intended. "But I'm the thief. Not you."

"I can be helpful," David insisted.

"No offense," Lucifer said as she checked the contents of her trick bag, "but you're not really cut out for this kind of thing."

"Okay, so I may have made a few mistakes when we were casing the joint."

"Ugh . . ." Lucifer said, rolling her eyes.

"But," David continued, "I can be helpful. Look at me. I came prepared."

"David, you look like a mime."

He was wearing jet-black from head to toe with thick, heavy boots and a ridiculously conspicuous black beanie cap. Not to mention he had more pockets in his cargo pants and field jacket than there were in a Las Vegas pool hall.

"That's so people won't see me."

"It's not just about no one seeing you. It's about no one *noticing* you. And people are going to notice a Call of Duty cosplayer skulking around in the middle of the night." She reached up and pulled the beanie from his head. "You know your hair is already black, right?" And Lucifer desperately wanted to run her fingers through it.

So. Distracting.

David turned in his seat and said, "I get it. I'm not a thief. But I want to help. I need to help. I know I'm a liability, but I also know I can be of some use to you. I can be your lookout." He put his hand on her arm, sending an electric thrill straight to the base of her skull. "I promise, I won't get in your way and I'll do everything you say, no questions asked."

"David . . ."

"I want to do everything I can to help Gina. But . . ." He paused for a moment, then said, "I'm not going to lie. Your world fascinates me. Magic, being a thief, all of it. I want to know more about it, about you." He slid his hand down her arm and took hold of her hand. "I like being around you."

Lucifer watched his eyes in the soft light leaking into the car. Was he being serious or was he using his charm to get his way? Letting David tag along in the cemetery had been a bad idea, but letting him come along on a real job was the pinnacle of rank stupidity.

So why was she going to allow it?

"No questions asked?" she asked.

David raised three fingers and said, "Scout's honor."

"All right, then. From here on out, you don't ask me what I'm doing or why. You don't speak unless I ask you a question. You just follow me and do as you're told. Understand, David, this is what I do. This is my *job*. But I'm doing this to save Gina. If things go wrong and you get yourself busted, you're on your own. You're not my priority, Gina is. Understand?"

David nodded.

"Good boy. Now let's go. And try not to wake up the neighborhood with those clod stompers."

Lucifer found the night's overwhelming silence soothing. There was no wind, very few cars, and any other errant sound of the sleeping city was swallowed by the fog. Lucifer had chosen this particular time of the morning to minimize the chances of being seen. It was a golden hour just after the local bars and clubs closed but before the restaurants started their morning operations.

Lucifer led David down an alley and on the sidewalk toward the gallery. This was going to be more difficult than she thought. She knew it was a mistake letting him come along, but she just couldn't say no. She enjoyed having him around, but more importantly, he enjoyed being around her. That is, if he was telling her the truth.

That thought made her head swim. Who knows, maybe he could be good at this. Maybe he had innate thieving abilities. She could teach him, help him improve until, eventually, they could start their own little enterprise. The two of them, working together, being together—

"Stop sneaking and walk normally, David," Lucifer whispered. "You look like a hunchback who needs to pee."

Or maybe not.

Lucifer could see him blush with embarrassment even in the morning dark. It was impossibly cute.

Dammit, girl, focus.

They passed through another alley behind several restaurants and down the street until they reached the edge of the gallery grounds. Lucifer pulled David under an overhang of thick tree branches looming over the sidewalk. The tree itself was behind the tall wrought iron fence that surrounded the grounds, but its branches stretched out almost to the street. The fence was thick with vines, but they were too weak to support Lucifer's weight, let alone David's. They'd have to go over another way.

Lucifer opened her trick bag and pulled out a rope with a stout metal cylinder about four inches long attached to the end. She pressed a button on top of the cylinder, and three short tines fanned out, creating a small grappling hook. After a quick toss, Lucifer had the rope secured to a branch overhead and climbed into the tree.

Without a word, David scrambled up the rope behind her. She watched him pull himself up with his powerful arms so quickly and quietly she honestly wondered if he had ever done this before. Of course, what should she have expected from the school's star athlete?

Headlights broke through the fog as a car rolled along the street toward them. Lucifer quickly coiled the rope and tossed it back into her trick bag. Lucifer put her hand on David's knee, bidding stillness as they let the car move past. Between the cover of the leaves and fog, she knew they were practically invisible.

It was a taxi, aimlessly trolling for fares. Once it passed, Lucifer and David climbed down the tree and kneeled in the wet grass. "Now you can sneak," Lucifer whispered.

David smiled in the dark.

They made their way along the fence until they reached the back of the gallery's labyrinth. Lucifer found the small opening of a rabbit trail at the bottom of the hedges and climbed through. Here, David didn't fare as well as he did with the rope. He was almost too broad, and his dozens of pockets caught on the hedge's branches. Eventually, Lucifer helped pull him through.

The high walls of the labyrinth provided the cover they needed to get close to the gallery itself without being seen by the cameras. The labyrinth wasn't terribly difficult to figure out. It was really more decoration than brainteaser. Still, it took longer than she would have liked.

When they reached the entrance, Lucifer stopped and motioned David next to her. She pulled a small silver case from her trick bag and opened it with a soft click. Inside were three almond-shaped crystals.

"Hold out your hand, palm up," she whispered. David did as

instructed, and Lucifer placed one of the crystals in his hand. "Don't move."

She tapped the fingers of her right hand to the fingers of her left hand in an odd but deliberate pattern. Right ring finger to left index, right middle to left thumb, twist, right thumb to left pinky, tap tap. She repeated the pattern but this time started with her left ring finger. When she finished, she touched the crystal with her index finger. The crystal cracked down the center of its length. The two halves separated and unfolded themselves into diaphanous glass wings paired to a small sphere. The wings fluttered and rose from David's hand. The crystal butterfly flapped its way toward the gallery, where it landed on a camera and wrapped its wings around the lens, filtering any person from view.

David sat motionless, his palm still upturned and his mouth agape. Lucifer lifted his chin, closing his mouth with her fingertips, then gave him a gentle pat on the shoulder. "Stay directly behind me. C'mon."

The window directly beneath the magicked camera was tall and narrow, divided into three equal panes of glass, one on top of the other. It wasn't designed to open, which made it perfect. Most thieves who work windows recommended finding one that opens or cutting through the ones that don't. But Lucifer found that if you completely remove the pane, a curious glance won't raise suspicions where a hole in the glass or an ajar window would.

It took Lucifer less than thirty seconds to disable the pressure sensors, remove the lowest pane, and get both her and David inside.

The gallery was quiet and dark, with only the dull blue glow of the auxiliary lighting system overhead making it possible to see. Lucifer took out another crystal almond from the silver case. This one fluttered into several smaller pairs of wings that each moved off into separate directions.

"Motion sensors," she said.

David nodded. Lucifer was impressed. She could tell he had a million questions, but he was keeping true to his word and staying silent. No, he shouldn't be here, but Lucifer liked that he was. She was enjoying his presence and, if she was being honest with herself, loved showing off for him.

She bit her lip in an attempt to focus on the task at hand. "Follow me."

The exhibits looked different in the dark. Everything became more ominous, more haunting in the dim blue light. Still, she would have loved to sit down and enjoy the empty gallery's still beauty.

As they approached the Swan Room, Lucifer stopped and crouched low. Across the main vestibule, a security guard sat behind a desk, the harsh light of monitors reflecting off his shiny bald head. Lucifer quietly pointed him out to David and put a finger to her lips. David winked, but Lucifer could see the vein in his neck pulsing rapidly. His heart was racing. That was both good and bad. Good because it meant he was nervous and had a proper appreciation for what they were doing. Bad because nervous people made mistakes.

Lucifer crept toward the Swan Room with David in tow. She froze when the security guard suddenly laughed. She turned to see he was watching an old sitcom on one of his monitors. Quickly, she and David moved through the archway and into the room.

The Swan Room was completely empty.

All of the paintings that had been on display earlier that day were gone. The only evidence of the earlier celebration were several bare tables and a single plastic champagne flute sitting on a window sill. Beyond that, the painting she wanted was nowhere to be found.

This was a problem. Lucifer had a feeling they were still somewhere in the gallery, but where? "Upstairs," she said.

The upper floor of the gallery was mostly office space that overlooked the open expanse of the Swan Room. There were no official exhibits, but a few paintings and sculptures were on display much like one would find in any office. Lucifer scanned the rooms, peering into their windows until she came to the large corner office. This was no doubt Ms. Brisendine's. Lucifer could see the paintings through the frosted glass, each carefully leaning against the far wall.

Lucifer examined the lock then reached into her trick bag. She pulled out a screwdriver, but instead of having a typical standard or Phillips tip, the screwdriver had a key welded to the end. The notches along the length of the key were filed down so they were now nothing more than dull nubs.

She held it up for David to see. "Bump key. It's a pretty basic tool that can open most simple locks. All you have to do is slide it in and . . ."

Lucifer put the bump key into the lock and slammed the back of the handle with the palm of her hand. There was a dull thud followed by a click. She handed the bump key to David and then swung open the door.

Val's office was large but minimalist. Her desk was organized, and the shelves that lined the back wall held as many masks and figurines as they did books. For Lucifer, the hardest part of the job was fighting the urge to explore. But wasting time by looking around was a good way to get caught. So she made a beeline for the paintings. There, at the back of the stack, was *Night on 47th*. Lucifer really did find it to be beautiful.

Such a shame she was going to destroy it.

There was a desperate tap on her shoulder. When she turned, David was pointing to the doorway. Outside in the hall, Lucifer could see the unmistakable beam of light coming from the security guard's flashlight as he walked toward them.

Lucifer pulled a knife and a telescoping poster tube from her trick bag. She quickly cut the painting from the frame, relying on experience to guide her hand while she watched the approaching light. Once it was free of the frame, she extended the tube with a flick of her wrist, rolled the canvas and shoved it inside.

The light flashed across the open door but then swung back and held.

"Oh my God," David murmured. His eyes were wide as he stared at the light searching out in the hallway. "I can't get caught, I just can't. I'll lose my scholarships. We have to run—"

"Listen," she whispered as she slung the tube's shoulder strap over her head. "Hide behind the desk, count to thirty, then head for the window. I'll meet you by the tree. Go back exactly the way we came. If I'm not there in three minutes, leave without me."

"But—"

Lucifer shot him such a withering stare that he blanched. "They're going to know something's been stolen," her whisper sounding more like a snake's hiss, "but I want them looking for one thief, not two, now hide."

David hesitated, his mouth twisted in nervous frustration. But as the security guard's footsteps came closer, he ducked behind the desk in a crouch and waited.

Lucifer didn't.

She raced toward the door and, without skipping a step, burst into the hallway, up over the railing and out into the open air. It was fifteen feet to the floor of the Swan Room below. As gravity pulled her down in what seemed an interminably slow arc, Lucifer heard the security guard yelp in surprise then follow it with a string of quite colorful curses. She tucked the tube and her trick bag under her chest while in midair. Finally, she slammed into the floor. She used her momentum to propel herself into a roll and minimize the inertial impact on her feet. There was a split second of dizziness before her roll brought her back to her feet and she was racing toward the archway.

Lucifer was slight enough that, in the dark and with her hair tucked into her hood, she would most likely be suspected of being a small man. Ask anyone to describe a thief, and the first thing they'd say is *he*. Lucifer liked to use that prejudice to her advantage.

She needed to draw the security guard away from the open window to give David a way to escape without detection. Instead of running left back toward the way they entered, Lucifer pivoted right. She slowed down when she noticed the labored steps of the security guard trying to chase after her. She could have easily outrun him, but she didn't want to get too far ahead of him. Lucifer wanted to stay in his sights. The more he was focused on her, the less likely he'd see David.

When she heard the guard's plodding steps round the corner, she picked up her pace. "Stop!" the man yelled, but she kept going. Lucifer ran past several glass cases housing a dozen pieces of ancient pottery and into a small room at the end of the hallway. A center wall bisected the room, allowing more display space for paintings, but there were no exits. The only way in or out was the way she just came in, and the guard was getting closer.

She slid into the corner of the room, hoping the shadows would hide her long enough. The guard stopped in the room's entrance. He flashed his light around in erratic arcs. "I know you're in here. There's no way out. Cops are on their way so just make it easy on yourself and come out. If I come in here and find you, I'm not going easy on you. So get out here, now!"

Lucifer carefully reached into her trick bag and pulled out the final crystal almond. She whispered the small activation incantation then huddled tight into a ball in the corner.

Though she had her head down, completely hidden under her hood, she knew the guard's light was on her.

"Stand up," he said. "Slowly and let me see your hands."

There was the recognizable snap of a buttoned leather strap. Mace. Lucifer began to shake. Though she was fully recovered from her attack a few days earlier, she was in no hurry to experience the horror of being maced again.

"Hiding your face isn't going to help. Okay, you asked for it—"

Lucifer looked up into the blinding beam of his flashlight. The guard gasped when he saw her, dropping his mace can and nearly dropping his flashlight as well. The crystal had formed into a horrific mask of jagged fangs that covered Lucifer's face. Before the guard could recover, she whispered another word, and crystal wings sprouted where the ears should have been. The mask flew from her face and straight toward the guard, its terrible jaws wide and snapping.

The guard fell over backward, struggling to get his billy club free. Lucifer jumped over him as the mask nibbled at his ineffectual attempts to fight it off. The only damage it could really inflict were a few paper cuts, but no one in the mundane world would know that. As far as the guard was concerned, a winged shark-face demon was trying to eat his face off.

Lucifer was at the window when she heard the guard smash the crystal mask into a thousand pieces. The crystals were only one-use since they lasted no more than an hour before dissolving into pretty sand, but she was hoping the guard would have struggled with it a bit longer.

She was through the window and running toward the labyrinth when she saw flashing red and blue lights reflected off the side of the gallery. The cops were there. She didn't bother to use the Labyrinth as cover. She raced straight toward the tree at the back of the grounds.

David was there, crouched behind the trunk of the tree and watching with eyes so wide Lucifer feared they were going to fall out of his head. "Climb," she said. They were up in the tree when two cops came barreling toward the labyrinth. David dropped to the sidewalk, but before Lucifer could follow, a cop's flashlight trained on her.

"Freeze!"

There was a short pop of gunfire. The turning leaves above Lucifer's head rustled as the bullet screamed past. She fell from the tree more gracefully than she was expecting.

"The cops are shooting at us!"

"I know, David. That's what they do," she growled as she grabbed his sleeve and pulled him into a run.

The two ran down the sidewalk. David started to cut left when Lucifer shouted, "No! This way!"

"But the car's this way!"

"Not yet. C'mon!"

David ran after her. Lucifer heard the sirens of a police car one block over. When she looked back, she saw one of the cops still on foot and gaining ground. The police car was moving ahead to block their path. Lucifer knew that more cops would be on their way. She might be able to hide in the shadows or get to the rooftops and wait them out. But not with David with her. They had to get to safety. Now. But she knew this might be a possibility. And every good thief knows to come prepared.

Lucifer pushed David into the alley behind the row of restaurants. The air was filled with the smells of their kitchens preparing for breakfast. A single lamppost filled the alley with harsh light and deep shadows. Lucifer pulled David to a stop.

"Take off your jacket. Hurry."

"But—"

"No questions!"

David yanked off his jacket like it was on fire. Lucifer took it and tossed it along with the painting tube behind a nearby Dumpster. She grabbed a handful of items from her trick bag and handed them to David: a pack of cigarettes, a lighter, and a hairnet. "Put that on and light two cigarettes."

As David did what he was told, Lucifer pulled off her hoodie and turned it inside out. The inside was a bright, incandescent red, and when she wore it reversed, it looked like a cardigan. She quickly rolled her jean cuffs to give the vague appearance that she was wearing capri pants. Lucifer could hear the cop's thundering steps on the sidewalk getting closer.

Lucifer hid her trick bag with the other items behind the Dumpster then fluffed her hair as much as possible. She took one of the lit cigarettes from David and said, "Relax, lean back against the wall, and look that way." She pointed to the far end of the alley in the opposite direction the cop was coming from. "Don't turn to look at the cop until he comes into view. We need him to think we saw someone run that way."

David nodded, his black hair mashed against his skull by the hairnet.

The two were staring at the far end of the alley when the cop ran up. Lucifer and David turned to see the cop, gun drawn. The cop froze for a second, quickly scanning Lucifer and David. Lucifer just raised her hand and pointed to the far end of the alley.

"Suspect heading east down the alley behind Culver," he barked into his radio. Without another word the cop started running again. After a moment, he disappeared in the dark. The cops were looking for a man in dark jeans and a black hoodie, not a bus boy taking a smoke break with his garishly dressed girlfriend.

Lucifer retrieved their things from behind the Dumpster. "Let's get back to the car before they realize they're looking in the wrong place."

Sunlight was creeping over the horizon by the time they were safely far enough away from the crime scene. David hadn't said a word since the alley. "Are you all right?" Lucifer asked.

David slowly turned to her with a look of such amused shock, she almost laughed. "I don't know. That was the most exciting thing I've ever done. And you . . . just, wow. With the magic and the window and then jumping over the railing! It was like watching an action movie."

"So you had fun." Lucifer knew she shouldn't be encouraging him, but she liked entertaining him.

"Fun? Yeah, until the cops started shooting at us. With guns. And bullets."

"Technically, it was one gun with one bullet."

"Sorry, I can't be as cavalier about it as you. I've never been shot at before."

"And you still haven't been. The shot was at me. Not you."

"True. Are you okay?" he asked.

"I'm fine." *It's not the first time someone tried to shoot me.* She patted David on the arm and said, "You did well, David. You didn't get arrested."

"That will look great on a college application. 'Never arrested.'" They both chuckled. "Now that we've got the painting, what happens next?"

Lucifer watched the blood-red streak of sunrise creep over the horizon. "Next comes the hard part."

CHAPTER 18

"**A**re you sure you can do this?" Lucifer asked.

"Of course," David said. "Why wouldn't I?"

Lucifer fingered the rubber strip that protected the passenger window inside the car door as she looked out into the darkness. Clouds blanketed the sky, but the nearly full moon glowed behind them, turning them silver against the black.

"I don't know. Aren't you supposed to be in school or something?"

"It's ten-thirty at night."

"You know what I mean," Lucifer said, knowing he could see her scowl.

"My parents are in Costa Rica until next week and my school doesn't care. I'm a senior and I'm so far ahead on credits I only have to go two days a week. All my teachers will think I'm out scouting colleges or something. And basketball conditioning doesn't start for a couple of weeks yet so none of my coaches will wonder either. It's fine."

Lucifer nodded. Ever since their close call at the gallery, Lucifer didn't want David around. It wasn't that she didn't enjoy his company. She did, more than anything. It was that what they were doing could get him in serious trouble. It was bad enough that David could have been arrested after the cemetery, not to mention that he would be facing serious jail time if they had been caught at the art gallery. But what they were doing now could get him killed. Or worse.

Much worse.

But the allure of magic was intoxicating. Lucifer knew that all too well. She also knew that when things went south, they went by bullet train. David didn't. And the close call at the gallery didn't seem to convince him of the danger either. He spent most of the ride home peppering her with questions. What were those crystals? How did you know the trick in the alley would work? Was that magic too? Why steal *that* painting? And on and on and on. They were all perfectly natural questions, questions she would have asked herself in his position. But it was the enthusiasm with which he asked them that made her nervous. Curiosity didn't just kill cats.

Lucifer tried to dissuade him from coming, but he was insistent. After the heist, Lucifer was simply too tired to argue with him, so she just told him to pick her up later that afternoon after they both had a chance to get some real rest.

They had been driving for almost four hours, stopping only once for food and a bathroom break. They followed the coast toward Cape Vale or, at least, what used to be Cape Vale before the great hurricane of '36 wiped the small coastal town from the face of the earth. Now it was a quiet resort where the wealthy could park their seafaring playthings for the winter.

They pulled off of Highway 95 and headed east toward the ocean. Even with the windows up, Lucifer could smell the salt in the air. David's headlights illuminated the lonely road. The darkness of the night seemed to swallow the entire world except for the tiny sliver of asphalt directly in front of them. Even the silvery moon couldn't break through the blanket of clouds enough to offer any respite from the swallowing darkness.

After another twenty minutes, orange light broke through the black veil of night. Oldport Marina was just ahead.

Lucifer had David drive past the marina first to get a better idea of what was there. Google Street View had given her a pretty good idea of the marina's layout, but she still preferred to see things firsthand before making a plan of action.

The marina was thick with boats. Most were sailboats, though there were a few trawlers and yachts scattered among the masts that stretched across the calm water like a dense forest of pale, naked trees. Many of the smaller crafts were covered with protective tarps, while a handful of smaller dinghies and rowboats were stacked in dry dock on the various piers, all recently stored away for the season. It didn't take long for Lucifer to spot exactly what she needed.

David parked in a small lot where his car wouldn't be conspicuous. Lucifer grabbed her trick bag and the tube with the painting. She said, "You should wait here."

"No way."

"David—"

"Lucifer, I've already committed a felony with you. What's one more?"

She sighed. "This is going to be different. If things go wrong here, you won't get arrested. You'll die."

"I know how to swim."

"You'd be lucky if it was drowning that killed you."

David gave her a playful smirk and said, "What else would it be? Sharks?"

"A witch." Lucifer watched his smile evaporate.

"Is it the witch that took Gina?" he asked.

"No," she said. "It's Minnie Hester, the Witch of Cape Vale."

"Okay, but how dangerous could a witch named Minnie be?" His smile returned, irritating the hell out of her.

"Dangerous enough to kill both of us with a thought if we aren't careful. This isn't the gallery, David. We're not trying to avoid cops and cameras and security guards. I'm going to talk to a witch. Do you get that?"

David's smile was replaced by a stern resolve. "Then I'm definitely coming with you. If witches are as dangerous as you say they are, then you'll need protection."

Lucifer rolled her eyes and said, "How very Cro-Magnon of you. I can protect myself, David. But that's the problem. I don't know if I can protect you. Witches are bad, bad business. Their magic is beyond deadly."

"But you have magic."

"No, I don't. I can *do* magic, but I don't have it. Think of magic like flying. If I want to fly, I need an airplane. And I know enough to pilot a small Cessna. Witches can fly without a plane because they *have* magic. It's a part of them, like immense and agile wings. And their magic is powerful. I mean, they murdered their own children to get it. Imagine what they've been given in exchange for that kind of sacrifice."

"Given? Given by what?"

Lucifer sighed. "We can have that conversation when I get back."

"When *we* get back."

Lucifer sat in silence for a moment. They were running out of time, and she knew the only way David was going to stay in the car was if she knocked him out with a quick punch to the head. Since she wasn't willing to do that, she nodded and opened the car door. "C'mon."

The air was cool, but it hinted at the biting cold of autumn every time a subtle breeze blew in off the water. Lucifer chided herself for not wearing something warmer or better insulated.

David was wearing dark jeans, a heather gray Henley and an army-green jacket. Lucifer was impressed. He had obviously paid attention after she scolded him for his ridiculous outfit at the gallery heist and chose clothes more appropriate for sneaking around in the dark. And though his jacket was unlined, he didn't seemed bothered by the bitter cold hiding behind the soft ocean breeze.

Lucifer led him toward a small black dinghy that was moored to the side of one of the wooden piers. She pointed and said, "Untie the lines." As David did as he was told, she hopped inside and began pulling items from her trick bag.

The sounds of the creaking pier beneath David's footsteps echoed across the still water. As the dinghy bobbed beneath Lucifer's minimal weight, small waves lapped against the hulls of nearby boats, adding to the quiet cacophony.

Once the lines were untied, David jumped in next to Lucifer. "They have cameras here."

Without looking up, Lucifer said, "Yes, they do. But we're returning the boat when we're done. So they won't have any reason to review the footage."

"Aren't there security guards?"

She nodded, "They don't pay much attention, though."

"How do you know?"

"When I first came to America, I didn't have any place to stay, so I'd find a marina just like this one. Most of the boats are unlocked, so I'd snoop around until I found one and then crawl inside and sleep there for the night. If security ever noticed me, they never bothered me because nothing ever went missing. I suspect security here will be the same. Now grab that paddle and start pushing us out."

David did so but then said, "Why not use the outboard motor?"

"Too much noise. But don't worry, you won't have to paddle far."

She grabbed a couple of life vests from the back of the boat, tossed one to David, and then put hers on. After she had it securely fastened, Lucifer leaned over the side of the boat and scooped up some water into a small plastic cup she had in her trick bag. She then placed her hand over the top of the cup and turned it upside down. Etched on the bottom of the cup was a symbol made of flowing lines and intersecting circles. "*Tella mar undeulla,*" she whispered. The symbol glowed with a soft green light. The water inside the cup leaked out over the side of her hand, the drops hitting the floor of the boat with tiny thuds. When the water was gone, the glowing symbol faded and Lucifer lifted the cup. There, in the palm of her hand, was a nyriandran. A small creature similar to a jellyfish but with long wing-like fins and large lavender eyes that stood out in stark contrast to its green, bioluminescent skin.

David stopped rowing to get a better look at the creature that Lucifer was holding. "It's beautiful," he said.

"She is. But also very fragile. I need to get her in the water soon, but I want us clear of these boats first."

David took the hint and started rowing again, but he kept a mesmerized eye on the nyriandran. Once they were past the docks and out in the small bay, Lucifer gently placed the creature in the water. She could see its tiny body glowing beneath the surface of the water. The nyriandran swam to the bow of the boat. There, tiny lines of light grew from its body and attached themselves to the bottom of the boat. Soon the creature was guiding the boat silently out of the bay, pulled by its illuminated tendrils.

"She's called a nyriandran. Sort of an aquatic bloodhound. She can sniff out magic and get us close to where we need to be. Closer than I could get us, anyway."

"You keep saying magic is this horrible thing," David said, leaning over the bow to watch the graceful nyriandran. "But all I've seen is beauty and wonder."

Lucifer stared out in the endless dark of the ocean beyond the breakwater and said, "That's about to change."

The air grew cooler, and the breeze started to cut through Lucifer's thin hoodie the farther out they went. When the boat finally moved past the breakwater, it rose and fell in the small, gentle swells. The stillness of the night was replaced with the soft hiss of wind and the lapping of water against the side of the dinghy.

Lucifer fought back a wave of fear as she stared out into the impossible darkness of the ocean beyond. It was endless. Only the dim light of the sheltered moon peeking through the haze of clouds overhead was visible. Beneath it was nothing but a vast, swirling emptiness waiting to swallow her whole.

Lucifer and David suddenly hitched forward as the nyriandran stopped pulling the boat. She looked down to see the creature retracting its gossamer tendrils and slipping deeper into the water until her green light disappeared into the darkness below.

"What happened?" David asked.

"This is as close as she's willing to get. We'll have to go the rest of the way ourselves."

"And which way is that? I can't see anything."

Lucifer scanned the dark horizon. The moonlight was penetrating enough to show thin whitecaps crashing against a small island of rocks about a hundred yards away. "There," she said, pointing. "I'll get the motor started."

After a quick bit of tinkering, Lucifer hotwired the outboard motor. The engine was annoyingly loud after the serene calm of the nyriandran. She twisted the throttle and steered the boat toward the rocks. The water grew choppier the closer they came. The boat rose above the crest of a wave and slammed back down into a trough, sending a shock of pain up her spine. She slowed, but it did little to help. Black water sprayed into her eyes, and the refreshing smell of salty sea air was being encroached by the sour stench of rotting fish.

Lucifer brought the boat to a stop about twenty yards from the barren island. Any closer, and the waves could smash the boat against the rocks and rupture the bladders that kept it afloat. The island itself was only about fifty yards across but just tall enough that the waves didn't roll over the top. That was where she needed to be.

There was a small anchor in the corner of the boat. Lucifer quickly tossed it overboard and killed the motor. "What time is it?" she asked.

David pulled out his phone. "Eleven fifty-two."

Lucifer reached into her trick bag and pulled out a large brass bell and a steel mallet. Thick patches of green bled over the ancient bell, but the angular symbol etched into its face was still clearly visible, even in the hidden moonlight. "At exactly midnight, ring this bell four times, then toss it in the water." She then took off her life vest and started untying her shoes.

"What are you doing?" David asked.

"I have to get to the island and I don't want my clothes weighing me down."

"You're going into the water? Are you nuts?"

She unzipped her hoodie. "Any closer and the boat will crash into the rocks and sink. I'd rather swim a hundred feet to those rocks than a quarter mile back to shore."

Lucifer slipped out of her hoodie and then took off her jeans. She was now wearing nothing but pink and blue striped boy shorts and a thin spaghetti-strap tank top. Even in the dark, she could see David was trying to avert his eyes.

"David, I'm going to need you to keep an eye on me."

"But you're . . ."

"More covered than I would be in a regular bathing suit. Stop being such a prude and focus." She slipped her life vest back on and asked, "What are you going to do at exactly midnight?"

He stared at her and said, "Ring the bell four times."

"And then?"

"Toss it in the water," he said. "Lucifer, shouldn't I go with you?"

"Only if you want to die."

Lucifer tossed her clothes and shoes into a garbage bag she had brought to keep everything dry. When she slung the painting tube over her shoulder, David said, "I didn't know you had a tattoo."

Lucifer froze. Her mark. "Yeah, I've got a tattoo."

"Why an 'h'? Shouldn't it be an 'L' for Lucifer?" he asked.

"It's not a letter. It's . . . something else. And not important right now." She turned around and faced him. "David, whatever you do, do not come to the island for me. You stay in this boat, no matter what."

"I've got a bad feeling about this. Let's at least get the boat a little closer—"

"We can't, I told you. Now remember, exactly midnight," Lucifer said before jumping overboard.

The water was painfully cold. Lucifer clamped down her teeth to keep from suddenly inhaling a mouthful of seawater. The ocean roared around her, lifting her then lowering her, over and over again as she fought the current toward the rocks. The island was only a few yards away but felt like miles now that she was in the frigid water.

She dropped into the trough of a wave, and her foot touched rock. She was close. She gave one final kick and reached a slimy outcropping, but a wave pulled her hand free and she was sucked back out into the ocean. Again, she fought her way to the island and this time was able to hold on. She pulled herself out of the water and onto the slippery rocks. The rocks were ice cold, making her skin crawl with goose pimples.

When she was finally able to stand, the wind cut through her as easily as an arctic blast. Instantly, her teeth began to chatter. Lucifer wanted nothing more than to huddle in tight and warm herself, but she didn't have time. She did her best to ignore the cold and made her way to the flat center of the island.

Lucifer opened the tube and pulled out the painting. She unfurled the thick canvas and laid it facedown on the rock. On the back, she had already inscribed a series of glyphs and symbols in a deliberate arrangement. There was just enough moonlight to allow her to inspect what she had drawn, making sure the pattern was correct. Everything looked to be in order, not that there was anything she could have done about it if it wasn't.

A tiny chime echoed across the water. Lucifer turned to see David floating in the dinghy, his face lit by the light of his phone as its alarm bleated across the water. The light disappeared. Then she heard four dull *klangs* as David rang the bell, one right after another. After the fourth, Lucifer watched him hurl the bell into the water.

The ringing of the bell hung in the air for a moment, like an echo trapped in the wind. But as it started to fade, she could feel it thrumming in the wet rock beneath her feet, as if the bell were still ringing, sending its haunting chime to reverberate through the water as it sank. There was no mistaking it now. The rock was vibrating. Though Lucifer stood still, the island was shaking enough to slide her across its surface.

Lucifer couldn't hear the bell any more, but she could feel its chime growing more intense in the water and stone beneath her. The soft breeze turned into a gust strong enough to cause the excess fabric of her shirt to whip against her shivering skin with loud, wet slaps.

Suddenly the water on the far side of the island fell away as if the bottom of the sea had disappeared. Lucifer could see a whorl of black barnacles and twisted anemones that clung to the jagged base of the island. She could make out movement among the rocks. Irregular shapes with slimy limbs glistening in the sparse moonlight slipped over the suddenly exposed stone, reaching and crawling up the edge of the island.

The gusting wind became a gale as the ocean rushed back to fill the void it had left just a moment ago. Lucifer grabbed the painting as the swollen wave crashed across the island with such violence that it knocked her down and sluiced her to the edge of the rocks. She coughed up a mouthful of saltwater and was able to catch her breath before another wave pummeled her. She clutched at a small crevice between two rocks, letting its sharp edge dig into her fingers to help keep the water from pushing her off the island.

What had once been a relatively calm sea just moments before was now a raging hurricane. The black waves burst into white foam that disappeared in the howling wind that screamed across the lonely rocks. The water lashed at Lucifer's bare skin. Each wave was a stinging, relentless claw that threatened to pull her off the sanctuary of stone and into the deep.

The canvas hung limp in her hand, a heavy, wet thing that flapped in the torrential wind like a sad and hopeless flag. Thankfully, the image wasn't yet a ruined mess, but Lucifer wasn't sure how long it could survive. She had chosen *Night on 47th* primarily because it was painted in acrylics and not watercolors like so many of the other paintings in the gallery had been. So far, it seemed to have been the right choice. But she doubted anything could withstand this storm for very long.

Lucifer kept low, searching for handholds to pull herself inland. A lull in the waves allowed her to quickly scrape across the rocks, but as she was just about to reach the center of the island, she looked up and felt her heart seize in her chest.

Standing before her was Minnie Hester, the Witch of Cape Vale.

The sight took Lucifer's breath away. The witch was the physical embodiment of voluptuous perfection, a beauty the creature had no doubt purchased along with her dark pact of magic. Though naked, she appeared completely unaffected by the wet and cold. Her alabaster skin glinted in the smothered moonlight, and her black hair flowed with the same slow, unstoppable inertia of the mighty waves that crashed around her. But it was her eyes that terrified Lucifer more than anything.

They were as dark and empty as night.

Lucifer slapped the soaked canvas facedown on the rock. She wasn't looking at the witch, but she could feel her reaching for her, her extended claws dripping with the eternal sea. With every ounce of strength she had, Lucifer shouted into the deafening wind. "*Ech rost! Ton d'kallar von rost!*"

The symbols on the back of the painting erupted in a blinding pastel light that shattered the darkness. The light engulfed the island, growing in intensity. Lucifer knew the witch was close, her dreadful hand about to grab her. She wanted to look, to see just where the threat was, but the light was too bright. She couldn't open her eyes without the searing pain of her pupils squeezing impossibly tight.

But the hand never came. Lucifer heard the roaring wind calm to nothing and felt the spraying seafoam dissolve into a light, drizzly mist. Lucifer opened her eyes. The light was gone.

So was the island.

Lucifer was now standing in the middle of an empty city inter-section: 47th Street. The lazy rain pattered against the parked cars that lined the streets in all directions, and the streetlamps glowed with a soft, surreal light. Tall buildings rose all around her with all but a few of their windows dark.

The witch was there with her, standing calmly across the street. Her hair continued to undulate with the same speed and force of the waves that were no longer there. She was still naked, looking almost comically out of place in the sudden urban setting. Lucifer almost laughed until she realized that she herself was in nothing but her underwear and a bright-orange life vest.

When the witch spoke, her voice scraped like the chitter of talons clawing across the ocean deep. "What manner of sorcery is this, witchling?"

Lucifer bristled at the insult. "I call it a skip spell. A temporary little pocket dimension. It won't last long, but it's the only way I knew I could talk to you on neutral ground."

The witch glided forward, her delicate feet moving with relaxed but deliberate intent. "And why would such a fragile young thing wish to speak with me?"

"I need answers."

"I need flesh," the witch growled.

"Yeah, that's not happening."

"No?" The witch smiled, the void of her eyes pulling at Lucifer like the gravity well of black suns. "It's true, you are a tiny thing without much meat on your bones. But that delicious boy floating at the edge of my island . . . now *he* would be a meal to savor." She moved closer, leaving perfect footprints in the watery street behind her. "Perhaps a deal could be made."

Lucifer had no idea just how long this little pocket dimension would last, and she didn't want to waste time bantering with the witch. Fighting the instinct to run away screaming into the imaginary city, she stepped forward and said, "I want to know how to get to Witchdown."

The witch stopped. Her smile melted away in the gentle rain, but the black holes of her eyes grew. "Why would any mortal wish to travel to Witchdown?"

"One of the Seven Sisters has kidnapped a girl. A living girl. I need to get her back."

"Kidnapped how?"

Lucifer shrugged. "A book. She used it to Bloody Mary the girl right through a mirror and into the Shade."

The witch stood motionless. "A living girl in the Shade. My, but the Sisters are ambitious."

"Yeah, they're real trailblazers. But how do I get there?"

The witch let out a wet, diseased cough that took Lucifer a moment to realize was a laugh. "Simple, child. You *die*."

A shiver ran through her, though Lucifer couldn't tell if it was from the cold or the way the witch relished the word. "The girl they took was alive," Lucifer said. "There has to be a way."

"No. Only the dead may travel to the Shade. The Sisters themselves gave their lives to travel to the Shade."

"But one of them brought a living girl into the Shade."

"Because the Sister is a *witch*. The Sisters of Witchdown can craft complex sorceries that take lifetimes to perfect, where one wrong incantation or misplaced stroke of a symbol could bring all their magics crumbling around them like a house of cards." The witch waved a dismissive hand at the city around her. "You tinker with cantrips and sleight of hand like an inept child miming the actions of its parents. All while my sistren and I wield true power, power gifted to us for our loyalty. Our sacrifice. What have you sacrificed to deserve such dominion over life and death?"

"So that's it then? The only way to get to the Shade is to become an eyeless, infanticidal sea hag. . . . I'm sorry, I mean a witch, like you?"

"Yes." The witch took one step forward. Lucifer could smell the fetid stench of rot and decay bleeding off of her perfect skin. "You play with such trivial spells, girl. But the Sisters' book holds their secrets. Find it. Follow its path. Then you will know magic as only a woman can."

The book. Of course the answer was in the book. There was no way Lucifer would even entertain the idea of becoming a witch, but she wouldn't have to. If the book held the secret of getting into the Shade, she might be able to cheat her way in. She just needed to find the damn thing.

"But your time is short," the witch said.

"How do you know that?"

The creature looked up at the fabricated sky and said, "The moon is nearly full. And a witch's power is always at its greatest when it shines wholly swollen overhead. Whatever intention the Sisters have for this girl, it will come to fruition when the full moon is at its zenith." The witch extended her arms. "But do not waste your concern on her. Come to me, witchling. Let me guide you on your path to the sisterhood. We will feast upon the floating boy as I show you dark and terrifying wonders."

"As much fun as cannibalism sounds, I'm going to pass. I've already seen too many dark and terrible wonders as it is. But thanks for pointing me in the right direction."

"You reject my offer?" the witch asked, sounding genuinely offended.

"Of course I reject your offer. What, do you honestly think I'd go to all this trouble to help a girl if I was willing to drown a friend then go play little mermaid with some monstrous cow like you?"

The witch blanched. "What did you say?"

Lucifer waved her hands. "Oh, I'm sorry. I meant monstrous *sea* cow. So I guess that would be manatee then, wouldn't it. Yes, I think it would. Minnie the monstrous manatee. It has a certain ring to it, don't you think."

The witch's hair floated in the air around her face, creating a black halo. She smiled and said, "You will know the horrors of the deep in a way no human ever has."

"Witch, please. I call this a skip spell because I can skip out of here any time I want. You, on the other hand, not so much."

The wet, coughing laugh returned, only louder, more menacing. "Let me show you just how weak your little spell truly is."

The witch didn't move, but the soft rain grew heavier. Thick drops of water dotted the empty streets. When they fell against the parked cars, they began to run like paint smearing on a canvas.

Lucifer turned to see the buildings themselves melting. Tiny lines of yellow from the windows swirled inside the thick rivulets of black that oozed along its sides. Heavy wind blew coagulated chunks across the sky in a kaleidoscope of color. Everywhere she looked, the world was dissolving.

The wind grew stronger, the rain harder. The lampposts wilted and dripped into the dull puddles that had once been cars. The street tilted beneath Lucifer, causing her to stumble to her knees. When the street rose up again, it burst apart in a blast of black seawater and green foam.

Lucifer was on the rocky island again, the pocket dimension of 47th Street now nothing more than a melted memory. She desperately tried to hold onto the rocks, but wave after wave pounded her. Above the sound of the wind and the roaring waves, even above the witch's rheumatic laugh, she could hear David screaming her name. Somewhere in the distance. Somewhere a million miles away.

Lucifer looked up and saw the witch standing on the rocks, her arms wide, as the storm raged around her. The woman's black eyes bore into her. Lucifer could feel the terrible gaze holding her, lifting her. She was suspended above the rocks, though Lucifer couldn't tell if it was magic or the rush of water flowing over the island that held her aloft. All she knew was that her limbs were growing numb and useless from the overwhelming cold.

The witch howled into the storm. It was an impossible screeching, like white noise funneled through a distorted guitar amplifier. Lucifer struggled to reach into her trick bag for something, anything that might be able to help, but it wasn't there. She had left it in the boat with David. Not that it mattered. Her arms wouldn't obey. She was too cold, too tired.

Suddenly, the witch brought her hands together in a thunderous clap that sent a wall of water crashing into Lucifer. She tumbled through foam and fear as she was pushed clear of the island. Dark water danced all around her. Lucifer opened her eyes and winced at the sting of salt-water. The briny liquid filled her mouth when she tried to scream.

Now that she was submerged, the light on her life vest began to blink, giving Lucifer quick glimpses of dark shapes moving toward her.

Blink

She tried to swim to the surface, but up was now an abstract concept.

Blink

There was no up, no down, only the sea and the things that were coming to take her.

Blink

Scales flashed in the dark, then disappeared.

Blink

Tentacles groped for her through the muddy swirl.

Blink

Faces with eyes of black glass leered at her.

She squeezed her eyes shut. Things brushed past her in the current. The water in the back of her nose burned. Her lungs pleaded for air.

Blink

A hand. It reached for her, wrapped itself around her neck and pulled her into the dark.

CHAPTER 19

I t was David. He pulled Lucifer up out of the water with one hand while using the other to keep himself from falling overboard. "Lucifer!"

The biting wind cut through her like chilled knives slicing at her sodden skin. Lucifer maneuvered one of her arms over the edge of the boat. The rubbery fabric of the dinghy offered enough traction to keep her from falling back into the water, but it also rubbed her armpit raw. David let go of the boat and grabbed her life vest with both hands. He held her for a moment before timing his lift with a large swell to help her inside.

She plopped to the bottom of the boat like a dead fish and sucked in lungfuls of wet, salty air. Precious, precious air. David hovered over her, screaming her name, though she could hardly hear him over Minnie Hester's otherworldly screech commanding the raging storm.

Lucifer coughed, willed her hand into a fist, and gave David a thumbs-up.

"Oh thank God," he shouted. He moved to the far side of the dinghy and lifted the anchor out of the water, his sinewy arms straining with each pull of the rope. The dinghy rose and fell in the rolling waves. It tilted to its side and almost capsized before slamming back in the opposite direction. The violent movement twisted Lucifer's stomach into knots, but she was too cold and too weak to care.

She heard the outboard motor sputter to life. "Hang on!" David shouted, though the order was pointless. Lucifer didn't have the strength to hold onto a thought let alone the boat. All she could do now was hope that gravity kept her from being tossed overboard.

Mercifully, the dinghy began to move toward the shore instead of just the constant up and down caused by the angry swells. Lucifer lay on the bottom of the boat and watched the lightning streak across the inky sky, occasionally interrupted by the foamy spray misting over the dinghy whenever the bow would crash through a wave.

The frigid wind against her wet skin finally spurred her into action. Lucifer fumbled around until she found the garbage bag with her clothes. The plastic bag had done little to keep her clothes dry, however, and her shoes were missing. Thankfully, her trick bag was still there and all of its contents accounted for.

Lucifer had fought her way out of the blinking life vest and into her clothes by the time David had steered the dinghy past the break-water and into the calmer waters of the marina. The wind had died down to a lazy breeze, and the rain was now only a mild drizzle. Still, Lucifer felt as if she were stranded in the Arctic. She shivered uncontrollably, and her teeth chattered so hard that she worried they would break.

"Lucifer?"

She turned to David and tried to give him another thumbs-up, but her fingers were too numb to obey. "I-I-I-I-I'm f-f-f-fin-n-n-ne, David-d-d-d." Lucifer did her best to smile, but her chattering teeth made her feel like one of those ridiculous wind-up toys.

David's concerned expression melted into one of worry. "You're freezing!"

"J-j-j-ust g-g-get me to the c-c-c-car."

David steered the dingy back to the pier. Before they had even stopped, he hopped onto the pier and lashed the boat secure. It took Lucifer a full minute just to get her trick bag over her shoulder. What limbs still had feeling in them were stiff and only moved with the greatest concentration.

David saw her struggling and reached into the boat and pulled her onto the pier with one powerful movement. He put his arm around her shoulders to help steady her. "Where are your shoes?" he asked.

Lucifer couldn't feel the warped, wet wood beneath her bare feet. "G-g-gone."

Without a word, David scooped her into his arms and half marched, half ran his way back to the car. She vaguely remembered David putting her in the passenger seat before they were on the road with the heat blasting.

"I can honestly say, with absolutely no sense of shame or embarrassment, I have never been that scared before in my entire life." David was shaking himself, though probably from adrenaline and not from cold. "I mean, holy crap, Lucifer! She was *real*! That witch was real! I know you already showed me magic and all, but part of me still thought . . ." He wiped sweat from his brow with the back of his hand. "At first I was worried you were going to drown or be eaten by sharks or something. But when she appeared on that little island, I swear, Lucifer, I thought I was going to have a heart attack." He chuckled. It was a quiet burst of nervous energy tinged with relief. He looked over at Lucifer in the passenger seat and asked, "Did she tell you what you wanted to know?"

"The b-b-book. I have to find the b-b-b-ook-k-k-k." Lucifer's teeth chattered like machine gun fire.

"Lucifer, are you all right?" he asked.

She shook her head. No matter how much hot air the vents were blowing over her, the cold wasn't leaving.

"Your lips are blue," David said. "I'm taking you to a hospital."

"N-n-n-nothing they c-c-can d-d-do." Lucifer said. "It's m-m-m-magic." She could feel the spell's tendrils pulling at her. A consequence of getting too close to a witch who made her home at the bottom of the sea.

David gripped the steering wheel so hard his knuckles were white. "Magic? Oh, Jesus. What do I do, Lucifer? Tell me what to do."

"It'll p-p-p-pass."

"It'll pass? Before or after you die from hypothermia?"

Lucifer didn't respond.

David said, "Okay, we just need to keep you warm until the magic wears off, right?"

Lucifer managed a nod.

"Right," he said, pressing his foot down hard on the accelerator. In a few minutes, David pulled the car off the highway and toward a rest area where dozens of semitrucks huddled together against the night. David parked his car in an isolated corner of the lot. He stepped out of the car but left it running with the heat on high.

While David rummaged through the trunk of the car, Lucifer concentrated on the hot air blowing over her. No matter how warm the air was, it couldn't get through her skin. The witch's magic had left it as heat resistant as the underside of a space shuttle. Nothing was getting through.

David got back into the driver's seat with a blanket in one hand and a duffel bag in the other. "Take your clothes off," he said.

Lucifer wanted to retort, make some kind of sarcastic remark, but she was shivering too much to think. But David must have seen a questioning look on her face because he said, "Magic or not, you're never going to get warm in those wet clothes." He unzipped the duffel bag and pulled out a pair of gray sweatpants, T-shirt, and his letterman's jacket. "My gym clothes. Don't worry, they're clean." He sniffed a rolled-up pair of white tube socks. "Ish."

Lucifer managed a chuckle. David helped her undress and fumble into his gym clothes. He did a rather masterful job of looking away and affording Lucifer some modesty. The shirt was the same gray as the sweat pants, but with his school's orange and blue mascot, the Spartans, emblazoned across the front. The clothes were way too big and not even remotely clean. But Lucifer didn't care.

David handed her his letterman's jacket and said, "Put this on." As she did, David pulled the socks over Lucifer's blue toes still puckered from the water. Once she had the jacket on and buttoned, David wrapped her in the blanket like a chrysalis. He then produced a small candle. It was a yellow thing with a picture of daisies laminated on the side of the frosted glass. "Winters here can be a bit nasty," he said. "I keep an emergency kit in the trunk in case I ever break down in the snow."

Every few minutes a semi would roll into the rest area and park while another would lumber back out onto the dark, waiting road. Rain pattered softly against the windshield as the candle flickered, filling the car with its soft orange glow. Finally, now that Lucifer was dry, bundled, and sitting in a car with its heat blasting and a candle warming the air, she could feel a hint of warmth breaking through the witch's spell.

"I thought you were dead," David said, his voice barely more than a whisper. "I watched you disappear. You were there with the witch, but then there was this bright light. And you were gone." He looked over at her with a playful scowl. "Really wish you had let me in on that particular part of the plan."

Lucifer didn't entirely trust her voice, but at least her shivering was no longer measurable on the Richter scale. "A skip s-spell," she said. "I tried to t-t-trap her in the p-painting. Didn't w-work." The candle flame moved in a slow, lazy dance.

"Are you getting warmer at all?" he asked.

Lucifer could feel the slightest hints of warmth sliding through tiny cracks in the icy spell. "A b-bit," she said.

David rubbed his hands over her shoulders, creating as much friction heat as he could. Then he pulled her close and wrapped his arms around her. Lucifer leaned into him, trying to soak in his body heat. They sat watching the candle flicker as she shivered against his chest.

It was a strange sensation, being this close to someone. Lucifer couldn't remember the last time anyone had held her, not even in the fading and distant memories of her mother. Affection was never something Lucifer thought she needed. She lived in a world of witches and rituals and grand larceny. What was she going to do with a hug? But the tenderness of David's embrace, the calmness, the warmth, was so natural, so perfect, Lucifer couldn't imagine wanting anything else.

David broke the silence and said, "That was the bravest thing I've ever seen anyone do, Lucifer. I don't know how you do it."

Lucifer shrugged her shoulders but doubted David noticed through her shivering. She nestled in closer. She liked this. She liked being in his arms. She didn't want to think about witches or paintings or anything magical at all. She just wanted to think about David and being here in his arms.

"I don't mean just summoning the witch," he said. "I mean everything. Being shot at by cops at the gallery, the graveyard, the Worcester House. You're so calm about it all. Like it's nothing. Like it's just another day that ends in 'Y.' Nothing scares you."

"Everything s-s-scares me, David. You have no idea how terrifying it is to do what I do."

"I believe you. So why do you do it?"

"Because . . ."

"Because what? You can tell me, Lucifer."

Lucifer wasn't sure what to say. Part of her wanted to keep her mouth shut, to drop the conversation and go back to pretending they were just two kids in a parked car. But another part wanted more than anything to tell him everything. She wanted him to see her for everything she was. And maybe, just maybe, he wouldn't hate her for it.

"There are things out there, David. Dark things. Dangerous things. Even more dangerous than witches. And one of those things is known as the Harlot. A few years ago I did something very, very stupid. I traveled to the Aether where she lives and I stole something from her. Eventually she caught me and . . ."

When Lucifer didn't speak, David said, "And? Did she hurt you?"

"Yes," she whispered. Lucifer trembled in David's arms, but not from the icy chill of the witch's spell. "She was going to kill me," Lucifer said. "Instead, she recruited me. At the time, the Aether was overrun with demons and demigods all fighting over who would rule that dimension. So instead of killing me, the Harlot used me as her pawn."

Lucifer curled in tighter. "I ran from death squads in the favela. Saw so many of my friends just disappear into the night and never come back. I know about death. I know about suffering. But that war, David. The things I saw . . ."

"It's all right," David said, smoothing her hair. "You're safe here." David's voice was calming. He spoke to her in soft words that soothed her until, eventually, Lucifer stopped trembling.

The candle had burned halfway down by the time Lucifer found the will to speak again. "When it was over," she said, "the Aether was a wasteland and the Harlot was the only one left standing. But she wasn't done with me. Putting me through that hell wasn't punishment enough, so she did the worst thing possible: she marked me as her *heir.*"

David gently stroked the side of her head, brushing her tangled hair smooth with his fingertips. Lucifer could feel the heat from his hand slowly penetrating the icy spell that gripped her. "There are worse things than inheriting someone's money," he said.

"I'm not inheriting her money. I'm inheriting her position. The Harlot is the Keeper of Secrets. Which is exactly what it sounds like. She knows everything, David. I mean everything. She's trapped in the Aether, driven mad by all that knowledge being magically sucked into her brain. And someday that will be me."

Lucifer sat up and stared out the foggy window. Trucks slipped in and out of the dark, their lights fading like fond memories in the mist. "I should be worried about getting good grades in school or wearing the right clothes, having the right friends. Instead I worry about pict-magic and dimensional shifts and filcher demons. When

I finally find myself in a parked car with a boy it's so I don't slip into hypothermia from a witch's spell."

She reached out from under the blanket and wiped away a small patch of condensation from the window, a hint of feeling coming back into her fingers. "I'm not a good person, David. But I never thought I was a bad person. But I must have done something to deserve this, right?"

"Lucifer, I can't even begin to imagine what it was like to go through what you did, but I can say for certain that you didn't do anything to deserve it."

"Why else would all of that have happened to me? There has to be a reason." Lucifer sighed. "I always thought that if I can help enough people, save enough people, maybe that will make up for whatever it is that I did."

"I don't believe that for a second."

Lucifer turned to David and said, "Oh, well, thanks."

"You misunderstand. I don't believe that you help people because it might, someday, help you. You help people because it's the right thing to do. If you knew, for a fact, that all the good you do would do nothing to help you, I believe you would still help. Because you know what it's like. What it's like to be at the mercy of others, to be helpless. You help because you're the only one who can."

David reached out and put his hands on Lucifer's shoulders. "Lucifer," he said, "*that* makes you a good person."

"Oh, please, David, I'm a professional thief. How good could I be?"

"Robin Hood was a thief. And it's not like you're out robbing banks or holding up liquor stores. You keep bad things out of the hands of bad people. You risk your life for people you've never even met. Look at what you've done already to help Gina."

Gina. The mention of her name filled Lucifer's stomach with an icy guilt colder than the witch's spell. If Lucifer was such a good person, why was she in a parked car with Gina's boyfriend desperately hoping he would hold her again?

Lucifer turned away from David. She couldn't look at him. The guilt was too much. But David reached over and gently turned her back to him. He held her face in his hands. She could feel the heat emanating from his fingers, struggling to break through the weakening spell.

"Lucifer," he said. The flickering candlelight reflected in his eyes, turning their winter blue into infinitely deep pools of perfect black. They pulled at her just like the witch-tide that threatened to swallow her a few hours ago. Only now she wanted the current to wash her away. She longed to breathe in his sweet waters and let them fill her lungs until she could no longer breathe and she was drowning in him.

David leaned forward, slowly, cautiously. When their lips met, a wave of delicious heat rolled over Lucifer's body, shattering the spell. Her mind raced in a thousand directions at once, but as the warmth of his kiss spread through her, peeling away the frozen remnants of the spell, all of her thoughts melted away until there was nothing left but static.

When they finally separated, David looked at her with his half-smile that Lucifer found so incredibly irresistible. "You're sweating," he said.

"The spell's worn off. And it's really hot in here." Lucifer slipped from under the blanket and out of David's jacket.

"Lucifer, I—"

"Let's not . . . talk about this now. Please, David. I'm a little confused and, quite honestly, exhausted beyond words."

David sat back and said, "Yeah, you're right. I'm pretty tired, too. But it's another three hours back to the city. You cool if we just rest here until morning?"

Lucifer nodded. She leaned her seat back and rested on her side, using David's bunched-up jacket as a pillow. Without a word, David pulled her close and rested her head on his chest. As she lay there with her eyes closed, he gently stroked her hair until she fell asleep.

For the first time that Lucifer could remember, she didn't dream.

CHAPTER 20

"**W**here are we?" Lucifer asked, rubbing the sleep from her eyes.

"Just now pulling into the city," David said.

Lucifer stretched then leaned against the window. The sun was up, and most of the rain from the night before had already evaporated. "Why didn't you wake me up?" she asked.

"You needed the sleep. Besides, it's really funny when you snore."

"I don't snore."

"Lucifer, you sound like a bandsaw cutting through Bubble Wrap."

"Two words, David." Lucifer scowled and said, "Throat. Punch."

David chuckled. "Okay, okay." But after a moment, he said, "It was pretty cute, though."

She gave him two quick hits on the shoulder, almost causing him to steer out of his lane. That only made him laugh harder. She liked his laugh, the way its soft bellow filled the car, how it widened his crooked smile into a beautiful imperfection. But as they drove into her neighborhood, Lucifer's own smile faded as the guilt welled up in the pit of her stomach. Gina was in danger and running out of time. The moon would be full in a couple of days, and here Lucifer was, flirting with her boyfriend the morning after kissing him in a parked car. What was worse was that Lucifer was beginning to resent Gina. Why should Lucifer feel guilty for enjoying David's presence? Shouldn't she be allowed to have friends too?

But people who are just friends don't kiss in parked cars.

Lucifer looked over at David. There was a sadness behind his smile. She could tell that the guilt was eating at him too. Their kiss from the night before sat between them like the proverbial elephant in the front seat of the car, perched on the cup holder wedged between them. Lucifer couldn't get the memory of it out of her head. She remembered the softness of his lips and the incredible warmth that spread over her as the kiss finally broke the witch's spell. As wonderful as it was though, she didn't want to talk about it. She didn't want to be reminded that she had kissed the boyfriend of the girl she was trying to save while she was trapped in a hellish death dimension. But it was hard not to be reminded of it when all she could think about was kissing him again.

David parked in front of her apartment building. "So. Now what?" he asked.

Kiss me, she thought.

Lucifer pinched the bridge of her nose in an attempt to focus. "Now we find the book," she said.

"How? We don't know who mugged you."

"Whoever he was, he came to Olivia's house looking for it. He knew she had it and that I came to get it from her. So chances are he knows someone Gina knows. Someone who knew about the book and what happened at the Worcester House. So I want to talk with her friends again. Maybe I missed something, some clue that will lead me to him."

"Gina's dad might have caught him already."

"I hope not," Lucifer said. "He's the only human link we have to Gina and I'm afraid Buck would probably kill the guy if he ever found him." Lucifer gathered up her damp clothes and opened the car door. She said, "I have to run up and get some clean clothes and a pair of shoes. You mind waiting?"

"Not at all."

Lucifer stepped out of the car but turned back before closing the door. "I might be a while. So, you can come up if you want."

It didn't occur to Lucifer what she had done until they were halfway up the stairs to her apartment. She just wanted him close because she was afraid that he would leave if he waited in the car. However, inviting him up to her apartment might give him the wrong impression. But David was nice. He wouldn't think that's what Lucifer meant. Would he? He was a high school senior, handsome, star athlete with a beautiful girlfriend. Even though Lucifer didn't know anything about dating or boys or sex, she knew that it was foolish to believe David didn't have at least *some* experience with girls.

Lucifer kept running the possible scenarios through her head. What would she do if he did think that's why she invited him up? What would she do if he didn't?

She stopped in front of her door and gritted her teeth. Lucifer was preoccupied with David when she should be thinking about helping Gina. She had to get her back from the fabled city of Witchdown. Daydreaming about a boy wasn't going to help her with that. She had to stop. It was time to get serious.

But what if he wanted to get serious?

Just stop!

"Lucifer? You all right?"

She looked back at David. "Huh?"

"You've been staring at the door for a while. Just wondering if you're going to open it."

"Oh, yeah." Lucifer fumbled through her trick bag for her keys. She turned the lock and said, "Don't touch anything. Most of the things in here are a bit dangerous."

After they stepped inside, Lucifer became acutely aware of just how strange everything must have looked to David: the lack of furniture, the overabundance of books, the ancient artifacts, and a handful of stuffed animals, each marked with various symbols on various appendages, strewn about in a chaotic system that Lucifer had to admit she only pretended to understand. Lucifer thought to ask David to sit down since she assumed that's what hosts were supposed to do, but there was nowhere for him to sit other than her leaky beanbag chair. She had never had company before, so there was no need to waste money and effort on nice furniture. One of the only benefits of not having any friends.

Lucifer draped her clothes over the horns of a Culler Demon skull she had slipped over the head of a punching dummy. "I'm going to take a quick shower. My skin is itching from the saltwater."

David nodded, seemingly too distracted by the wealth of curiosities Lucifer had throughout the apartment.

After Lucifer quickly rinsed herself off, she threw on a pair of worn-in jeans and a faded T-shirt with the British Union Jack across the front. As she dried her hair, she stepped into her bedroom and said, "You really don't want to touch that."

David looked back at her like a toddler caught with his hand in the cookie jar. He was holding a bedsheet in one hand and standing in front of Lucifer's standing mirror: the doorway into the Aether.

Lucifer wasn't sure what she was expecting when she came out of the shower, but it was obvious that David wasn't planning on anything physical happening between them. Though part of her was relieved, part of her was a little disappointed.

All of her was thoroughly confused.

"I was just going to see if I was the fairest of them all," he said, flashing his crooked smile. Lucifer didn't need a magic mirror to tell her that, yes, he was indeed the fairest of them all.

"Ha ha, funny," she said. "But unless you want to talk to the Keeper of Secrets, you might want to take a step back. That's a portal to the Aether."

David took two steps back, his smile gone. "What do you mean, 'portal'? You're saying this actually goes to other dimensions?"

Lucifer took the sheet from him and draped it over the mirror. "No, just the Aether."

"That's the place where the war took place. The one you were telling me about."

"Yep. That's the place."

As Lucifer finished toweling her hair dry, David said, "And the Harlot, the Keeper of Secrets lives there." The way he said it made the hair on the back of Lucifer's neck stand up.

"Yes," she said, not bothering to hide the edge in her voice.

He turned to her and pointed to the mirror. "Lucifer, if the Harlot knows everything, we can ask her how to get to Witchdown." The look in David's eyes turned Lucifer's stomach. She had seen that same look a hundred times, that hunger for impossible answers. It was the same look gamblers had when they were convinced the next turn of cards or spin of the roulette wheel was going to bring them the fortune they so desperately needed to turn their lives around.

"No, David."

"No? Lucifer, she could tell us what we need to know."

"Yes, she could. But not for free. See, that's the trick with the Harlot. She sells her secrets to anyone willing to buy them, but the price is always too high. Always." She grabbed a pair of sneakers and slipped them on. "Besides, I already asked her."

"What did she say?" David asked.

"Nothing. I didn't pay. I told you, the price was too high."

"I can get us money, Lucifer," he said. "I have some saved, and my parents will give me a loan. Hell, I'll start a Kickstarter if I have to."

Lucifer needed to nip this in the bud. She had seen countless people give away too much for too little too often. She wasn't about to let that happen with David. "Listen to me," she said. "The Harlot doesn't take money. Why would she? She has no use for it. She takes other things. It could be a kidney, a favorite memory, or your ability to use verbs. Whatever it is, it's something that you're going to miss."

"What was the price, then?"

"David—"

"Tell me, what did the Harlot want?"

"My emotions. All of them. I would have had to give up all my feelings. Forever."

David stood in silence as the lustful look in his eyes slowly dwindled. Lucifer was thankful he was smart enough to know just how awful paying such a price would be.

"David," she said. "We don't need to ask the Harlot because we already have the answer. That's why we summoned the Witch of Cape Vale. The book will tell me how to get to Witchdown. I find the book again, I'll get Gina back." She grabbed his hand and squeezed. "You have to trust me, David. This is my world. I know what I'm doing."

He stared at the covered mirror for a moment before nodding in acquiescence. "Where do you want to start?" he asked.

"Isis. She blew me off pretty hard when I talked to her at the mall. I'm sure it was because I was the one who shinned her boyfriend in the balls, but I don't want to take any chances. Can you take me to her house?"

"Yeah, but she won't be there. She'll be at Ethan's house. They drive to school together. At least I assume she'll be there. She and Ethan are on-again off-again every few months. Right now I'm pretty sure they're on-again."

She tossed her trick bag over her shoulder. "Let's go."

Ethan's place was modest compared to the larger homes in the tiny subdivision, but a half-finished addition sticking out of the side of the house indicated that its modesty would be short-lived. When Lucifer and David reached the front door, David turned the handle and walked inside.

"What are you doing?" Lucifer asked.

"Ethan's a good friend of mine. I'm practically family. Come on."

David led her through the house into a back den where Ethan sat on a leather sofa, eyes glued to a nature program on the widescreen TV in front of him.

"Hey, Ethan. Is Isis with you?"

Isis walked into the room from a hallway on the far side and said, "Uh, not for long if he keeps acting like an ass."

David leaned over to Lucifer and whispered, "And about to be off-again."

Isis looked at Lucifer with absolutely no expression before smiling at David. "Hi, David."

"Hey, Isis. Got a sec?"

Isis glared at Lucifer. "For you, David, yes. Her? Hell no."

"Ethan, have you seen my briefcase anywhere?" a voice shouted from upstairs.

"It's on the kitchen table, Mr. Sinkowicz!" Isis shouted back.

"Thank you," the disembodied voice responded.

"Hey, Ethan. David's here. Ethan!"

Ethan yanked his gaze from the TV and said, "Why are you shouting? I can hear you. Damn, girl, give a guy a chance to respond."

Isis rolled her eyes. "All morning like this." Isis turned to Ethan as he walked over. "Did you hear your dad shouting at you?"

"Oh, I've been tuning him out since I was twelve. What's up, brah," he said as he gave David a bro-hug. When he saw Lucifer he said, "What's nut-punch devil skank doing with you?"

Lucifer chuckled. "I was in a band called Nut-Punch Devil Skank once. Had to break up when the accordion player left, though."

Ethan mockingly sneered before turning to David and asked, "How's Gina? Hear she's got the plague or something."

"She's . . . getting better."

Lucifer turned when she heard footsteps. Ethan's father walked into the den and said, "Ethan, I'm heading to work. Don't be late getting to school or I'll—"

Lucifer went at the man with a spinning back-fist that connected right on his chin. Ethan's father fell into a heap at her feet. Ethan was on her in an instant, putting her in a full nelson and dragging her away from his father. "What is your issue, bitch?"

Lucifer brought her heel up into Ethan's groin. When his grip loosened, she spun out and drove the flat of her palm into his solar plexus. All the air went out of his lungs, and Ethan fell to his knees. But as soon as Ethan was down, Isis was on her back, clawing at her hair.

"Keep your hands off my boyfriend you filthy—"

Lucifer grabbed Isis by the shoulder joint and tossed her head-over-heels on top of Ethan, who was struggling to catch his breath. Isis yelped when she landed. She and her on-again off-again boyfriend were tangled in a terribly unflattering arrangement. David lunged forward and grabbed Lucifer by the shoulder but let go and put his hands up when she readied to put him down as well.

"Whoa, whoa, Lucifer, be cool! What's gotten into you?"

Lucifer turned and saw that Ethan's father was gone. She broke into a run, but David grabbed her by the arm, stopping her. "Lucifer! What the hell are you doing?"

"David, that's him!"

"Him who?" David asked. "What are you talking about?"

"That's the guy who mugged me!" Lucifer pulled her arm free and started running down the hallway. "Ethan's father has the book!"

CHAPTER 21

Lucifer was out of the house and running just as Ethan's dad was backing his car out of the driveway. The tires screeched, and thick billows of blue smoke rolled into the front yard. Lucifer ran into the smoke and made a beeline for the silver sedan. It was a Mercedes-Benz with way more power than anyone ever needed in a car, and Ethan's dad was whipping every horsepower it had into a frothing stampede. The tire smoke stung her eyes, giving her a painful reminder of what Ethan's dad had done to her. But this time, the pain was bearable. Nothing was going to stop her getting her hands on him and that damn book.

A mail truck skidded to a halt just as the Mercedes-Benz backed out into the street. Ethan's dad accelerated, fishtailing the back end of the car into a pickup truck parked on the side of the street before screaming down the block. Lucifer didn't lose stride as she ran out into the middle of the street, chasing after the swerving car.

Ethan's dad was around the corner and out of sight in a matter of seconds, but Lucifer didn't slow down. She could hear the roar of his engines echoing through the neighborhood. She cut across a perfectly manicured lawn and parkoured over a redwood privacy fence, using the car's roar to guide her. She passed two gardeners bent over a flower bed and rolled through a gap under a row of hedges to find herself back in the middle of the street. She ran, ignoring the honking and yelling behind her. She didn't care how much she slowed traffic. She was going to catch this guy or get run over trying.

HONK!

"Dammit, Lucifer, get in the car!"

Lucifer turned at hearing her name. David was behind her, leaning out the window of his car and waving at her. She jumped into the passenger seat. "Drive!"

"Which way?"

"That way! Go go go!" she shouted as she pointed.

David rounded the corner onto a main thoroughfare. Lucifer spotted the Mercedes-Benz a few hundred yards ahead. Ethan's dad had slowed down, obviously assuming he had easily outrun a girl chasing him on foot. "There he is."

David pressed the accelerator. "Do you want me to ram him?"

"The man nearly melted my eyes from my sockets. Of course I *want* you to ram him. But don't. He can barely control that car as it is. You ram him, somebody's going to get killed. Just get closer. I have an idea."

As David pulled up to a few car lengths behind the Mercedes, Lucifer fished her phone out of her trick bag and dialed.

"Hello?"

"Buck? It's Lucifer. Listen to me—"

"Tell me you have something."

"I found the guy who mugged me. It was Mr. Sinkowicz, Ethan's dad. He has the book and I need it to get Gina back."

"*Mark* Sinkowicz? That doesn't make any sense. Why would he have the book?"

"As soon as I have my hands around his throat, I'll ask him. But he's in his car and I'm afraid if I try to stop him he'll run somebody down. I need you to pull him over, Buck, so I can search his car."

"Where are you?" Buck growled the question.

Lucifer peered out the window and said, "Crossing Eighth Street now. He's heading north toward Graeae Towers."

"On my way," he barked.

"Buck, wait . . . dammit."

"What is it?" David asked.

"I think Buck is going to kill Mr. Sinkowicz."

Mr. Sinkowicz turned and pulled into a parking garage. He flashed an ID to the guard sitting in the small booth next to the gate. The guard nodded, the gate lifted, and Mr. Sinkowicz drove through.

David pulled up to the gate and smiled at the guard. The guard didn't smile back. "This is a private garage. Graeae Industries employees only," the guard said. "There's public parking two blocks south. You'll have to back up."

Lucifer was about to try to talk their way into the garage when she heard sirens approaching in the distance. "Back up," she said.

David backed out and pulled off to the side of the street just as a police cruiser came screaming into view, sirens blaring, lights flashing. Lucifer hopped out and waved her hands as the cruiser came into view. The cruiser's brakes locked up, and the car slid to a halt just behind David's parked car in a cloud of shredded rubber.

When Buck stepped out of the car, Lucifer could tell he still hadn't slept. Heavy black circles rimmed his eyes, and thick stubble covered his granite jaw. When he spoke, his deep voice crackled with exhaustion. "Where is he?"

The passenger-side door of the cruiser opened, and another police officer stepped out. He was big, though nowhere near the size of Buck. He had military tattoos running the length of his arms, though they were difficult to see on his dark skin. Lucifer could tell by his expression that he had no idea what was happening. He was going along for the ride simply because that's what partners did.

"He went inside the garage, but only employees are allowed—"

Buck brushed past her and made a beeline for the guard shack at the entrance of the garage. Lucifer grabbed his arm. "I can't get answers if he's dead—"

In a flash, Lucifer was facedown on the ground with one arm pinned behind her back. But it wasn't Buck who put her there, it was his partner. "You're under arrest for assaulting a police officer," he said, pressing all of his weight between her shoulder blades with his knee. Buck kept walking.

David stepped back and held up his hands, "Whoa, whoa, what's going on?"

"Dammit, Buck, I can't save Gina if I'm in jail!"

Buck stopped, took a deep breath, then turned back. "Let her up," he said.

His partner kept the pressure on her back. Lucifer could feel the vertebrae of her spine compressing under his considerable weight, and what little air she had left was being squeezed out of her lungs.

"She put her hands on a cop," the partner said.

"I said let her up, Ty!"

After what seemed like an eternity, Buck's partner Ty lifted Lucifer off the ground and put her back on her feet. "Don't move from that spot," he said, pointing to the ground at Lucifer's feet. Lucifer was itching to get to Mr. Sinkowicz, but she had a feeling Ty wouldn't hesitate to fill her face full of mace. And she was never going to let that happen again.

Ty walked over to Buck and pulled him to the side. "You going to tell me just what the hell is going on with you? Past few days you've been . . . *off*, man."

"You have to trust me on this," Buck said, his eyes carrying a faraway stare that said more than any words could.

Ty put his hand on Buck's shoulder and said, "You don't want to tell me, that's cool. But remember what happened with Valdez. I should have told you about that mess, but I didn't. Don't make the same mistake I did, partner."

Buck nodded but said nothing.

Ty turned and gave Lucifer a sour glance before saying, "I'm going to go get some coffee. I'll be back in fifteen." He got behind the wheel of the cruiser and sped off.

"Let's go," Lucifer said.

As Lucifer, David, and Buck ran toward the guard station, the guard yelled, "Officer, this is private property! You can't come in here without a warrant!" Buck stuck his head through the plexiglass window and snarled something at the guard. Lucifer couldn't hear what it was, but the guard went pale.

Threat successfully delivered, Buck caught up to Lucifer and David running up the concrete ramp toward the upper levels. But the parking garage was huge, and it seemed like every other car was a Mercedes. David paused every once in a while, double-checking to make sure he hadn't missed it, but Buck was like a mad bull. He charged through the parked cars, swiveling his thick head back and forth like a gun turret as he scanned the garage. Lucifer, on the other hand, was following the smell of scorched tire and over-revved engine.

She was beginning to lose hope until she found Mr. Sinkowicz on the top level, getting out of his car with his briefcase clutched to his chest.

Lucifer bolted toward him like a shot, her tennis shoes squeaking on the concrete of the garage floor with her every stride. As soon as Mr. Sinkowicz saw her rushing toward him, he fumbled with his briefcase, desperately trying to get it open. Lucifer had no desire to see what kind of face-melting device he had inside, but she was too far away, too slow to get to him before he pulled out whatever he was reaching for.

Sinkowicz's hand disappeared inside the briefcase. When it reappeared, Lucifer was expecting to see another can of mace or even a gun. But what Sinkowicz held in his hand was the last thing she was expecting: a Light King. The Light King was a mass of writhing disembodied electric tentacles that slithered between his fingers, spitting and hissing sparks of blue light that dripped to his feet. Lucifer took a step to dive behind a nearby car as Sinkowicz held out the ball of snaking light toward her.

Before he could release it, Buck tackled him from the side with such force that Sinkowicz's briefcase flew from his hand and into the air, sailing over two parked cars.

The mass of snaking lights hit the ground with a sound of light-bulbs breaking. It split into dozens of individual tentacles, each flicking and sparking with electrical hisses. Buck had Sinkowicz facedown, but before he could get handcuffs on him, the tentacles had wrapped themselves around Buck's ankles. There was a flash of silver light, and Buck stiffened, a scream of agony caught in his bull-sized throat.

Sinkowicz pulled himself out from under Buck's seizing mass and struggled to his feet. The tackle must have knocked the wind out of him because he still wasn't fully upright when Lucifer reached him. She hit the ground and slid between his legs like a runner stealing second base. As she passed through, she thrust her arms out, taking Sinkowicz out at the knees. He fell forward and hit his face against the concrete with a dull, wet thud. Lucifer flipped and was on his back before the man could lift his face from the puddle of blood pooling beneath his broken face.

Lucifer turned to see David rushing up. "Oh, god, what's wrong with him?" David asked. He bent to help Buck as the huge cop trembled violently from the shocks of the Light King tangled around his ankles.

"Don't touch him!" Lucifer shouted. She turned Sinkowicz on his back. "What element did you use?" she asked.

Blood poured out from his broken nose and down his sagging cheeks. He coughed, and a line of bloody phlegm slowly slid down his chin.

"What element?!" she screamed.

Sinkowicz's eyes slowly began to focus. "Fire," he muttered before coughing up another mouthful of blood.

Lucifer was up and digging into her trick bag. She looked at David and said, "If he tries to stand up, hit him."

"Lucifer, that's Ethan's dad."

"Hit. Him."

Lucifer found the small velvet pouch she was looking for and dumped its contents into the palm of her hand. They were orange gaming dice ranging from four- to twenty-sided. But instead of numbers, they had symbols of the four elements, air, earth, fire, and water carved into each side.

She took the pyramid-shaped four-sided die and placed it on the ground, making sure the symbol for water was showing. She then took a twenty-sided die and spun it on the tip of the pyramid.

"What is that?" David asked.

"It will neutralize the Light King, but whatever you do, don't touch Buck until it's completely gone."

David nodded but said nothing. Lucifer was happy that he was learning to keep his questions to himself when she needed to concentrate.

The die spun faster and faster, perfectly balanced on its tip. The bright, pulsing light from the Light King began to fade. The tentacles themselves deflated like bad party balloons until they were nothing more than an oily mess on the concrete. As soon as the last tentacle disappeared, the spinning die shattered into dust.

Free of the Light King's biting energy, Buck took in a sharp breath and sat up.

"Are you all right?" Lucifer asked.

Buck nodded and turned to the bloody man lying on the ground next to Lucifer. The look he gave Mr. Sinkowicz sent a shiver down Lucifer's spine.

Buck was on his feet faster than Lucifer would have expected. The cop lifted Sinkowicz off the ground and slammed him into the side of a beige minivan parked nearby.

Lucifer heard something crack. Sinkowicz howled in agony, but his scream was cut short when Buck threw him back down to the ground and put his knee between the man's shoulder blades. In a flash, Buck had him handcuffed and up on his feet again. He shoved him back into the minivan. Sinkowicz yelped again, nearly collapsing from pain. "Ah! You broke my ribs—"

"*Where's Gina?!*"

"Please, I—"

SLAM!

"WHERE IS SHE?!"

Lucifer stepped forward and said, "We already know where she is. And the man can't talk with a punctured lung."

"He only needs one lung to talk."

"Buck, I want to hurt this guy just as much as you do." She pointed and said, "But I need you to get his briefcase. Then stand right there until I'm done. No arguments."

The cop's herculean chest heaved as he struggled to calm himself. He turned on his heel and said, "Hurry up."

Lucifer turned to Sinkowicz. "This is how this is going to work," she said. "It's really easy. I'm going to ask you questions, you're going to give me answers. If you don't answer my questions, you'll have to answer his." Lucifer thumbed over her shoulder toward Buck.

The blood drained from Sinkowicz's face, leaving his already pale expression even more ghostlike.

Buck came back and opened the briefcase, dumping everything on the ground at his feet. There were some papers, a notebook, a tablet, and various pens and pencils, but no Light Kings or other magical items. And no book.

"Where's the book?" Lucifer asked.

"I don't have it."

"That isn't the question she asked you," Buck growled.

Lucifer shot Buck a withering glance before turning back to Sinkowicz. "Where?"

"Please, you don't understand what will happen to me—"

"And I don't much care. Where?"

Sinkowicz dropped his chin to his chest. "In the office."

"Let's go."

Sinkowicz chuckled through his broken nose. "You can't go up there."

"You're going to get me in," Lucifer said.

"I can't."

Buck pulled his gun and pressed it to Sinkowicz's head.

"Whoa, Mr. Pierce! Calm down," David said.

Sinkowicz squeezed his eyes shut and whimpered. It was a stuttered wheezing that reminded Lucifer of someone trying to play a clarinet underwater.

Sadly, this wasn't the first time she had seen someone held at gunpoint. And if Buck pulled the trigger, it wouldn't be the first time she had seen that either. Growing up in a favela made one a witness to all manner of horrors. But even though it was eerily familiar, Lucifer had absolutely no desire to watch anyone die. Not even the guy who emptied a can of mace in her eyes.

"Buck," she said in a calm, even-toned voice. "You don't want to do this."

Buck didn't speak. His jaw was clenched so tight that the muscles in his jaw popped with the tension.

"If you kill him, then Gina is going to come home to a father in jail. Is that what you want?"

"I want my daughter home and *this* son-of-a-bitch is the one that took her!"

Sinkowicz yelped and nearly collapsed to his knees. A warm puddle of urine trickled out of his pant leg and pooled beneath him. "Please," he begged.

Lucifer gently reached out and touched Buck's arm. "I've got this. Trust me."

Buck let loose with an indecipherable howl then holstered his gun. He bent down so close to Lucifer's face that she could feel the heat radiating from him. "If he doesn't give you the book in the next thirty seconds, I'm calling in SWAT," he spat before walking away.

"SWAT won't do him any good," Sinkowicz murmured.

"Why not?" Lucifer asked. "Do you have a few more magical

surprises up your sleeve? Why's a middle manager like you playing with magic anyway?"

"I have to. Everyone in the office . . . dabbles."

"What are you talking about?" Lucifer asked.

Sinkowicz wiped a trickle of blood from his chin with his shoulder. "You have no idea what Graeae Industries is, do you?"

"A company that steals from the rich and gives to the richer. What does that have to do with magic?"

"Everyone in upper management is a member of the mystical community. Or at least knows about it. It's the only way to get promoted to those positions." He winced. "Please, can you get him to take these handcuffs off?"

"No." The idea of an entire company being run by people with knowledge of magic terrified her. There had always been vague stories surrounding Graeae Industries, but Lucifer had never seen anything to indicate that it was the dark and ominous enclave rumor said it was. To hear that those rumors might be true made Lucifer's skin crawl.

Lucifer folded her arms and leaned in close. "What does any of this have to do with you and the book?"

"Office politics. I overheard Carey from accounting talking about a new executive position opening up, that he would be great for the job. But he knew the company was leaning toward someone outside the company. So he had a plan to use the book to curry favor with a coven of witches. In exchange for helping them, the witches would give Carey the power he needed to get the job. The problem was, the book belonged to the COO, and he kept it locked in his office. So Carey was going to have to steal it."

"But you decided to steal it first," Lucifer said.

Sinkowicz nodded and hung his head. "Yeah. I made some bad investment deals and needed money. With the new addition on the house, the car, Ethan's college fund, I couldn't keep up. I thought if

I could get the book, I could get the promotion. It was just a fantasy, really. But one day when I was going over budgets with the COO, he was called out of his office for a moment. The book was just sitting there on his shelf. No one was around. So I took it."

"Then what did you do?" Lucifer asked.

Sinkowicz shrugged his shoulders. "I read it. I didn't understand half of it, but the basic instructions were pretty clear. All I had to do was get the book into the hands of someone young, younger than me anyway, and the witches would take care of the rest. So I gave the book to Ethan."

"You gave it to your own son?" Lucifer asked.

"I told you, I didn't understand half of it. I didn't know what was going to happen. It didn't matter anyway."

"What do you mean?"

Sinkowicz chuckled. "Ethan isn't what you would call a reader. I told him we were experimenting with new marketing strategies and needed a teenager's perspective. I asked him to take a look at the book, but he just tossed it aside and went back to his video games."

"Then how did it get to the library?"

"When it became obvious he wasn't going to read it, I asked him to give it back. That's when he told me he took it to the library. Apparently, because that's where books come from." Sinkowicz frowned, the drying blood on his face cracking with the gesture. "I love my son, but he isn't much of a thinker, either."

"So Ethan takes the book to the library. That's where Gina's friends pick it up to use it for their little Bloody Mary party at the Worcester House."

Sinkowicz nodded. "I swear, I didn't know Gina would be taken. Please, you have to believe me."

"What did you think was going to happen?"

"I don't know. Not . . . this."

"Guess Ethan isn't the only one who isn't a thinker," Lucifer chided. "So why did you attack me? Gina was already taken. The book already served its purpose."

"Carey from accounting." Sinkowicz's voice began to tremble. "The COO discovered the book was missing. It didn't take long for him to hear about Carey wanting it. Apparently, I wasn't the only one to overhear Carey talking about his plan. But since Carey didn't take it, he denied everything. So they brought him before the CEO."

"Did they fire him?"

Sinkowicz laughed. "No. He went up to the CEO's office and never came back. The next day all of Carey's things were gone and someone else was using his office. They just . . . disappeared him." Tears formed in the man's frightened eyes. When he spoke, his voice was barely more than a whisper. "You don't know these people. They would find the book eventually and know that I took it. So I had to get it back. When Ethan told me some new girl came to school asking about Gina, I thought you were some PI the company hired to find it. Ethan told me Olivia had the book. But when I got there and saw you got there first, I . . . I panicked. I'm really sorry—"

"Don't," Lucifer sneered. "Just tell me what you did with the book."

"Carey's car was still parked in the garage. They hadn't towed it yet. So I stashed it in there. The next day the car was gone and the book was back in the COO's office. That's why I can't help you. I don't have access to the executive floor any more. Even if I did, they have stronger security measures now. Magical security measures."

"You let me worry about those."

"You're going to break into Graeae Towers?" Sinkowicz asked. "That's insane."

"No, it's a felony. Now tell me what's waiting for me up there."

Sinkowicz did his best to describe the layout of the executive offices and what he knew of their security systems. When he had finished and Lucifer was confident he had told her everything he knew, she pulled out her cellphone, tapped her glyph app, and held it up to his face. "What do you see?" she asked.

"Uh, some squiggly lines and a spiral."

Lucifer turned to Buck and said, "I'm done with him."

The cop's temper had cooled somewhat, but Lucifer felt there was still only a 50 percent chance Sinkowicz would make it out of the garage alive.

"Promise you won't tell anyone it was me," Sinkowicz said as Buck grabbed his arm. "If they found out I was the one who took the book—"

"Don't care," Lucifer said. "This is what happens when you *dabble*. Other people get hurt. From now on, learn to live within your means."

Mr. Sinkowicz protested as the cop pulled him toward the exit. Buck ignored the man's blubbering as he read him his rights. David, who had been silently watching events unfold, stepped to Lucifer. "I can't believe Ethan's dad is the one who maced you. He would make pancakes in the morning for me and Ethan whenever I would stay over. I always thought he was a pretty cool dad."

"A pretty cool dad until he started playing with magic," she responded.

They followed Buck outside where his partner was waiting with a cup of coffee. Without a word, Buck's partner opened the back of the police cruiser. "Do I want to know?" his partner asked.

"Assaulting a minor, larceny, resisting arrest."

"I never resisted arrest—"

"Keep your mouth shut." Buck pushed Mr. Sinkowicz's head down and shoved him into the backseat. Buck turned to Lucifer. "What now?"

Lucifer looked up at the imposing height of the building looming above them. "Now," Lucifer said. "I break into Graeae Towers and steal the book."

"What did you just say?" Ty asked.

Buck motioned for his partner to give him a moment then led Lucifer away from the police cruiser. "Dammit, Lucifer, I'm a cop. You can't just announce your intentions to commit a crime."

"Then I probably shouldn't mention that I'm going to need your help," Lucifer said.

Buck sighed.

Lucifer said, "If I'm going to get Gina back, I need that book. And there's no legal way to get it. If that makes you uncomfortable—"

"Just stop talking for a sec," the cop bellowed. Lucifer could see he was on the verge of breaking down. Whatever resolve he had was quickly deteriorating. Buck looked over his shoulder to make sure his partner was out of earshot. "Answer me this, Lucifer. And be honest," he said. "Did you have anything to do with the break-in at Brisendine Gallery?"

Lucifer said nothing.

Buck shook his head and said, "What do you need me to do?"

CHAPTER 22

"You're not coming, and that's final," Lucifer said, stuffing a Pantouk crystal in her trick bag.

David leaned against the wall of her apartment, his mouth twisted in disapproval. The faux-leather sleeves of his letterman's jacket skiffed against the wall like a sigh. "Why not? I helped you in the cemetery. I helped you at the gallery. I even helped you with the witch! How can this be worse than that?"

Lucifer had to admit that if it hadn't been for David, she would have drowned. But it was her selfishness that let him tag along with her. She loved being around him, showing off for him, but it nearly got him killed. And this wasn't a singular threat like the witch. She was breaking into an office run by a group of people with intimate knowledge of the mystical underworld. It was doubtful any of them were witches, but that was the problem. She had no idea what to expect. And that was the absolute worst way to start a job. If half of what Lucifer had heard over the years about Graeae Towers was true, she was going to have her hands full. And having her boy-crush along for the ride would be too much for her to handle.

"It's worse because it is, David. You know the story about Perseus? He visits three old ladies to learn how to kill Medusa. Those three old ladies were the Graeae. The book is in Graeae Towers."

David shrugged his shoulders. "So? It shares a name. What does that have to do with anything?"

"Any company involved with magic and has the stones to share that name should be approached with extreme caution. And if Sinkowicz is telling the truth about the people with heavy-duty magical mojo running the place, caution might not be enough. I haven't done any recon, any dry runs, nothing! I'm going into this job blind. I have no idea what is waiting up there for me. Taking you along would get us both killed."

Lucifer rifled through a pile of stuffed animals in the corner of her room. She found a few to her liking and crammed them into her trick bag as she continued.

"I don't believe it," David said, crossing his arms. "There's no way Graeae Towers is more dangerous than the Witch of Cape Vale."

Lucifer said, "That's just it, David. I don't know. Probably not, but it sounds like there's enough sorcery in that place to give Minnie Hester a run for her money. For crying out loud, the COO of the company keeps the book on a shelf in his office like it's a dictionary." Lucifer rummaged through her closet until she found the pair of dark gray sneakers she was looking for. "All I know is that there's going to be a whack-ton of mystical muscle guarding that place. It's too dangerous for you to go with me."

David stepped forward and put his hand on Lucifer's shoulder. He looked down at her with his crooked smile and said, "That's exactly why you *need* me to go with you."

That smile made Lucifer's knees buckle. How could she say no to such a beautiful thing? She pried her gaze away from his magnetic smile and said, "No. David, the security is going to be more than just cameras and guards on patrol."

"But you said you haven't done any recon. You never break into a place without knowing everything you can about it first. Let me help you case the joint, at least."

Lucifer hated herself for not cringing when he said it. Even the little things he did that annoyed her were starting to seem cute. "We don't have time for that," she said. "Minnie Hester said that whatever it is the Sisters are planning to do with Gina, it's going to happen under the full moon. That's in two days. There's no time for recon. I have to do this blind and I can't if I have to keep one eye on you."

David tapped his chest and said, "I was the one who saved your

life with the witch, remember. And I think I can take care of myself."
He squeezed Lucifer's shoulders. "We make a good team, Lucifer."

Lucifer looked up into his eyes, stared at the sweet curl of his
smile, remembering the way his kiss finally broke the witch's spell.
He gently pulled her closer and leaned down. Lucifer put her hand on
his chest, the pointed corner of one of the many sports patches that
adorned his jacket biting into her palm. "Stop."

David straightened. "Sorry, I . . . sorry."

"I never should have let you come with me to Cape Vale. Hell, I
should have never let you come to the cemetery with me. But I . . . I
like it when you're near me. And that's a problem."

"Why is that a problem?"

"Because I can't concentrate when you're around, David! This
is dangerous work and I have to be focused because when I'm not
focused, people die. And you make it very hard to focus." Lucifer
slipped her trick bag over her shoulder.

"But I like being around you, too, Lucifer."

Lucifer's heart swooned, but her stomach twisted into a giant
knot. It was if her internal organs were being pulled by opposite
forces of gravity. She had never felt anything like this before. How
could she like being around him so much yet feel so horrible about it?
"That doesn't help," she said. "We're supposed to be helping Gina.
Your *girlfriend*, remember?"

David looked as if he had been slapped in the face. "I know, I
know. But I can't help the way that I feel. I like you, Lucifer."

"What about Gina?"

David paused, his crooked smile now wilted into a twisted frown.
"I don't know. She's my girlfriend, yes, and we have to save her. But
. . . none of that changes how I feel about you." David shrugged his
shoulders. "I'm not sure what else I can say."

Gina isn't real, Lucifer thought. *Say that she never was and all this
was just a bad dream and the two of us are going to wake up from a cat-nap*

in the park, under the rustling leaves of an oak tree while swans splash and swim in a nearby duck pond.

"I have to go," Lucifer said.

David gently grabbed her arm to stop her. "Please, let me help."

"Not this time. I'm sorry."

"I won't let you face that kind of danger alone. Don't expect me to sit around and do nothing," David said with a firmness in his voice she had never heard before.

"You can do whatever you want. You just can't come with me."

"Lucifer—"

"David. You know how much I like you. But don't think for a second I'm not above knocking you out and tying you up in the closet."

He chuckled, but his laughter faded when he saw Lucifer wasn't even cracking a smile. She was dead serious. Breaking into Graeae Towers was going to be one of the most difficult things she'd ever done, and the last thing she needed was David constantly distracting her by being so . . . so . . . *him.*

Lucifer and David stepped out into the hallway. As Lucifer was locking her door, David said, "I'll drive you there. Let me at least do that much."

Lucifer slipped her keys into her trick bag. "I already have a ride. Just go home, David. I'll call you when I have the book." She left him standing in the hallway and went downstairs.

Buck was waiting for her on the street. She got into the cruiser and asked, "Where's your partner?"

"Taking the night off. Family issues."

Lucifer had no idea if he was telling the truth or not, but she didn't much care.

As they pulled onto the street, Buck said, "Sinkowicz is in jail. He wouldn't let his lawyer post bail. He thinks he's safer there."

"He probably is, though I don't think anyone is looking for him. The book is back where he found it, and someone else took the fall for it. He's in the clear."

"Not with me, he isn't."

Lucifer knew that there was nothing Buck could do to him for his role in Gina's kidnapping, but he would nail Sinkowicz to the wall for everything else.

"You should also know that we rounded up a couple of guys as possible suspects from the gallery theft," he said.

"Guys?"

"The security guard on duty and the pursuing officers described the suspect as a male."

Lucifer smiled to herself.

"But all their alibis check out. Just thought you'd like to know no one is going to jail for you." When Lucifer didn't respond, he continued. "I'm not comfortable with this, Lucifer."

"Plausible deniability. Just go in, ask if they saw anything the night of the gallery theft, and leave. You'll never notice me."

"This makes me an accessory."

"For doing your job?"

"I'm not on the gallery case. So, no, it's not my job."

Lucifer wrapped her hair in a hair band. "Security isn't going to know that. Look, all you have to do is distract them long enough for me to get past them. I can take it from there."

"How? I've seen their security system before. It's state of the art."

Lucifer gave him a sideways smile. "You'll see. You'll be embarrassed by how easy it is."

He grunted.

Lucifer reached over and put her hand on his obscenely large bicep. "We're going to get her back, Buck. I promise."

They drove a few blocks in silence before Buck said, "When Gina was five, the neighbor's dachshund chased her up a tree. It was a loud, obnoxious thing, but harmless. Still, Gina was terrified. She shied away from dogs after that. Every time she would see one, she would run into my arms to protect her. The way that sweet little girl trembled . . ." Buck trailed off. They drove another block before he finally said, "I would tell her that she didn't have to be afraid. That I would never let anything bad happen to her. Ever." The tendons in his elbows popped as he squeezed the steering wheel. "I don't know how much longer I can take this," he said. "My little girl . . ."

"Is going to be fine," Lucifer finished. "This book will tell me how to get to the Shade and bring her back. But to get the book, I need your help."

Buck glanced at her and gave her what she could only assume was a smile. But the anguish and exhaustion etched on his face made the gesture come across as a grimace. "Whatever I need to do," he said.

"Good. Drop me off a couple blocks away."

"I'll leave you at the alley behind Eighth Street. The cameras on the corner haven't been working for the past three weeks. Budget cuts."

"Perfect," Lucifer said.

When Buck stopped in the alley, Lucifer got out but turned back before closing the door. "Buck," she said. "I would give anything to have had a dad like you. Gina is a very lucky girl."

The big man nodded, the yellowed light of streetlamps glistening in his eyes. "Maybe if I had spent less time protecting her and more time showing her how to protect herself, this wouldn't have happened. Maybe if she were more like you . . ."

Lucifer shook her head. "Trust me, Buck. Of the two of us, I think Gina got the better deal." She tapped the hood of the car and closed the door. Then she walked into the shadows of the alley and made her way toward Graeae Towers.

CHAPTER 23

The city of South Haven was a mass of concrete and steel with the clustered buildings of downtown rising high above the urban sprawl. Many of the buildings had been built in the mid-twentieth century when the city was thriving in the postwar economy. And though most of the buildings didn't rise much higher than forty or fifty stories, they left a rather stunning skyline that meandered over the horizon like a lazy serpent basking its fluorescent scales under the moonlight. But the serpentine rise and fall of building tops was interrupted by a single spire that towered above its curving line like a silver arrow pinning the great serpent to the ground: Graeae Towers, the grand jewel of the city.

The building stood in stark contrast to the blocky structures that surrounded it. While the other buildings were dark, bland slabs of brick and stone, Graeae Towers was bright and sleek with long strips of windows between the clean, minimalist lines of its supporting frame. The upper floors tapered into a point, leaving a pyramid of deep-tinted glass and steel perched on top of the great silver column. Its shining surface reflected the lights of the city like a mirror ball.

Lucifer stepped onto the salmon marble of the courtyard in front of the building and waited underneath a flaking birch tree planted in a golden cistern. Buck had parked his cruiser across the street and was walking toward the glass doors. Lucifer mindlessly fingered the drawstring of her hoodie while she watched a pair of security guards through the windowed walls. They were sitting behind a vast maple desk, reclined in comfortable black chairs that looked to make it that much harder to leave for rounds.

Buck pulled his nightstick and tapped on the door. One of the guards looked up at the dull, klacking sound, annoyed at the intrusion. But when he saw Buck in his police uniform, the guard pulled his feet from the desk and walked over to unlock the door.

"Yeah?" the guard asked, doing little to hide his annoyance.

Lucifer tied her hair up into a bun and walked toward them. Once she was done with her hair, she reached into her trick bag and pulled out an ID card. It was an expired card used to get into a cable network office across town, but Lucifer didn't need it to unlock any doors. She just needed it to *look* like it could.

"There was a robbery at the Brisendine Art Gallery a couple nights ago," Buck said. "I'm canvassing the area to see if anyone saw anything that might help us catch the guy who did it."

"Unless the thief came in here—"

"*Desculpe*," Lucifer said, quickly flashing the ID card. "*Limpeza.* Cleaning."

"You sure you didn't see anything?" Buck asked, moving aside to let Lucifer through. "Maybe your partner saw something."

The guard glanced at Lucifer for a second before stepping back to let her past. "Hey, Johnny. You see anything odd the other night?"

Johnny, the guard still seated, didn't even bother to look up from his tablet hidden under the desk. "Wasn't on duty."

Lucifer walked to the elevators as Buck peppered the guard with more questions. She couldn't hear exactly what he was asking, but it was obvious by the guard's responses that he was annoyed and wanted to get back to whatever it was he and his partner were watching on YouTube.

As Lucifer waited for the elevator, she scanned the large plaque of names on the wall. There were hundreds, but it didn't take long for her to find the COO of Graeae Industries: Isaac Haldis.

The elevator doors opened, and Lucifer slipped inside. She pulled out a homemade master keycard she had made by tethering a third-generation smartphone to an expired Starbucks rewards card. She slid the card into the control panel and tapped an icon of a monkey covering its eyes on the phone's screen. Lucifer had toyed with the idea of stealing Mr. Sinkowicz's card and using that to get around the building, but the security system would have logged it in its records. That would have left a big neon trail leading right to him. And as much as she hated that man for attacking her and for his role in Gina's kidnapping, she didn't think he deserved to be disappeared for it.

Well, maybe a little.

Lucifer's master keycard would let her get to any floor in just about every building in the city, but before she wandered through Graeae Towers, she needed to look the part. She pressed the button for the basement floor.

The basement was mostly a collection of small maintenance offices and supply closets wedged between cold concrete walls. Thankfully, the basement was empty with only the sound of humming fluorescent lights overhead to keep her company. It didn't take long for Lucifer to find a cleaning uniform that fit and a handful of supplies to finish off the costume.

Sufficiently disguised, Lucifer stepped back in the elevator and pressed the button for the executive floor. She glanced up at the small, dark sphere of glass hiding the security camera in the corner of the elevator. That particular security measure didn't worry her. Chances were the guards were too interested in whatever they were doing to pay her any attention. Lucifer had learned pretty quickly that if she ever wanted to get around unnoticed, just dress like a member of the cleaning staff, and no one would pay you a second glance.

As Lucifer rode the elevator up to the executive floor, she couldn't help but think of David. Was he mad at her for not letting him come? It was certainly for his own good, but she was devastated by the thought that he might be angry with her. She wanted nothing more than to make him smile. It was such a beautiful smile. The way one corner of his mouth curled just a bit more than the other, how his teeth flashed like ivory rose petals in sunlight. . . .

Dammit!

Even without being there, David was still a distraction. Lucifer needed to concentrate on the job at hand, otherwise she was going to get herself killed.

She wondered if David would be sad if she died. Probably not, at least not really. And even if he was, he'd still have Gina to comfort him.

Gina.

Lucifer took a deep breath. Gina was in Witchdown and most likely terrified beyond the imagining of it. It was time to stop daydreaming about such ridiculous fantasies and focus on the job. Get the book, get to Witchdown, bring Gina back.

But . . . what if she didn't?

What would happen if Lucifer didn't steal the book? She could come out in a couple of hours and tell Buck and David the book simply wasn't there. It's gone forever and so is Gina. To be honest, it would be all Gina's fault since she was the one foolish enough to stand in front of the mirror in the first place. There would be no one to blame but herself. She would disappear just like Carey from accounting. So how bad would that be, really?

Buck would be inconsolable. And Lucifer had no doubt that he would kill Mr. Sinkowicz the first chance he had. Both of their lives would be over. And whatever plan the Sisters had would come to pass. Lucifer highly doubted the plan was to give the world more puppies and rainbows. But David . . . Lucifer could comfort him in his moment of loss. She could be the shoulder he cried on, the person he clinged to in his sadness, and the one who would ultimately make him smile again. And why not? Why shouldn't she know what it's like to have a boyfriend? A month ago, that idea would have seemed completely absurd. But now Lucifer had to admit that it was something she wanted. It was something she wanted badly. And all she had to do to get it was hide in a broom closet for a couple of hours, let a girl die at the hands of a witch, and wait for her father to murder the man responsible.

Lucifer rolled her eyes. As if she would ever let that happen.

When the elevator doors finally opened, the presence of magic hit her like an ocean wave. Lucifer's thoughts quickly came into sharp focus. She was back in her world, doing what she did best. Playtime was over.

The aura of magic was so thick that the air practically crackled with it. But the magical energy didn't seem to be coming from a single direction. It was as if the entire space was infused with sorcery. It was obvious to Lucifer that Mr. Sinkowicz had greatly undersold just how much his coworkers "dabbled" in the arcane.

Lucifer stepped out onto the immaculate navy carpet, the sound of her footsteps lost in the soft fabric. There was a large mahogany receptionist desk in front of a wall fountain that dribbled silently into a narrow pool. Lucifer was impressed by the engineering that must have gone into designing a completely silent fountain. Most people installed fountains specifically *for* the sound. It can be relaxing, calming, and welcoming. But here, it only served as a visual. The quiet was unnerving, lingering in the office like an invisible fog.

She suddenly realized what it was that was responsible for much of the magic she was feeling: a silence spell. As a test, she cleared her throat. She felt the familiar rumble in her throat, but what she heard was a muffled and distant cough that she would have missed had it not come from her.

Scientists had once designed the quietest room in the world by making walls that absorbed every sound so nothing reverberated back to the listener. The effect was so unsettling that the longest any one person could stay in the room without going insane was forty-five minutes. Lucifer suspected the quiet spell served the same purpose. She was already feeling uncomfortable.

Lucifer ignored her discomfort and moved through the office, searching. Grand abstract paintings lined the walls, each with a host of colors that perfectly accented the navy decor. On the floor next to those paintings were large leafy plants in lavender vases, giving the sense that the office had been carved out of the wilderness and Mother Nature was slowly trying to reclaim her territory.

Lucifer pulled out a feather duster from the cleaning supplies she took from the basement and began dusting. Though she doubted the bored guards monitoring the security feeds would pay her much mind, it didn't hurt to be too careful. She made a show of moving vases, telephones, even reaching for the tops of the paintings as she scanned for Isaac Haldis's office. She also kept a sharp lookout for any other security measures in place. She wasn't so much concerned with mundane measures like pressure-sensitive floors or fingerprint-ID locks on the office doors. It was the magical security that worried her. Before long, the silence spell would make it as difficult for Lucifer to concentrate as if David was around.

Well, *almost* as difficult.

She moved past a large conference room. The Graeae Industries logo was frosted on the glass walls that separated it from the rest of the offices on the floor. Each of the offices had similar glass walls allowing Lucifer to look inside. They each had the same minimalist design with a sturdy desk, ergonomic chair, a single piece of art on the wall, and not much else.

Lucifer turned a corner and found a short hallway that ended abruptly with the ladies' room on one side and the men's on the other. At the end of the hall was a small table underneath a large mirror attached to the wall. Resting on the table were a handful of objects that Lucifer didn't recognize. She stepped closer and wiped them with her duster. A glass sphere sat on a short pedestal with what looked like a dinosaur tooth resting at its base. It made sense for a company named after the three old crones of legend who shared an eye and tooth among themselves. That the company felt compelled to adorn the office with a tiny shrine to their memory only added to Lucifer's discomfort.

Outside each office was a small plaque with the name and position of the person who used it. It didn't take long for Lucifer to find the COO's office. Unlike the others, its walls were solid wood. Isaac Haldis did not seem to have the same desire for transparency his colleagues were required to have. And Haldis's apparent need for privacy extended beyond just having solid walls to his office. His office was also out of view of any security cameras, so Lucifer didn't bother to hide her actions.

Before she touched the door, she carefully examined every aspect of it: the handle, the hinges, the wood, the lock. Most office doors, even executive offices, only had a single lock in the handle of their doors. This door was no different. But Haldis had more than just a basic lock. Etched in the brass of the bottom door hinge was a small symbol. A symbol Lucifer didn't fully recognize. She quickly grabbed her smartphone and punched up her database app. She found it in the hybrid sub-folder. The core symbol was Mesopotamian but had been modified with a dash of Corsican pict-magic to give the spell some added punch. It was impressive work and not easily done. Lucifer doubted she even had the skill to craft that kind of spell without it blowing up in her face.

Lucifer knew that if she opened the door, the spell would activate. The symbol would emit a burst of energy that would bind anything in its path, like catching a fly in amber. But because the symbol was on the bottom hinge, it would only lock the trespasser's feet. It would be enough to immobilize them yet keep them alive until someone happened along, allowing the company to deal with the would-be thief any way they wanted to. Clever.

Lucifer thought she might be able to use her own brand of hybrid symbols to counteract the trap, but she wasn't familiar enough with Corsican pict-magic to trust herself. There was a good chance it would just make things worse. So she decided to go with the easier option.

Lucifer grabbed a set of lock picks from her trick bag and began on the lock. She had to work completely by feel since there was no sound to guide her. Eventually, she felt something give way. But before she opened the door, she reached up and curled her fingers on the top of the door jamb. Digging in, she pulled herself up off the ground and used her feet to manipulate the handle.

When the door opened, there was a quick flash of sickly yellow light followed by a small concussion wave that Lucifer felt deep in her chest. The lush navy carpet directly beneath her was now a brittle mass of melted green. She slowly pushed the door open with her foot and dangled for a moment before falling to the ground. Lucifer could feel the binding magic gripping the tiny fibers of the carpet, making it feel as if she were walking on gravel.

Lucifer quickly stepped inside. The office was larger than the others she had seen and more ornately decorated. Statues, vases, and several masks sat atop the long shelving units that lined the far wall while a handful of midcentury modern chairs formed a make-shift meeting area. But what caught Lucifer's attention was the huge painting hanging behind the dark mahogany desk.

It was a portrait, expertly done as far as Lucifer could tell. A woman in a yellow dress sat with her hands folded across her lap, her face composed and demure, but there was a hint of something unpleasant behind her eyes.

Most people had photographs of loved ones on their desks, but the portrait of the woman was the only image in the office. There was something unsettling about it. Lucifer dismissed it as jitters from the memory of trapping the Witch of Cape Vale inside the 47th Street painting. That was, until she noticed something unusual at the bottom of the frame: a pair of manacles etched into the wood.

This was a binding frame.

It was a cruel and terrible thing, the worst of what magic could do. A binding frame trapped its subject inside an image, forever, frozen in a state of full awareness. It allowed a particularly cruel person to look upon their captive indefinitely. It was a trophy, much like a moose head on the wall. Only in this instance, the moose was alive and fully aware of its suffering.

Lucifer's stomach turned. If she knew how to free the woman, she would. No one should be tortured like that. But the binding frame was at a level of magic beyond what Lucifer could manage.

The book, Corsican pict-magic, binding frames . . . the people at this company did not mess around. From what little she had seen so far, it was obvious that they were some serious players in the mystical underground. One of these days Lucifer was going to have to come back and investigate just what kind of magical shenanigans were going on here at Graeae Towers. But one job at a time.

Lucifer rummaged through the bookshelves. Most of the books were mundane business manuals, but a few were definitely of the arcane. The book she came for, however, was nowhere to be seen.

She went to Haldis's, desk but there were no drawers or shelves. There was no place to hide the book. Lucifer went through the office again, wall to wall, floor to ceiling, but the book was nowhere to be found.

Lucifer turned to the portrait on the wall.

Very carefully, she pulled the frame away from the wall. When she peered behind it, she could see a safe recessed deep into the wall. Lucifer had to admit that she was disappointed. A wall safe? How boring.

Lucifer pulled the portrait off the wall and leaned it against the desk. When she saw the safe in the full light of the room, she took back her disappointment. The dense green metal of the safe had been etched with dozens of intricate picts and symbols, each infused with particularly nasty magic.

Before even touching the safe, Lucifer consulted her symbol app again, making sure she knew exactly what each could do. It was a knot of chained magic that would take an expert hours to untie. And simply changing the symbols by adding elements or dissolving ones already there would only set off the rest of the magic in the chain. It was so complex that only the person with the right spellword could open the door to the safe without meeting an untimely and unpleasant demise.

This was going to be easy.

The problem most practitioners of magic had when it came to securing their valuables was that they relied too much on magic. Isaac Haldis was no exception. He had every magical safeguard set to prevent a would-be thief from opening the safe. But a safe is a box. And every box has six sides. Yet so many people put all their mystical booby traps on only the one side with the door.

Lucifer reached into her trick bag and found the tools she needed: a ball-peen hammer and an antique metal syringe. She took advantage of the silence spell and took to smashing the wall with relish. She hammered away, knocking off thick chunks of drywall until the underneath of the safe was fully exposed. The metal box was welded to metal supports within the wall to prevent anyone from just taking the entire safe to someplace where they could take their time opening it with a blowtorch. Lucky for Lucifer, she had the magical equivalent of a blowtorch with her.

Lucifer took the syringe and carefully squeezed its contents along the bottom edges of the safe. Too little, and it wouldn't work. Too much of it, and it would melt the entire safe and everything inside. It was a special mix of chili powder and bile from the snot-gland of a fire salamander. Lucifer had ruined three perfectly good practice safes perfecting the formula.

Her eyes began to water from the acrid smoke of the melting metal. When the smoke finally dissipated, Lucifer used the hammer to bang on the bottom of the safe. The rectangular hunk of metal along with the contents of the safe all fell to the ground in uncharacteristic silence. There, at the top of the pile, was the book. Lucifer grabbed it and tossed it in her trick bag.

Then something shattered.

The sound came from outside the office. But that wasn't possible. The silence spell was still in effect. But there was no mistaking it. Lucifer had heard shattering glass.

Lucifer instinctively dropped into a crouch. That's when she saw a summoning symbol on the piece of metal in the pile on the ground. If disturbed, the symbol summoned whatever big and nasty was bound to it. It had been etched on the inside of the safe where she never could have seen it. Isaac Haldis was an exception after all.

Now that she had what she came for, it was time to go. Slowly, she made her way to the door and peered out into the hallway. No movement. And no sound. Lucifer crept out into the hallway and started toward the elevator. When she crossed the hall toward the restrooms, she saw the Graeae shrine beneath the mirror. Only now the glass sphere of the shrine was in a thousand pieces and the tooth was gone. She caught her reflection in the mirror and saw something lurking behind her:

A witch-hound.

The witch-hound was a swirling cylinder of orange and pink flesh that coalesced into a cavernous maw of wicked, slathering teeth. Lucifer had never seen one before, but she had read about them. The great sorceress Ro' Ember was rumored to have used them to defeat her brother in the 1356 War of the Twins, only to be devoured by them moments after her victory. Any person who used one for security had to be either incredibly powerful or incredibly crazy.

Lucifer dove to the side just as the ethereal beast lunged at her. She could feel the sheer mass of the creature as it slid overhead and slammed into the wall with such force that the wall disintegrated in a flurry of dust and debris. The bits of drywall that had come into contact with the witch-hound's amorphous skin sparked and smoldered.

Lucifer was up and running. The silence spell muted the cacophonous riot of destruction the witch-hound was leaving in its wake as it chased her. All she could hear was the rapid pulsing of her heartbeat echoing in her ears.

She looked back just as the witch-hound lunged. This time, the monster dove low, but Lucifer was able to jump up and avoid the full brunt of its attack. However, she was too off-balance to get the height she needed to get fully clear of the creature. It slammed into her leg, the muscles of its roiling body feeling like hundreds of angry ferrets under its diaphanous skin desperately trying to claw their way free. The witch-hound bucked and sent her flying high into the air. Lucifer hit the fluorescent lights in the ceiling directly overhead and came down behind a gray partition that separated a bank of cubicles away from the main offices. Shattered glass from the long thin bulbs rained down amid a flurry of sparks.

The lights of the entire floor flickered then winked out. Immediately, the backup generator came on and the floor was filled with the cold lunar glow of the emergency lights. Lucifer knew she had to get to the stairwell since the elevator was most likely shut down along with the power.

As she scurried on her hands and knees into the next cubicle, an office chair sailed overhead. The witch-hound had torn through the partition and was thrashing away in the tight space. The monitor, desk, and other little odds and ends all turned to dust in the maelstrom.

Lucifer rolled and sprang to her feet. She leaped over the next partition and sprinted down the narrow hall between the two rows of cubicles. She couldn't hear the witch-hound barreling behind her, but out of the corner of her eye she could see its reflection in the long line of windows she was running next to. It turned and twisted in on itself, the witch-hound's body rolling after her like a pastel pyroclastic flow that devoured all in its path.

The entrance to the stairwell was just off from the reception area. Lucifer pulled one of the paintings from the walls as she sprinted past and tossed it at the witch-hound. The beast was delayed by the large painting just long enough to shred its heavy frame into splinters within its whirling jaws.

She reached the stairwell, but the door wouldn't open. The mystical alarm that Lucifer tripped when she cracked the safe must have put the entire floor into lockdown. If she had a minute to spare, she could open the door easily. But there was no way the witch-hound was going to leave her be long enough to get it open. And now that the door was locked, that meant security would be on its way here to find out just what was going on. She was going to have to find another way out.

The witch-hound charged. As it lunged for Lucifer, she planted the palms of her hands against the wall and flipped herself up and over the creature, using her hands as the pivot point. The monster slid underneath her, its horrid fangs scarring the wall as it went past.

Lucifer needed time to think, to formulate a plan, but it was going to be near impossible with the witch-hound on her heels. She made her way back to the cubicles, hoping to use the partitions to hide long enough to think of a way to escape. This was *exactly* why she never started a job without knowing all the ins and outs of a place.

The cubicles were now twisted piles of gray and black rubble. As she jumped over one pile, she saw the witch-hound's reflection in the window. Instinctively, she shifted her weight to change her direction, but her ankle caught on a jagged piece of cubicle frame and she went tumbling. The creature soared overhead, crashing into the windows. The impact was so great that the entire window was punched free of its frame and fell out into the open air.

Lucifer was up and moving again, ignoring the sting of pain in her ankle where the twisted frame had torn into her flesh. She made her way down the hallway toward the restrooms, doing her best to staunch the terror of seeing the pursuing monster's reflection in the mirror at the end of the hall. It was relentless. It was never going to stop.

She ducked into the men's room. The smell of disinfectant was overwhelming. The rich mahogany walls looked black under the blue of the emergency lights in stark contrast to the pale marble floor tiles sparkling like a summer lake in moonlight. Lucifer hid in one of the stalls and stood on the toilet. She didn't hear the witch-hound come in, but she saw its swirling shadow moving across the floor from underneath the stall door.

Lucifer could feel her heart racing inside her chest. At that moment, she was grateful for the silence spell. Without it, she knew the witch-hound would be able to easily hear her heartbeat. She knew that she wouldn't be able to outrun the monster forever. Eventually, it would have her. She was as good as dead. But if she was already going to die . . .

Her sudden escape plan was beyond dangerous and would most likely get her killed, but at this point she really didn't have anything to lose. Quickly, Lucifer reached into her trick bag and pulled out a slim black lipstick case. She watched the creature's shadow slide across the floor, searching. Lucifer pulled the cap off the lipstick and rolled it under the stalls toward the far end of the restroom. When the cap rolled out from under the far stall, Lucifer saw the monster's shadow dive in the direction of the cap. Lucifer wasted no time.

She kicked the stall door open and ran. Out in the hallway, she reached up and yanked the mirror from the wall. It was slightly too big to carry under one arm, so she put the lipstick between her teeth, gripped the mirror in both hands, and bolted toward the ruined cubicles.

Lucifer didn't bother to look back. She knew the witch-hound would be behind her. This time when she came to the mangled partitions, she didn't turn toward the executive offices but continued straight toward the gaping hole where one of the windows used to be.

She stepped on the wall and leaped.

A crushing wave of sound hit her now that she was outside of the silence spell's affected area: distant sirens, the soft hum of nighttime traffic, and the impossible rush of air as she plummeted down the side of the building. But there was another sound. It was deep, guttural, feral. The witch-hound had followed her out the window. It didn't matter. Lucifer had to follow through with her plan and just hope that gravity kept her ahead of the trailing witch-hound gnashing its horrible teeth above her.

She straddled the mirror, using her knees to keep it steady as she drew symbols and picts along the frame with the lipstick. Air caught the mirror and flipped her, but her ankles were scissored, preventing the air from ripping the mirror free. Her hair lashed against her face, nearly blinding her. As she drew, she couldn't help but notice the reflection of the ground beneath her, getting rapidly closer as she fell.

Again, she flipped. Lipstick smeared. Lucifer stifled a curse and wiped away the mangled symbol with the back of her hand and drew it again. Only a few more symbols to go, though she doubted she could finish before she hit the ground. She saw the glow of streetlights beneath her and the gnashing form of the witch-hound reflected in the mirror. The mirror was slowing her descent, allowing the witch-hound to get closer.

The sirens were closer as well. Out of the corner of her eye, Lucifer could see the gathering police cars surrounding the building. Directly beneath her was the courtyard, its pink limestone swelling in her peripheral vision.

Another symbol.

The witch-hound snapped its jaws so closely that it caught several of her whipping hairs and ripped them free. Her scalp burned. Her ankle throbbed. Her ears were filled with roaring air, the swelling whine of sirens, and the vicious growl of the witch-hound above her. She swiped the lipstick in a violent arc, finishing the final symbol. The witch-hound's reflection filled the mirror, its open maw about to swallow her whole. Lucifer closed her eyes, but not before she saw the horrified expressions of watching police officers as the ground came up to meet her.

CHAPTER 24

There was no impact. Lucifer was expecting to feel her body smashed into jelly before death took her, but instead she only felt a shift in gravity and a wave of nausea as she fell through the mirror and into the Aether.

She was still traveling at terminal velocity, only now in a vertical rather than horizontal direction. When she finally hit the ground, it was only from the harmless height of a few feet. Easily survivable. But the speed she was traveling wasn't so harmless. She slid across the burgundy carpet. The fabric of her cleaning outfit shredded, and her skin burned from the friction until she began to tumble. Lucifer ducked into a ball and covered her head. She crashed into a series of mirrors that created a domino effect with the myriad other mirrors in the great room. By the time she finally came to a stop, the cacophony of shattering glass was still echoing through the chamber.

Silence finally came. She ached everywhere. But as much as she hurt, Lucifer could tell that her injuries were superficial. Still, she hesitated to open her eyes. When she finally did, she saw dozens of scratches on the backs of her hands. Blood welled up in tiny streaks along the length of her right arm, and she could see the blistered skin of her left hip through the melted hole of her pants. But she was alive.

She couldn't say the same about the witch-hound.

The creature's amorphous head lay fifty feet away with a trail of blood and broken glass in its wake. It must have been only halfway through when the mirror hit the ground and shattered, thus closing the portal with only its head here in the Aether.

She stood, taking care to go easy on her ankle. Lucifer smiled when she heard the crunch of broken glass beneath her feet. It was nice to be able to hear again.

Lucifer searched for her trick bag but was unhappy when she found it. It had flown off her shoulder as she tumbled through the mirror room and was now dangling from the hideous chandelier overhead. If she hadn't just plummeted seventy stories into a field of glass and wood, she would have entertained the idea of somehow climbing to get it. But now she could only stare at it in hopeless apathy.

"Would you like a hand, darling?"

Lucifer turned to see the Harlot at the edge of the room. The woman strode toward her, ignoring the ruined mess crunching beneath her feet. When she reached the center of the room, the Harlot reached up with her gangly arm and plucked the trick bag from its perch. With a mild flourish and modest smile, she handed the bag to Lucifer. But the Harlot's smile faded, and she crinkled her nose when she took sight of her.

"What is that ghastly thing you're wearing?" the Harlot asked.

"It's a cleaning uniform." Lucifer looked down at the shredded clothing. "Well, it was, anyway."

"You look like an urchin. Come to the sitting room where you can clean yourself. I'll not have you soiling my home with such filthy attire," the Harlot said as she moved through the debris of the broken mirrors. If the Harlot was willing to overlook, or was simply unable to see, the mess Lucifer had made, she wasn't about to bring it to her attention.

As they stepped into the sitting room, the Harlot motioned toward a porcelain washbasin. She then sat down in her chair, smoothing the dark folds of her dress. Lucifer stripped off the ragged cleaning uniform and set to washing herself. By the time she had finished cleaning her wounds, the water in the basin was the dull hue of bad borscht.

"I must say, you are spoiling me, darling," the Harlot said. "To have you come so soon after your last visit is indeed a treat, regardless of that bitter parting. But to do so and bring such a gift . . . apology accepted."

Lucifer pulled her street clothes from her trick bag. "What gift?"

"The witch-hound's head, of course. That is why you're here, isn't it? To apologize for your insult?"

Lucifer had no doubt that the Harlot knew exactly why she was there, but Lucifer wasn't really in the mood to play games. "Uh, yeah. That's why. I hope you like the color. I didn't keep the receipt."

"Oh, I would never return such a lovely gift," the Harlot said, pouring herself a cup of tea. "Though I'm shocked at the over-whelming effort you went through to obtain it. Especially when, with just a bit of modification, witch-hounds can be trapped much in the same way as filcher demons."

"I'll remember that next time." Lucifer winced as she pulled her jeans on over the giant raspberry on her hip. "I don't suppose you have any aspirin here, do you?" she asked.

"What need have I for aspirin? But then again, I don't go jumping out of office windows. Perhaps you would have brought some medication yourself, had you heeded my warning."

"Warning? What warning—" Lucifer remembered. The Harlot had said she would jump from an office window, just like that man Karl. "Oh," she said, zipping up her hoodie. "I guess you were right about that."

"I'm right about everything, darling," the Harlot said, sipping her tea.

"No, you're not."

"Oh? I also remember expressing sympathy regarding your shoes. Did you not lose them at Cape Vale?"

"Yes," Lucifer huffed, "but you also said I would kill myself and I didn't. I wasn't even *trying* to kill myself. Unless I'm actually dead right now, but I kind of doubt that since I don't think I would ache this much if I were dead."

"You're not dead," the Harlot scoffed.

"See then? You were wrong. You said I would jump out of an office window to kill myself."

"No," the Harlot said. "I told you that you would toss yourself from an office window *and* kill yourself. I did not tell you the two were one and the same."

"That doesn't . . ." Lucifer threw up her hands in frustration. "I'm not killing myself and I'm not going to talk about it with you anymore."

The Harlot held the cup of tea close to her mouth, steam curling around her raptor-like nose. "Then what *would* you like to talk about?"

"How about removing this hex from me."

The only response was the gentle clink of the Harlot's teacup against the saucer she held in her other hand.

"No? Then there's nothing I want to talk to you about," Lucifer said.

The Harlot exhaled, dissipating the rising steam. "Are you sure there's nothing else you wish to discuss?"

Lucifer slipped her trick bag over her shoulder and said, "I have the book now. I can get to the Shade without your help." But when Lucifer turned to leave, she froze in her tracks. There was something draped over the arm of the nearby sofa that made Lucifer's heart seize in her chest.

It was David's letterman's jacket.

"What the hell is that?" Lucifer asked, pointing to the familiar coat.

"So there *is* something else you wish to discuss," said the Harlot, not trying to hide her smile.

"Answer me!" Lucifer rushed over and pulled the jacket from the sofa. When she grabbed it, her bump key fell from the jacket's pocket.

"A souvenir he kept from your clandestine evening at the gallery," the Harlot said. "He used that to break into your apartment, though it did take him several attempts to succeed. Once inside, he used your mirror to come here. Oh, but he is a pretty one."

"What did you do to him?" Lucifer said. Her throat tightened as terror pulled at her like the waves of Minnie Hester's horrid storm.

"I did nothing to him," the Harlot said as she placed her tea on the table before her. "I simply answered his question. As I do for all people who come to see me."

Lucifer's mind was reeling. She had the book. She was going to save Gina. She had everything under control. What was David thinking?

"It doesn't make sense! Why would he see you? Why?" she asked.

The Harlot rose from her chair and towered over Lucifer. The Keeper of Secrets' rictus smile faded into a sympathetic frown. "David is a prized athlete, a brilliant student, a truly remarkable boy. But he is still a boy."

"What does that mean? He thought I couldn't get Gina back because I'm a girl, but somehow he could because he's a boy? David's not like that." Lucifer looked up, her eyebrows crinkled. "Is he?"

"No. In that regard, he is above most. But he is a boy, and boys do foolish things when they fall in love."

Right now Lucifer didn't want to be reminded of how much David loved Gina, and she hated the Harlot for bringing it up. "But David doesn't know this world. Even if he loves her, why would he try and go after Gina by himself?"

"Again, you misunderstand my meaning. David was afraid for *you*." The Harlot stood and glided next to Lucifer. "After the Witch of Cape Vale, he truly understood how dangerous it would be for you to get Gina back safely. And he didn't want to see you get hurt. Don't you see, darling? Gina isn't the one David fell in love with," the Harlot said.

"You mean he fell in love with me?" Lucifer asked.

The Harlot brushed Lucifer's hair behind her ear with a long, sharp finger. "Is that so hard for you to believe?"

Lucifer collapsed down onto the couch. David loved her. She

knew he liked her, but she thought it was because of his fascination with the world of magic more than anything having to do with her. Yes, there was the kiss that broke the witch's spell, but that was something that just kind of sort of happened. Wasn't it? She didn't think he could actually be in love with her. Of course, Lucifer would have no idea. She had zero experience with this kind of thing. The only way she would know is if there were a giant neon sign over his head saying, *Hey, Lucifer, I Love You!*

But she knew she loved him.

It was strange to finally admit it, but Lucifer knew that's what she was feeling. How she was so distracted when he was near, how she couldn't stop thinking of him when he wasn't. He consumed her thoughts. It was now suddenly obvious that she loved David. And part of her was thrilled that he loved her too. But that thrill immediately turned to horror.

"Where is he?" she asked the Harlot.

"Witchdown," the Harlot said very matter-of-factly.

Panic fluttered through Lucifer on sharp, rusty wings. She suddenly realized she was clutching David's jacket so tightly that her fingernails were threatening to tear themselves from her fingertips. She stood, but her knees wobbled so badly she fell back onto the couch. The idea of a girl she had never even met trapped in Witchdown was bad enough, but a boy she loved? Lucifer felt like she was going to throw up.

"How could someone so smart be so *stupid*," Lucifer said.

"Sadly, that is a question no one ever bothers to ask me."

Lucifer stood again, but this time found her footing. "So you told him how to get into the Shade. To Witchdown. There's a way a living person can get there."

"You know my price, Lucifer," the Harlot said.

"Is that what David paid? You made him give up all his emotions?"

"David didn't ask the same question you did. He doesn't have the same experience dealing with me that you do. Then again, no one does."

"Stop smirking at me!" Lucifer gripped the letterman's jacket even tighter to keep her shaking hands under control.

"Darling, David asked how he could get to Gina. So I told him. He played the same game that Gina did and was taken through the mirror at the Worcester House."

"So David is trapped, too!"

"Yes. And have no doubt, Lucifer," the Harlot said, all sympathy dissolving from her face, "the Sisters of Witchdown will find use for him."

Without another word, Lucifer turned and ran.

CHAPTER 25

Lucifer's legs couldn't carry her fast enough. She hurdled over the expanse of shattered mirrors, ignoring the jagged glass that threatened to cut her along every stride. Fortunately, the twin mirror to her own wasn't destroyed when she and the witch-hound's head came rolling through the mirror room.

The second Lucifer was through the mirror and back in her own apartment, she pulled the book out of her trick bag and started reading. It was nearly impossible for her to concentrate. David was in Witchdown. Who knew what kind of horrors he was having to suffer at the hands of the witch that took him. But there wasn't time for nightmarish speculation. If Lucifer couldn't find a way to Witchdown, David was dead.

She opened the book and examined its pages. The paper was so dry and brittle that it felt as if it were going to disintegrate between her fingers. For some reason, Lucifer was expecting fine, calligraphic script written inside, but much of the writing was jagged, rushed, barely legible. The words meandered across the page like drunken ants crawling away from some unseen threat.

Several sections had words clustered together, while others were so far apart it was difficult to determine if they were part of the same sentence or just random thoughts. There were dozens of scribblings and crude sketches of symbols throughout the book, and more than one page was stained with blood.

She scanned the book as quickly as she could, looking for anything that explained how she might get to the Shade. Most of the book was devoted to the history of the Sisters of Witchdown, a history that Lucifer was already familiar with. There was the small section on summoning that Gina and her friends must have used that night in the Worcester House. There was one on how to use the book to curry favor with the Sisters and another on filcher demons and how to use them as minions, followed by several blank pages.

There were small picts in the corners of the pages regarding the filcher demons. The ink used to make the marks looked very similar to the one Helen Peltier used to write her name on the cover. She must have been trying to neutralize the book so readers wouldn't become possessed by the demons whenever they read its pages. Only Helen must have passed away before completing the spell.

Thankfully for Lucifer, she was immune to that kind of possession. Most people were. But for the handful of people who weren't immune, like Olivia, they would become possessed by a filcher demon. And according to the book, the Sisters could use the demons to influence the possessed person into doing their bidding.

Lucifer had read countless magical texts in her life and knew their shorthand. She knew which pages were history, which were recipes for spells, et cetera. But there was nothing in the book that explained how to get to Witchdown. The way most of these older books were formatted, all the information she was looking for should be right after the section on filcher demons. Yet all those pages were blank. Perhaps Helen had figured out a way to remove them from the book, hoping to preserve it as a historical document without having the magic infused in the book be a danger to the person reading it.

But there was something about the blank pages that bothered her. They were blank. Completely blank. Helen had made small notes on just about every single page in the book, but these pages didn't have a single mark on them. They didn't even appear to be as aged as the rest of the book.

Lucifer grabbed her green butterfly glasses from her trick bag. When she put them on, she saw that the blank pages of the book were anything but. Without these special glasses, only a person possessed by a filcher demon could see what was written on the pages.

They were covered in symbols with lists of components for dark spells and instructions for even darker rituals. One of the darkest was a ritual to bring the witches themselves back into the world of the living. And the one thing they needed more than anything else for that ritual to succeed was a living girl.

The Sisters of Witchdown wanted to come back, and Gina was their ticket. But it was a complicated ritual, one that even Lucifer had trouble following. Which was actually a good thing. The more complicated a ritual, the easier it was to disrupt.

She turned the page and found exactly what she had been looking for. There, written in several different styles of handwriting, was the information on traveling to the Shade.

Finally, Lucifer had the answer, and she didn't have to give up all of her emotions to get it. She was going to be able to save David. But her excitement slowly faded to despair when she read what was required for a living person to travel to the Shade of their own volition: murder bordering on genocide.

Sacrifices. Dozens of them. The Shade was a realm of death, and death was its only currency. In order for Lucifer to travel there and survive, she would need to ritually sacrifice nearly a hundred people. She was willing to do almost anything to get David and Gina back. But killing innocent people wasn't one of them.

It wasn't fair. She finally knew what it felt like to be in love, to *be* loved. It was more joyous and painful than she could have ever imagined. And with the turn of a single page, it had all been taken from her.

She flipped through the rest of the book, desperately searching for another way, but there was none she could find. It wasn't until she started to close the book that she saw the symbol etched into the inside cover. Just like the blank pages, the symbol could only be seen by those possessed by filcher demons or with the aid of magical lenses.

The intricate glyph took up nearly the entire inside cover, and there were dozens of notes hastily scrawled in the margins around it. According to the text, it was called the Sister's Wheel. It was the core symbol the witches used to kidnap Gina in the first place. It allowed the witch to open a gateway between the Shade and the world of the living, provided a person in the living world performed the summoning ritual: the Bloody Mary game Gina and her friends played that night at the Worcester House.

Once summoned, the witch was able to shadow Gina wherever she went. It was only a matter of time before Gina stood in front of a mirror, allowing the witch to snatch her into the Shade.

As Lucifer studied the peculiar Sister's Wheel and the cryptic phrases surrounding it, she saw that there was another way into the Shade. A dangerous way. A way that would get her to Witchdown and, in theory, bring her back. The Harlot was right.

The Harlot was always right.

The sun had come up and was already dipping below the horizon by the time Lucifer had finished studying the book, memorizing all the symbols, glyphs, and picts she could. The full moon would be rising any minute now. It was now or never.

Lucifer reached inside her trick bag, feeling her way around its contents until she found the simple business card she wanted. She then grabbed her smartphone and dialed.

"Hello?"

"Trish?"

"Yeah? Who is this?"

"It's Lucifer. We met a while ago at your clinic. I came in looking to have a tattoo removed."

"Oh . . . oh, yeah, right. Lucifer. Hey, uh, what's going on?"

"Where are you right now?" Lucifer could hear the soft murmur of music in the background.

"Uh, at home," Trish said.

"Where's home?"

Trish paused for a moment before saying, "Not to be rude, but I don't think that's any of your business."

"It doesn't matter, I can find you. I need your help, so don't go anywhere. I'll be over in about half an hour. I'll be in the police car," Lucifer said.

"Police car—"

Lucifer hung up and dialed a different number.

"This is Officer Pierce."

"Buck, it's Lucifer."

"You're alive! Holy crap, Lucifer. What happened? I've got five officers that could have sworn they saw someone take a gainer off the of top Graeae Towers. There was nothing left but a wet stain on the pavement. I thought it was you."

"It was the witch-hound," she said.

"The witch what?"

"It doesn't matter, Buck. I have the book and I know how to get to the Shade. But I'm going to need help. Pick me up in twenty minutes."

"But—"

Lucifer hung up and tossed her phone back into her trick bag. As she headed toward the door, she grabbed an old emergency medical technician's manual from a stack of books she was using to prop up an old table lamp. The stack and the lamp crashed to the floor, but she didn't care. She knew how to save David and Gina, but she was running out of time.

"What the hell is going on, Lucifer?" Buck said when she jumped into his cruiser.

"Drive to 381 Pinewood Drive," Lucifer said before her door was even closed.

"What's there?" Buck asked, putting the cruiser in drive.

Lucifer double-checked the contents of her trick bag. "A girl named Trish. She's had training as an EMT, now c'mon! Hit the lights, man!" Lucifer shouted as she slapped the dashboard.

A few minutes later, Buck pulled into the driveway, killing the lights and sirens so as not to scare the entire neighborhood. Trish stepped out of her front door, her purple hair pulled back in a ponytail. "You weren't kidding about the cop car, were you? What exactly is going on?" she asked as Lucifer raced toward her.

Lucifer gently grabbed her arm and started pulling her toward the car. "I'll explain on the way."

Trish looked up at Buck's haggard and imposing frame standing next to his car and said, "Lucifer, uh . . ."

Lucifer held out her hand in introduction. "Trish, this is Officer Pierce. Officer Pierce, Trish. Now that we're all acquainted, let's go!"

"Am I under arrest?"

"No, ma'am, you're not under arrest. Lucifer—"

Lucifer held up her hand, interrupting and said, "Trish, this man's daughter and my . . . er, her boyfriend are going to die unless you come with us."

"Is that true?" she asked Buck.

Buck gave Lucifer a pained expression that broke her heart before turning to Trish and saying, "Yes." He waved to the back of his cruiser. "Let's go, ma'am. Now."

"Wait a second. I can't just leave. And I have no idea who your daughter is."

"Please," Buck said again, letting a hint of anger into his voice.

Lucifer helped Trish into the back and sat beside her.

"Will someone please tell me just what is going on here?" Trish asked.

Lucifer ignored her and said, "Head to the clinic on Elm and Braxton." She then pulled out the EMT manual and a highlighter from her trick bag.

"The clinic," Trish said. "It's closed. Seriously, what is happening?"

"I'm going to need to know what's going on, too, Lucifer. And I want you to tell me what happened at Graeae Towers. The report said it looked like a bomb went off on one of the upper floors."

"Somebody's pet got loose. And there are things we need to get from the clinic. When we're done there, we need to hit a gas station and buy every bag of ice they have. Seriously, Buck! Sirens! Lights!" Lucifer shouted as she smacked the back of the seat. She knew her own panic was only going to frighten Buck even more, but she didn't care. She had to hurry. Not only was the moon rising, but her courage was fading fast.

Buck flipped on his lights and siren and stepped on the gas, his tires barking as they struggled for traction on the road.

"Officer," Trish said, "What's wrong with your daughter and her boyfriend? Are they sick? I want to help, I do, and I have some training as an emergency medical technician, but I'm not a doctor."

Buck peered in the rearview mirror to look at Lucifer. The man's eyes were wide, bloodshot, with thick black bags underneath. "You said Gina and her boyfriend, Lucifer. What happened to David?"

"He's in the Shade now, too." Thinking about it made Lucifer's heart ache, and she didn't want to discuss it. Thankfully, Buck didn't either. "Here," Lucifer said, handing the manual to Trish. "Do you have these things?"

Trish hesitated before taking the manual and looking at what Lucifer had highlighted. "Someone you know have hypothermia?"

Lucifer started a quick web search on her phone. "Do you have them or not?" she asked.

"Yes."

"What about these?" Lucifer asked as she handed Trish her phone.

Trish looked at the screen and said, "Those are some heavy-duty meds, but yeah, we've got that, too."

"Good. Then there's a chance."

"A chance to what—"

Buck skidded to a halt in front of the clinic. All three were out of the car and heading toward the clinic door when Trish said, "You know I don't have my keys to this place, right?"

Lucifer looked back at Trish. Less than six seconds later she had the alarm disabled and the door open without ever taking her eyes off the girl.

"I'm pretty sure that's illegal," Trish said.

Buck gently nudged Trish inside the door. "Roll with it," he said.

Inside, Lucifer asked Trish, "How long to get all this stuff together?"

"I don't know, five, ten minutes?"

"Lucifer," Buck said. "You told me you had the book and you know how to save Gina. What are we doing here?"

"There are things here we need if I'm going to be able to come back."

Trish held up the EMT manual and said, "Things like a defibrillator? A heat blanket? Look, I don't know what's going on and I don't want to get in bad with the police. But I would really like to know what you all are talking about. How is this stuff going to help you get back from anywhere? Just exactly what are you going to do?"

Lucifer fixed her with a hard stare.

"I'm going to kill myself."

CHAPTER 26

The headlights of Buck's cruiser struggled to illuminate the dark and dilapidated walls of the Worcester House. The building sagged and wilted as if they were melting from the heat of the halogen beams.

"What are we waiting for?" Lucifer asked.

"This," Buck said, and he flipped on his flashing lights. As the blue and red lights flickered across the house, teenagers began pouring from the doors and windows, all in a mad rush to escape arrest. When no more came out, Buck looked back and said, "Clear."

Lucifer and Trish got out of the backseat. Lucifer said, "Thanks for doing this, Trish."

"Don't thank me," Trish said. "I'm only doing this because your friend there threatened to arrest me if I didn't. But if this goes wrong, this will be on you and him, not me. I won't be held accountable if you die."

"Dying is the point. You're just here to make sure I don't stay dead."

It took twenty minutes for Lucifer to convince Buck that this was the only way to save Gina and almost another hour for him to convince Trish to help them. If Lucifer wanted to go to the Shade, she was going to have to die. It was the only way to do it without becoming a serial killer. But if Lucifer had to die, she wanted to be able to come back to life. For that, she needed Trish. And, expectedly, Trish wanted nothing to do with them after hearing all the talk of magic and dimensions and dying. It wasn't until Buck threatened to throw her in jail that Trish finally agreed to help.

Lucifer looked up at the full moon, swollen and blinding against the black sky. It would reach its zenith in a couple of hours. Gina and David didn't have much time. David . . .

She shook her head trying to force the thought of him away. It was distracting enough imagining him holding her in his arms, but the thought of David at the mercy of a witch was too much to bear. If she wanted to help him, she couldn't be distracted. She needed to focus.

Buck opened the trunk of his cruiser and pulled out an armful of equipment. The rest of the trunk was filled with bags of ice. Lucifer pulled a flashlight from her trick bag and said, "Follow me."

The chaotic mess of the house was even more eerie in the dark. Lucifer couldn't imagine why anyone would willingly want to spend time here. Lucifer pointed to a small, claw-foot bathtub amid the cluster of furniture attached to the ceiling. "Buck, I'm going to need that tub."

The massive cop reached up with his free hand and tore the tub loose as easily as plucking an apple from a tree. Large chunks of the ceiling came down with the tub, and three of the four legs on a tattered lounge chair came loose, leaving the chair to swing like a mildewed pendulum.

Lucifer bounded up the creaky stairs, taking two at a time. At the top of the stairs, she kicked over several half-empty beer cans that the fleeing teenagers left behind in their hurry to get away from Buck's flashing lights. A single cigarette smoldered on top of an ashtray made from an old hubcap. "In here," she said.

The room was the same as when she had come here with David. Just as before, the squalor of the house didn't find its way past the doorway and into the room. The vanity mirror sat in the middle of the room, reflecting the moonlight shining through the perfectly whole windows.

Lucifer handed the flashlight to Trish. She then started pulling candles from her trick bag and placing them strategically around the room. Buck came in, dragging the bathtub behind him. The tub's claw feet left two long, jagged scars in the wooden floor.

"At least this room doesn't look like a snot pit," Buck said.

"That's only because of the magic," Lucifer said. "Now fill the tub with all the ice." Lucifer grabbed a small crowbar from her trick bag and walked to the corner of the room. "Trish, shine the light over here. I want to show you something."

Lucifer wedged the small crowbar into the space between the wall and the floor and yanked. One of the narrow floorboards came up, exposing the underfloor six inches beneath it. Clearly visible were the unmistakable markings of intricate gouges in the wood.

"What is that?" Trish asked.

"It's part of a symbol called the Sister's Wheel. If you pulled up all the floorboards you'd see that it's been carved underneath the entire floor. I can't believe I didn't think of that the first time I was here."

"Wait. So you're trying to tell me all this stuff about witches and whatnot is for real? Like, for real real?" Trish's voice was thick with skepticism.

Lucifer stood and took the flashlight from Trish. She aimed the beam of light at the bathtub and said, "Notice anything?"

"It's the bathtub," Trish said.

"Buck dragged it into the room."

"Yeah, so?"

"Look behind it. The scratches on the floor are gone."

Trish stepped closer to the tub to get a better look. She squinted, then took the flashlight from Lucifer's hand and knelt down. As Trish was feeling the smooth floor, Buck came in with several bags of ice.

"Not only does the Sister's Wheel open a pathway to the Shade, it has a mending element to it as well. That's why the scratches disappeared and why the windows are still intact." Lucifer placed the rest of the candles around the room. However, their warm glow did little to counteract the cold, harsh moonlight coming in through the window.

"When the Sisters of Witchdown crafted the symbol," Lucifer said, "they wanted to use it to preserve their bodies and anchor their spirits in the world of the living. That way they could return from the Shade. But, lucky for us, they were destroyed before they could use it." Lucifer lit the last candle then patted her trick bag. "Unlucky for us, though, they created this book and figured out a way to use it to bring filcher demons into our world. Once someone's possessed by a filcher demon, the witches can command them to do anything they want."

"Like carve that thing under the floor?" Buck asked.

"Exactly. They just needed to wait until the book fell into the right hands. Which, from the condition of that book, I'd say was a pretty long time. But then Mr. Sinkowicz got greedy and started the ball rolling."

Buck tore the plastic bags open and dumped the ice in the tub. "But why?" he asked. "Why kidnap anyone? Can't they just come through?"

Lucifer walked over to the tub and started undressing. "Because their bodies have turned to dust by now. If their spirits come to the living world, they'd be trapped here as ghosts with little or no power at all. They created Witchdown to keep their power intact and their spirits safe in the Shade, but what they want more than anything is to come back to the world of the living. In order to do that, they need a body. A living body."

"They want to possess her like one of those demons." Buck gripped the edge of the tub with a thick hand, his knuckles turning white as he squeezed.

"No," Lucifer said as she slipped out of her jeans. "Possession means there are two people in one body. That's not what they want. They want to sacrifice Gina's spirit, her soul, and then take over her body. Then they send the body back to our world, only it will no longer be Gina inside. It will be one of the Sisters. And with a Sister of Witchdown alive again, it'll only be a matter of time before she's able to get the rest of her Sisters back here as well." Lucifer reached out and grabbed his hand. "But I'm not going to let that happen."

Buck grabbed her hand and squeezed back, giving her a short nod. Lucifer could tell that he was barely hanging on. She knew the only reason he was even willing to entertain this crazy plan was because he was so desperate to get Gina back. That and because he hadn't slept in days and wasn't thinking very clearly.

The big man looked at Trish. "You know what you're doing? You know how to do this?"

Trish shrugged her shoulders. "Well, I've never killed anyone before if that's what you're asking. But yes, technically, I know how to do it. I've had plenty of training in CPR and I know how the meds work. But Lucifer, your brain can't go very long without oxygen. More than a few minutes and, even if I can bring you back, you'll have serious brain damage."

"That's what the ice is for," Lucifer said. "It should slow down my body functions enough so I can stay longer without that happening. Like when someone gets trapped under ice for a long time and they're still able to be brought back."

"I understand that, but your body temp needs to be brought down in a very deliberate way for that to work. Ice is just too variable."

"Ice is all we've got. I don't know what I'm going to find there and I'll need all the time you can give me. Five minutes, at least."

"Five minutes?" Trish said. She looked at Buck, but when he only returned a puffy-eyed stare, she threw up her hands in resignation.

What little Lucifer knew about the Shade came from texts that relied on speculation. Few people who traveled there ever returned. She knew the Shade was a ghostly image of the living world and that it served as a way station of sorts for the dead passing through on their way to whatever afterlife awaited them, but some of those spirits got lost along the way. Others chose to stay. Beyond that, all she knew was that the spirits of the Shade hated life and would do anything to destroy it. It was one of the reasons she had to die to go there.

Lucifer was now stripped down to her underwear and T-shirt. She wrapped her arms over her chest, though not out of modesty. She was cold. Her teeth were already beginning to chatter because of the unnatural coolness of the room. It reminded her too much of Minnie Hester's cold spell.

She took a note of the moon's position in the sky. It would be at its zenith soon. There wasn't any time left to find her courage. She was going to have to start without it. Lucifer took several deep breaths and then stepped into the tub.

Trish and Buck used their hands to scoop the ice over her body, encasing her until only her head was above the ice. Lucifer's teeth chattered together in a frigid drumroll. The cold was almost too much, but if she could handle the cold spell at Cape Vale, she could handle this. Only she didn't handle the cold spell. Not without help anyway. She had David. It was David's kiss that finally broke the spell. His kiss had saved her life.

Lucifer would have given anything to have him there at that moment, to look up and see his sweet, crooked smile. But all she saw now were the wavering shadows from the candlelight and the worried, mortified faces of Buck and Trish.

"Lucifer . . ." Buck said, his voice breaking before it trailed off.

"It's ok-k-kay, B-b-buck." Lucifer couldn't feel her fingers or toes, but the parts of her body she could still feel were in agony. Lucifer marveled at how freezing to death felt so much like burning.

The swollen moon kept on its steady march across the sky. Trish placed an electric thermometer in her ear. "Your core temp is dropping. Just a few more degrees and we'll be ready."

Buck was kneeling next to the tub, flexing his fists over and over again. His face was locked in a painful grimace, too ashamed to watch, too ashamed to look away.

"T-t-t-tell m-m-me ab-b-b-b-bout G-g-g-ina. Remind-d-d-d m-m-me why I'm d-d-d-doing th-th-th-this."

The cop nodded. He opened his mouth to speak but was only able to produce a sob. "I'm sorry," he mumbled. "I can't . . . I just can't. We have to stop this. We have to—"

"N-n-n-n-no . . . on-n-n-nly w-w-w-w-w-way. P-p-please, t-t-t-trust me." Lucifer did her best to smile, but she couldn't feel her face and had no idea if it looked reassuring or like a painful grimace.

Buck pressed his fist against his lips as if he were physically restraining a scream in his mouth.

Lucifer started getting sleepy. The burning of her limbs felt far away, like they were trying to remember the pain but could only recall a fraction of the memories. Every instinct she had told her to get out of the tub, find warmth, survive. But David was trapped in the Shade. She couldn't leave him there. He had rescued her with a kiss. If only she could do the same, she would have covered him with a thousand kisses, each with the power to gift him immortality.

Trish pulled the thermometer out of Lucifer's ear and said, "Okay, I think you're ready."

Lucifer was too tired, too frozen to respond.

"This is all levels of wrong," Trish said.

Lucifer felt a slight pinch in her neck and caught sight of Trish pulling away a glistening metal syringe. She saw Buck's twisted, tear-stained smile looking down at her. Lucifer wanted to smile back, but her mouth wouldn't obey. The weight of her eyelids became too much, and they closed, plunging her into darkness. All that was left now was the cold.

And then there was nothing.

CHAPTER 27

There was nothing.

And then there was . . . something.

Lucifer opened her eyes to darkness, but it was a darkness she had never known before. It was a darkness she could see. It had form. It had shape, substance, depth. It was the darkness of void, of emptiness, but it was neither of those things. It was something tangible, something familiar. She was in a world constructed of shadows.

Lucifer was in the Shade.

It took a moment for Lucifer to recognize the form around her. She was inside the room of the Worcester House, or at least the Shade equivalent of that room. The walls, the ceiling, even the floor appeared identical except they were all made from that ethereal darkness. But unlike in the living world, the Sister's Wheel was visible. It spread out across the floor in a vast circle, the giant seal of pale orange light glowing in defiance against the all-consuming blackness of the world.

Lucifer looked down at her body, only it wasn't her body. It was a Lucifer-shaped mass of the same nothingness that made up everything around her. She examined herself, noting the familiar contours and lines she always saw when she looked at herself. But now they were formed by this substance of absence.

Lucifer walked toward the vanity in the center of the room. When she moved, tiny wisps of dark drifted from the edges of her spectral body, trailing off like steam. As she gazed into the mirror, Lucifer expected to see her shadow-self in the glass, staring back at her. Instead, the mirror was a window into the world of the living.

She saw Trish sitting next to the bathtub, looking at the timer on her phone, while Buck knelt with his hands in his lap, his head hanging in defeat. But it was Lucifer's own body lying dead in the tub that terrified her.

The lips of her corpse were blue and its skin ashen. Black, limp hair floated next to the ice in the pooling meltwater. It was the most disturbing thing Lucifer had ever seen. But it wasn't simply seeing her own dead body that bothered her so much. It was how small she looked. How fragile. To see herself reduced to such a tiny, insignificant thing filled her with a profound sadness.

But Lucifer didn't have time for self-pity. The clock was running. If she didn't act now, both Gina and David would be just as dead. And as much as Lucifer wanted to be with David, she didn't want it to be as ghosts heading hand-in-hand into the great beyond.

She turned and headed for the stairs. But once outside of the house, Lucifer was taken aback. What she saw was like smoke poured into a mold of the world. Buildings rose in dark slabs against the darker sky as spirits meandered over the landscape in between the towering shapes. Most of the structures were just as they were in the living world, though several lay twisted or collapsed in defiance of any laws of physics. There were even a few buildings that had no living counterpart.

Lucifer watched as spirits floated through the air like aimless, sentient clouds. The denizens of the Shade were every form imaginable, from the horrible to the stunningly beautiful. Some appeared merely human, while others were vile and monstrous. Lucifer had no idea if it was a result of a violent death, a reflection of their inner selves, or simply how they chose to appear to the other spirits in this world.

The moon was high in the sky, ten times bigger than in the living world. It looked down on her like the engorged eye of a curious god, its light filling the sky with a cardinal glow. But the blood-red moonlight paled next to the blinding beacon rising to meet it. Not too far away, a spotlight of golden light rose straight into the air until it was swallowed by the impossible darkness directly above it.

The strange light originated from a collection of smaller structures that sat in a clearing just at the edge of the horizon. Each of the structures connected to the other with a strange latticework. Though the light prevented Lucifer from seeing all of the structures in the tiny village, she knew that there were seven.

She had found Witchdown.

The light rising from the town pulled at Lucifer, beckoned her, as if it were calling her home. Something about that incredible light made her want to bask in it, revel in it. The strange pull even seemed to be affecting the other spirits as well. Ghosts ambled and floated in the same direction, all heading toward Witchdown.

She ran, covering more ground than she could have in the living world. Part of her wanted to study her fellow spirits, examine them, study this world. But there wasn't time. The full moon was nearly overhead as it quickly approached the vertical beam of light. Minutes was all she had.

Lucifer stopped when she reached the edge of Witchdown. The town was protected by an invisible dome of magic, preventing the thousands of ghosts and spirits from getting inside. They swarmed over the magic dome, crawling over one another as they tried to claw their way inside. Lucifer understood their desire. The source of the light was coming from inside, and the light pulled at them, filling them with an incredible need. The closer they were to the light, the more desperately they wanted to feel its radiance.

The ghost of a man with impossibly wide eyes and very little flesh still left on his bones pushed past Lucifer and forced his way into the throng of swarming spirits. Lucifer couldn't see beyond the swirling mass into the town, so she followed his lead.

As soon as she approached the gathered mass, it swallowed her, pulling her under like an ocean current. It was odd, touching other spirits. Neither she nor they had actual bodies, but they all seemed to adhere to the same physical laws of the living world. But Lucifer could see that a few ignored those laws, allowing themselves to pass through one another, float, even fly. It made sense. Such physical laws didn't apply here, so why should she confine herself to them?

Lucifer relaxed. If she could fly, she could reach the top of the dome and get a better view of what was happening inside the town. She rolled and tumbled as spirits jostled to get a look inside, swimming closer only to be pulled away again. They moved in waves like the undulating thermal currents of a black star.

But as she concentrated, the unrelenting pressure slowly eased. Hands and arms now passed through her. She was a ghost among ghosts. With a thought, she was able to rise through the swirling mass until she was above it, floating at the top of the dome over Witchdown. Only a few other spirits were with her now, all focused on the source of the light beneath them. Lucifer could see it clearly.

David and Gina.

Lucifer's heart sang with joy at seeing David again, but his imprisonment in this hellscape filled her with horror. David and Gina huddled together in a cage made of bones, their bodies shining with blinding light that emanated in all directions. The force of their life burned like twin suns in this world of death and shadow. They were the source of the great beacon in the sky, the light that called to her and every other spirit in the Shade. At that moment, Lucifer realized that she had been wrong about the Shade. The spirits here didn't hate life. They *craved* it. Though she had been dead for only a few minutes, she could feel the undeniable need to be close to them, to be alive again, to bask in their light. She could only assume that the longer one stayed in the Shade, the stronger that need became. Any living thing that traveled here would be torn apart by all the ghosts desperately trying to feel life one more time.

From this vantage point, Lucifer could see the entire layout of the Sisters' grand spell, recognizing it from the book. The whole of the town was covered in symbols, seals, picts, every possible magical notation all intertwined to form an intricate design that glowed with the same pale orange light of the Sister's Wheel.

The latticework that joined the seven structures together were made of bones arranged in specific geometric patterns that connected to the glowing lines of the spell. Several whole specters were entwined in the bones to finish out some of the more intricate shapes, each writhing against their restraints and trying to free themselves so they could get closer to David and Gina.

The spell was incredibly complex, but something about that complexity tugged at her memory. It was something the Witch of Cape Vale had said to her while she mocked her inside the pocket dimension of 47th Street. Minnie Hester had said that only witches had the skill to craft a spell this complicated without it all falling apart. One wrong move, and it would all collapse like a house of cards. Though Minnie had been trying to insult Lucifer for her lack of innate magical abilities, she had actually given her the clue she needed to dismantle it. All she had to do was get inside the dome. But the Sisters had created the dome to keep their sacrifices safe within the confines of Witchdown. Gina had been here for days, yet none of the spirits had been able to breach the protective spell. How was she going to get through?

The swollen moon inched closer to its zenith. Lucifer didn't have time to study the dome. She needed to get through now. Her only chance was to break into the dome the same way she had broken into Isaac Haldis's safe. Lucifer could only hope the Sisters of Witchdown put all their efforts on safeguarding the side of the box with the door.

Lucifer floated down from the top of the dome. She descended far enough away that the host of ghosts wouldn't notice her. Again, she focused, concentrating on the lack of physical boundaries in this world. But this time, instead of flying, Lucifer sank into the earth beneath her feet.

Thick emptiness surrounded her. There were no spirits, no ambling ghosts, just the endless expanse of the Shade's shadow planet engulfing her. The light from David and Gina penetrated the earth like a golden spike through the world's black heart. She moved toward it, drinking in its warmth and vitality until she was directly underneath it. It was euphoric.

Slowly, she rose back aboveground and found herself next to the cage with David and Gina inside. They were surrounded by the seven structures, each really nothing more than a shack. They were simple abodes where the witches could sequester themselves away from one another while they worked to find their way back to the living world.

Lucifer was about to call to David and Gina and let them know she had come to help, but at that moment, seven figures emerged from each of the structures. The Sisters of Witchdown were coming.

The witches were horrible, beyond even Lucifer's worst nightmares. They were tall and emaciated, like diseased trees that shed their leaves only to replace them with unruly tumbles of black wire. Wicked rows of needle-sharp teeth lined their smiles, their obvious glee standing out in stark contrast with their gaunt features. Their tattered robes and dresses clung to their misshapen bodies, dragging behind them as they floated over the ground.

They glided to the center of their commune and gathered around a wide, squat seven-sided altar with heavy rings attached to each edge. They held hands. One of the witches turned to the caged boy and girl and her lustful smile swelled like a maggot fattening itself on rotting flesh. Together they chanted. The runes of the spell glowed brighter. One of the witches broke away from the circle and floated to a nearby platform. With a wave of her decrepit hand, the air above the platform shimmered.

What appeared truly sickened Lucifer. A row of humanlike creatures hung from a rusty scaffold shoulder to shoulder in a straight line, each with their hands and feet bound behind them. Every one of their heads were upturned with a single pipe-organ pipe of varying lengths rising up from their throats and out of their mouths.

The witch produced a cat-o'-nine-tails and lashed one of the crea-tures. It howled in agony, resulting in a deep, bowel-rattling tone that erupted from the end of the pipe. The conducting witch lashed an awful tune to the merriment of her Sisters. With every note, the magical light of their spell grew brighter. Their ritual was beginning.

As the music droned on, two other witches went to the cage. When they opened the door, David stood in front of Gina, doing his best to protect her, but one of the Sisters extended a finger and sent a bolt of black straight to his heart. David screamed and collapsed to the floor in pain, while the other witch grabbed Gina and dragged her from the cage. The girl fought and clawed to free herself, but the strength of a witch, even a dead one, was too much for her.

Lucifer came to the edge of the cage. David was on his side, clutching at the bone bars. Being so close to him, to life, was ecstasy.

"Gina! Gina!" David shouted.

"Quiet, David. Don't draw their attention."

David turned. "Lucifer? Is that you?" His eyes blinked in confu-sion. "What happened to you?"

"I'm . . . in disguise. But now isn't the time to talk about it. We have to get you back to the Worcester House."

Gina screamed. Lucifer and David turned to see the witches chaining her to the altar. Lucifer admired how Gina struggled and fought, though she knew she wouldn't win.

"We can't leave her here," David said.

"I don't plan to," Lucifer said. "But we need to get Gina back in the cage with you." Lucifer easily manipulated the rather primitive locking mechanism, opening the cage door. "When Gina runs this way, let her in and then lock this behind her. It's the only way you'll be safe."

"Safe? Lucifer, what are you—"

But Lucifer was already moving. The terrible music echoed through the black, aided by the raucous clamor of a thousand ghosts clawing at the magic barrier. The glowing lines and runes of the spell were everywhere. Thanks to Minnie Hester, she knew it wouldn't take much to destabilize the great spell. And from what she read in the book, Lucifer knew exactly which part of the spell she needed to alter to stop the ritual. There was a node on the great seal that would undo everything the witches had accomplished.

She found it next to one of the structures. It was infused with a dozen smaller symbols that linked together to form a larger pict that, in turn, connected with others to form larger ones still. The patience and attention to detail needed to craft such a thing was impressive. It had to have taken the witches decades to properly prepare for this. But like most magic this complex, it was built on a house of cards. Pull the right card, and it all came crashing down.

The music crescendoed into a single note that boomed across the Shade. The moon was directly overhead now. One of the witches floated above Gina as the others chanted around the altar. The light of Gina's life force faded as the moon siphoned it away. As her light went up into the moon, dark tendrils from the Sister's spirit floating above her drifted into Gina's body.

Gina howled then went silent. Her light was growing dimmer. There was no more time. Lucifer desperately scratched at the node in the ground beneath her, erasing the node until the lines and symbols slowly began to fade. Gina gasped as her golden light slammed back into her body and the hovering witch was thrown clear of the altar. The witches exchanged confused glances, trying to figure out what went wrong.

Then every witch turned to face Lucifer.

If Lucifer still had a body, she would have wet herself.

All seven Sisters were looking at her now with such malevolence that Lucifer couldn't bear to watch them. Instead, she focused on the node, reworking it, changing it. Lucifer could feel the witches closing in on her, their ancient guttural curses flooding her ears. They reached for her as she made one final swipe with her finger. The great, elaborate spell of Witchdown flashed and went dark.

Then the barrier collapsed.

Thousands of spirits poured in. Shocked, the witches turned to repel the oncoming hordes. If the denizens of the Shade got hold of Gina, they would tear her apart, and then the witches would need to find another sacrifice. Centuries in the Shade had, no doubt, made them impatient.

The Sisters of Witchdown ignored Lucifer for the moment and lashed out at the ghosts that swarmed down on them. Lucifer swept past them and reached the altar.

Gina pulled at the chains that held her to the black slab. "Get me out of here!"

"I'm trying, but you have to give me some slack in the chain."

Gina looked at Lucifer, her face riddled with terror and mistrust.

"I'm a friend," Lucifer said. "Your dad sent me." With a final heave, the chain came loose. Lucifer helped Gina off the altar and half led, half carried her toward the cage. Magic exploded around them as the Sisters pushed back against the rushing spirits. The ghosts burst into clouds of dust and black flame only to coalesce back into form and begin their charge once again. The Sisters couldn't kill what was already dead.

Lucifer and Gina tumbled underneath a scything line of energy that cut a swath fifty feet wide in the wall of ghosts crashing down on them like waves. David held the cage door open and yelled, "Hurry!"

As soon as they were inside, David slammed the door closed and locked it. Outside, shadows and witches warred among themselves. "Okay, Lucifer. Now what?" David asked.

"You know her?" Gina asked. Her voice was brittle from screaming, but there was still plenty of angst in her. She was tough. Definitely Buck's daughter.

"Yes," he said. "Long story. Well, Lucifer? Please tell me pissing off the Sisters of Witchdown was part of your plan."

"Not exactly. Look, I had to act or else they would have sacrificed you guys. I barely made it in time. But pretty soon they'll be able to hold back the spirits of this world long enough for them to spell another barrier."

"So what do we do?"

"A transport spell. I hope. I've never done one before," Lucifer said apologetically. "David, take off your belt."

"What?" David and Gina said in unison.

"I need the buckle."

David whipped his belt off in a single motion and handed it to Lucifer. Carving with her ghost hands was difficult and she hoped his buckle would make it easier. She took the buckle and began carving lines and symbols into the floor of the cage. "In case you haven't figured it out," Lucifer said, "the creatures that exist in the Shade have a thing for the living. I always thought it was hate, but it's not. It's desire. They crave life. They want to consume you. I bet it takes everything the witches have not to devour you themselves."

"How is scaring us going to help?" Gina asked.

"Sorry, that's not what I . . . what I'm trying to say is this. When you were pulled into the Shade, they had to bring you to Witchdown to prevent you from getting mauled by the locals. As you can see, that's a tough thing to do." Both Gina and David looked out at the spectral violence unfolding outside the cage. "So once you were in the Shade, they transported you."

"Like in *Star Wars*," David said.

"*Star Trek*," Gina corrected.

"It doesn't matter. There's something called the Sister's Wheel," Lucifer said as she continued carving. "It's a massive series of glyphs and symbols, like a giant seal. It's under the floor at the Worcester House. It's a multipurpose spell, and they included a transporting element to it. So if I can carve that element of the spell here, I can get us to the Worcester House. Once I get you there, I can get you back to the world of the living."

"Why not just use theirs? I mean, they've already built this thing, right?" David asked.

Lucifer looked out at the chaos. "A, we don't want to be going out there and B, I kind of sort of ruined it when I shut down their whole sorcery party."

"How long will it take?" Gina asked.

"Just about finish—"

Pain lashed at her. Intense, otherworldly pain. She watched her body disintegrate into dark snow, every black flake a searing agony. When she finally coalesced back into form, she was outside the cage and the witches were standing before her, malevolence radiating from their cold, hateful eyes. The spirits of the Shade swarmed past them and over the cage in such numbers that David and Gina's light couldn't penetrate them.

"Lucifer," one of the Sisters said. Her voice crackled like rocks over broken glass. "We know this name."

Another witch flicked a clawlike finger, and the mark on Lucifer's shoulder began to glow. "Hexerei!" the witch said. "You are heir to the Keeper of Secrets. We would very much like to speak with you."

As one, they extended their hands. Shadowy tentacles burst forth and wrapped themselves around Lucifer, squeezing her. Though she didn't need to breathe, the crushing pressure was still agonizing. Lucifer brought her mind into focus, past the pain, and dematerialized. She fell away and slipped under the earth.

The tentacles burrowed into the ground, pursuing her like the roots of an angry tree. Lucifer resurfaced under the cage, mingling with the other spirits in their chaotic attempt to reach David and Gina, but the Sisters' tentacles tore at the shadows, tossing them back into the air.

Lucifer was able to slip back inside the cage. David and Gina sat in the center, clutching one another just out of reach of the spirits clawing at them. It would only be a matter of time before the other spirits realized how to move through the bars like Lucifer had.

"Hold on," she said. "Just one last mark and we're going home." Lucifer reached for the buckle, but her hand passed through it. She was confused. She had been able to shift her spirit back and forth from solid to specter with relative ease. Why was she unable to do it now?

Gina had her face buried in David's chest. Lucifer swallowed her jealousy when David's face twisted in confusion. "Lucifer," he said. "You're fading—"

David winked away.

Lucifer's back arched, and she sucked in huge lungfuls of air. But how could that be? She didn't have lungs. But she could feel them filling, her chest rising and falling. Her skin was cold and wet, but her chest was burning. Lucifer blinked water from her eyes and saw Buck kneeling over her, holding a defibrillator paddle in each hand. Trish was next to her with a syringe in one hand and the heat blanket in the other.

"Lucifer, we did it!" Trish said. "You're alive!"

CHAPTER 28

Lucifer rolled to her side and tried to stand, but her body wouldn't obey. Her legs felt rubbery and thick, and her arms hung as uselessly from her shoulders as damp socks. Buck grabbed her and helped her sit.

"Lucifer," he said, his voice hoarse. "Did you . . . did you see her?"

Lucifer nodded. "I have to go back. I almost had them."

"Go back?" Trish asked. "Uh-uh. No way am I going through that again."

With Buck's help, Lucifer wobbled to her feet. "Yes," Lucifer sneered, "it must have been really hard for you."

"We need to get you to a hospital," Buck said.

"No. They're in trouble," Lucifer said. She slipped on the wet wood under her feet, but Buck caught her before she fell. Steadying herself against his muscled arm, she said, "I have to go back. Right now."

"Lucifer, Trish is right," Buck said, his voice all sand and gravel. "You can't do that again. I had to shock your heart for two full minutes before I got a heartbeat. You do this again, I don't think we can bring you back."

As much as she hated to admit it, they were right. And she was so close. One more line, and the transport glyph would have been completed. Now they were trapped in the cage, and once the Sisters were able to fight back the ghostly hordes, David and Gina would be at their mercy once again.

Lucifer found her trick bag next to the pile of her clothes. She reached inside and grabbed the book. "Buck, Trish, don't look while I read this. I need to see if there's something I missed. Something else I can try."

"Why can't we look at the book?" Trish asked.

"Because you might become possessed by a—"

"So this is where the party's at," a new voice said.

Lucifer looked back. It was Ethan. He held a wooden baseball bat in his hands, tapping the fat end against the palm of his hand. Isis was behind him, her arms folded across her chest, looking confused and angry.

"Go home, son," said Buck.

"Nah, I'm not doing that, Mr. Pierce," the boy said as he stepped into the room.

Isis pulled at Ethan's arm. "I told you, I don't want to be here."

Ethan pulled his arm free and bared his teeth at Isis. "And I told you to wait in the car!"

Isis blanched. She looked at Lucifer and said, "This is all your fault, you crazy bitch. Ever since you attacked his dad and got him arrested, Ethan's been a straight-up dick."

"Ethan just hasn't been himself lately. Has he, Isis?" Lucifer asked as she carefully stood. "You were the one who drew the Sister's Wheel," she said to Ethan. "Your dad said you never read the book. But you did, didn't you? You've been possessed this entire time. You put the book in the library knowing Isis would 'find it' during one of your little make-out sessions. Then it was just a matter of time before she and her friends used the summoning ritual."

Ethan smiled. It was a foul, violating expression that made Lucifer's skin crawl. "Oh, yes. But you've been a bad girl, Hexerei, and the Sisters are pissed. It took them a long time to prep for their little coming-out party and you done screwed it up. I'm here to put a stop to your meddling. And a little paprika and a stuffed bunny aren't going to help you this time."

"There's more than one way to skin that cat," Lucifer said.

Isis took a step away from Ethan. "What are you two saying? What sisters? Have you been dating the Schnyder twins behind my back?"

Buck pulled his gun but kept it pointed at the ground. "Ethan, drop the bat and turn around."

"Don't, Buck. I've got this," Lucifer said.

"You can barely stand."

"Put the gun away. That isn't Ethan. It's the filcher demon inside him."

Isis said, "Did everyone have meth-flakes for breakfast this morning? What the hell is wrong with all of you?"

"Isis, stand over there," Lucifer pointed to the floor next to Trish. "Buck, put the gun away. Now."

Reluctantly, the man holstered his pistol. "Do you know what you're doing, Lucifer?"

Lucifer slowly moved toward Buck, keeping her eyes locked on Ethan and said, "I have a plan of sorts. And you'll be happy to know, it doesn't involve me dying."

"Funny," Ethan said. "Because you dying is *exactly* what my plan involves."

Buck stepped forward, the floorboards creaking under his weight. "I've got a gun and a hundred pounds on you, son."

Lucifer gently nudged Buck to the side. "I've got this. You just stand over there and look intimidating."

"So what Olivia said was true? About tying her up or whatever," Isis said. "And now Ethan is possessed by one of those . . . sneeze monsters, too? Ugh! I can't believe I made out with you!"

Ethan didn't respond. He kept his oily smile on Lucifer.

The good thing about filcher demons was that they were stupid. That's what made them ideal minions. Their stupidity made them easily controlled. It also made them easily provoked. But that's what Lucifer was counting on.

The horrible sacrifices needed for a living person to travel to the Shade served to keep the denizens from tearing the person apart. But filcher demons were living things, too, in a manner of speaking, but they came from a dimension so corrupted and foul that Lucifer hoped the denizens of the Shade would want nothing to do with them. If Lucifer were possessed by a filcher demon, she might be able to move through the Shade without being torn to pieces. It was a horrible plan, but right now a horrible plan was better than no plan at all.

The problem was that she was immune to their possession. She could read the book cover to cover a thousand times, and it would never happen. If she wanted to be possessed, she was going to have to do it another way.

"Tell me, Ethan," Lucifer said. "What's it like knowing Isis is only dating you because she wanted to make David jealous."

"What the hell, bitch!" Isis said. Lucifer held up her hand toward Isis to calm her. Ethan was still focused on Lucifer. She was the reason he was there, and she didn't need anyone else distracting him.

"Think about it. Do you honestly think a girl like Isis would ever willingly go out with you?"

"Shut up," he said.

"Every time she kisses you, she's wishing she was kissing David instead."

Ethan came at her, ready to bring the baseball bat down on her head. Out of the corner of her eye, she could see Buck reacting to intercept. Lucifer had to be faster. She crouched and grabbed the defibrillators at her feet. As Ethan began his swing, Lucifer pounced forward and slammed the defibrillators against his chest. There was a ZAP! and the bat fell from Ethan's hands. His head fell back and he howled in pain.

And howled.

The howl gurgled in the back of Ethan's throat, growing in intensity until the filcher demon came crawling out of his open mouth. Paprika wasn't the only way to exorcise a filcher demon. It was just the kindest.

Ethan fell back, unconscious. Lucifer could hear both Isis and

Trish gasp in horror as the demon skittered on the ground, its lidless eyes fixed on Lucifer. The demon lunged for her so quickly that it only registered as a blur in Lucifer's mind. It hit her and knocked her back onto the ground, placing its hideous claws inside her mouth.

Lucifer didn't resist as the demon forced its way in, dissolving like bitter candy at the back of her throat. She swallowed, the monster now fully absorbed. She could feel its malice rolling in her stomach like bad sushi. Buck was hovering over her, his bloodshot eyes wide.

"Lucifer!"

"It's okay. I'm okay. That was intentional."

Buck helped her to her feet. She patted him on the arm and said, "Don't worry. It takes a few weeks for the possession to fully take hold. And I only need the demon for a few minutes."

Lucifer turned to Trish and Isis, both with their mouths open in mute shock. "Trish," Lucifer said, "check on Ethan. Isis . . . just try not to get in the way."

"Lucifer, what are you doing?" Buck asked. It was obvious from the look in the man's eyes that his hold on sanity was quickly slipping.

"I'm going to save your daughter." *And the boy I love.*

Lucifer quickly dressed. She slipped her trick bag over her shoulder then walked to the vanity and stood in front of the mirror, completely unsurprised by the disheveled mess she saw staring back at her. She had died, traveled to the Shade, fought with seven angry witches, had been brought back to life, and then possessed by a filcher demon. It was a wonder she didn't look any worse.

She looked over at Buck and winked. "Be back in a minute." Without another word, she dove through the mirror and into the Shade.

Lucifer tumbled into darkness. She was back in the Shade, though now she could feel how horribly cold the dimension was. Everything smelled of wet ash and rot, and the floor under her feet gave slightly, like walking on a stiff sponge. Instead of a spectral body, Lucifer now had her own, only it didn't have the golden light that David and Gina had. Because Lucifer was possessed by the filcher demon, the light emanating from her shifted from deep violet to a blistering hue of jaundiced green.

She ran. Lucifer was out of the house and racing down the dark streets toward Witchdown. This time, however, she had lungs that desperately needed air. Her body wasn't even close to having recovered from being dead just moments earlier, even with help from the mending elements of the Sister's Wheel. Everything ached, her limbs felt awkward and cumbersome. It was like running in a dream, always moving forward but never getting closer to the destination.

Several spirits converged on her only to turn away in haste when they felt her sickening light. In the distance, Lucifer saw a mountain of ghosts and specters rising up from the center of Witchdown. The occasional beam of light would break through the writhing mass, though Lucifer had no idea how much longer that cage would protect David and Gina.

Arcs of putrid magic sliced at the spirits, calving the mountain only to see it rise up once again. The witches were still struggling to keep the spirits of the Shade from stealing their prize. In the short time Lucifer had been gone, the number of spirits had grown tenfold, and the Sisters of Witchdown could not keep them at bay.

Lucifer reached the edge of the horde and burrowed straight ahead. Spirits dispersed at the touch of her foul light. Lucifer ran along the tunnel they created in their attempt to get away. Thankfully, they were also keeping her out of view of the Sisters.

When she reached the cage, she saw David and Gina together in the center. They were forehead to forehead with David's hands on the side of Gina's face as he spoke to her, obviously trying to calm her, to comfort her as ghosts battled to be the first to taste their life.

Jealousy cleaved Lucifer's heart. She could see the genuine affection in David's eyes as he looked at Gina. In that moment, Lucifer would have given anything to be the one trapped with him. Instead, she was the one who had to save him.

Without missing a stride, Lucifer unlocked the cage and slipped inside. Gina yelped as David put his arm protectively around her.

Lucifer pulled a knife from her trick bag and said, "You two ready?"

Not waiting for an answer, Lucifer carved the final piece to the transport glyph in the floor of the cage. The cage suddenly twisted, folding around them. When it morphed back into shape, they were inside the room of the Worcester House, the Sister's Wheel glowing beneath them.

David helped Gina to her feet. "Lucifer? How . . . I . . ."

"Less talk and more getting the hell out of here. Through the mirror, both of you. Hurry!"

David and Lucifer helped Gina up and through the mirror. Lucifer saw Buck on the other, his mouth noiselessly screaming Gina's name when the cop saw his daughter coming through the mirror. He grabbed her and pulled her through so quickly her shoe came off in Lucifer's hand.

She tossed the shoe through the mirror and said, "Okay, David." David looked at her and smiled. He was tired, frightened, confused, but he seemed grateful. Still, Lucifer couldn't help but think something was missing. Something about the way he looked at her seemed different. Of course, being trapped in Witchdown would change anyone, and now wasn't the time to think about it.

She laced her fingers together, allowing David to use her intertwined hands as a foothold. He was up and through the mirror. Lucifer was about to follow when seven dark figures suddenly appeared in the room, surrounding her.

"Lucifer," one of the Sisters said. "Leaving so soon? You must stay and tell us how you can be a ghost one moment and a living girl the next. That is a secret my Sisters and I would very much like to possess."

Lucifer rushed to climb up the vanity when another Sister said, "Stop."

Something inside Lucifer seized. She told her body to climb into the mirror, to get away, but the filcher demon inside her prevented her. Apparently it took less time to take hold than she thought.

"You have only delayed the inevitable," said the Sister. "Both the boy and girl have summoned us. Once summoned, we can find them anywhere, pull them through any reflection."

Lucifer nodded. She could feel that she still had complete control of her body, so long as she didn't make a move toward the mirror. "That's true. Unless I destroy the book."

All seven Sisters laughed. "How charming that you think you'll have that opportunity."

Their fiendish claws clasped each other, forming a complete circle around her. Horrible light filled the room.

Something smacked Lucifer in the chest. Only it wasn't the witches' spell. It was the defibrillator. Someone from the other side had tossed it through the mirror. As quickly as she could, Lucifer grabbed the paddles and pressed them to her chest.

Then the Sisters' magic hit her.

Lightning ran through her, igniting her. The pain was excruciating, so much so that darkness played at the edge of her vision. Lucifer knew that, for a moment, her heart had stopped, but she wasn't sure if it was the defibrillator or witches' magic that started it again. It didn't matter. The jolt was enough. She felt the filcher demon inside her rising like bile in her throat. She screamed, an awful gurgling sound. The filcher demon fell out of her mouth and spilled onto the floor. Its tiny head swiveled back and forth as it took in its surroundings.

Then it jumped at the nearest Sister.

The Seven Sisters of Witchdown unloaded on the creature, turning it into a cloud of acrid gas. But the distraction was long enough to allow Lucifer to half dive, half fall through the mirror.

She collapsed to the ground in the living world with a dull thud. Her arms twitched, and her legs didn't want to work. She looked up at the vanity to see the witches' hands reaching through the glass, their arms smoldering as they desperately grasped for anything.

Lucifer quickly rolled over and dumped the contents of her trick bag on the floor. She grabbed the book in one hand and a lighter in the other, but her thumb simply wouldn't work properly. She couldn't get it to light.

Lucifer felt something warm close around her hand. It was David. He held her hand in both of his and helped her flick the lighter to life. A tiny flame popped into existence. He looked at her with that perfectly crooked smile that would have turned her legs to mush if they weren't already useless. She put the flame to the pages of the book.

In an instant, the book was engulfed in fire. Tiny demonic faces rose into the air and then faded with the rising smoke as the pages popped and crackled in the unnatural heat. The witches howled and spat curses through the mirror. Lucifer could see their faces crowding together, all staring hate directly at her. And then, just as quickly, the mirror cracked and every window in the room shattered. The entire room of the Worcester House seemed to deflate as the floorboards dissolved into the same rotting husks found in the rest of the house. The Sister's Wheel that had kept the room whole was useless now that the book was nothing more than a smoking pile of ash.

Silence filled the room. Lucifer looked around, taking stock of the situation. Buck was holding Gina in his arms so tightly she was worried the poor girl would suffocate. But from what Lucifer could see of her face, Gina didn't much care. Ethan and Isis were next to Trish, all three appearing shell-shocked. Ethan gave Lucifer a nod and said, "Hey . . . sorry about, you know . . ."

"Were you the one who threw the defibrillator to me?"

"Yah, figured you'd need it," he said.

David put his hand on Lucifer's shoulder and said, "When you didn't follow me out, we knew you must have been in trouble. Ethan thought it had to be the witches using the filcher demon to stop you. So he tossed it in, thinking it could help."

"Uh, yeah, about that," Trish said. "Am I ever going to get that back?"

"I'll buy you a new one," Lucifer said. "So, everyone's alive? No one's possessed? No one's missing? We're all good?"

Buck looked at Lucifer. "Yes," he said, his broad face beaming through his tears.

"We're all good, Lucifer," David said. "You did it."

At that moment, David's smile was the most beautiful thing Lucifer had ever seen. But something about it was different. She couldn't tell what it was, only that there was something . . . missing.

Even so, she was overjoyed that it was the last thing she saw before she slipped into unconsciousness.

CHAPTER 29

"I 'll get it!" Gina shouted.

Lucifer could hear Buck's heavy footsteps heading toward the front door. He bellowed, "No you won't! Stay put!"

The cop opened the front door, looking odd and even more imposing in jeans and a T-shirt than his usual police uniform. Perhaps the oddest thing about him was his face. The tired scowl that he always wore had been replaced by a bright and cheerful smile. He was happy.

"Lucifer!" he said, swallowing her up in a bear hug.

When he finally let go, Lucifer said, "Not letting her answer the door?"

"I'm not taking any chances."

Lucifer looked back at the stack of mirrors and the demolished vanity in the trash bin out on the street. "No mirrors either?"

His scowl came back for the briefest of moments. "No. Chances." He stepped out of the doorway and said, "Come in, come in. When did they release you?"

Lucifer showed him the plastic hospital bracelet around her wrist. "A couple of hours ago. No frostbite, no brain damage. Just exhaustion and a little dehydration. Docs say I'm good as new. So I thought I'd stop by and say thanks for picking up the tab on that. Hospital says it was all taken care of."

Buck grinned. "Yeah, but not by me. Speaking of thanks . . ." He stepped into the other room then came back with a manila envelope thick with cash. When he handed it to her he said, "Thank you, Lucifer. I mean it. You gave my daughter back to me and I owe you for that. If there's anything you ever need, you let me know and it's done. No questions asked."

Lucifer couldn't help but smile. "Thanks, Buck."

"There's more than just money in there. My friend, the one that told me about you. Her number is in there. I think she can help you."

"Help me with what?"

"Well, getting you out of that rat-hole apartment you've been squatting in, for starters."

"But I like my rat-hole."

Buck put his hand on Lucifer's shoulder. "Lucifer, this woman can help you, whether you think you need it or not. You're not obligated to do anything, just give her a call. Talk with her. You've done so much to help me and Gina. Let someone help you for a change."

Lucifer tucked the envelope in her trick bag and said, "Fine, I'll call her. But I'm keeping that apartment."

"Hey, the kids are in the other room. You want to say hi?"

Lucifer peeked around the corner. A movie she didn't recognize was playing on the widescreen. David sat in a recliner with Gina curled in his lap, while Ethan and Isis tickled each other on the couch. They were all laughing and smiling as if nothing had happened. Gina grabbed David's face and kissed him. Lucifer's heart sank into the pit of her stomach. She wasn't sure what she was expecting. That David would come in, swoop her into his arms, and run off with her? It was foolish to think that he would just leave Gina behind, especially after everything that had happened. But Lucifer loved him. And he loved her? Didn't he? That's what the Harlot had said.

Lucifer scratched at the mark on her shoulder. As much as she wanted to be a part of David's world, she couldn't. She belonged to another. Yes, part of her had hoped that David could help her find a way to live in his world, but now that Gina was back . . .

"No," Lucifer said. "They look like they're having fun, and I'd just remind them of . . . unpleasant things."

"You sure?" Buck asked.

"Yeah. Just tell them I stopped by."

Buck nodded and showed her out. "You call that number," he insisted before closing the door.

Lucifer had made it to the sidewalk when David and Gina came walking out. "Lucifer!" Gina called. "You weren't going to say hi?"

"Oh, you were in the middle of the movie and I didn't want to interrupt."

"Oh, please," David said. "We've seen that flick a hundred times."

Gina wrapped her arms around Lucifer in a bear hug that rivaled her father's. "Thank you," she said, her voice near breaking. "I can't thank you enough for what you did."

Lucifer returned the embrace. "You're welcome. Though in fairness, your dad paid me."

"Money well spent," said Gina.

Lucifer adjusted her trick bag on her shoulder. "You two know not to say anything about any of this, right? About magic, Witchdown, and all the rest?"

"The sooner I forget it, the better," Gina said. She reached down and grabbed David's hand. There was a haunted look behind her eyes. Sadly, Lucifer knew that it was something Gina would never be able forget.

David said, "Ethan and Isis won't even talk about it. And since Mr. Pierce dropped the charges against Ethan's dad, I doubt they'll ever mention any of this again."

"What about Trish?" Lucifer asked.

Gina said, "Dad arranged to have the clinic stocked with all new equipment. He even gave Trish a literal get-out-of-jail-free card. I don't think she'll say anything. Hey, you sure you don't want to stay? We're going to order pizza."

Lucifer wanted to stay more than anything, but she wouldn't be able to handle seeing David with Gina. "I'd love to, but I've got some things to take care of. Rain check?"

"Gina?" Buck called from inside the house. "Gina, where are you, kiddo?!"

"I'm right here, Dad!" Gina shouted back. "I better go. He doesn't like it when I'm out of sight for more than a few seconds." Gina gave Lucifer another hug and a thank you before dashing back into the house.

"She's handling everything well," Lucifer said.

"She hasn't slept since she got back and she won't be alone in her room. It's all an act."

Lucifer gently touched David's fingers. "Is she the only one acting?"

David squeezed her hand but then promptly let go. "Lucifer, I don't want you to think I'm not grateful for everything you did. I truly am. But . . ."

"But?"

"It was wrong of me to lead you on like that. That night we kissed . . . I took advantage of you and I should not have done that. I'm ashamed of my behavior and I hope you can forgive me." He spoke like he was reading a speech, something he'd rehearsed in front of the bathroom mirror. His every word came at Lucifer like a punch to her stomach.

Lucifer ignored the tightness growing in the back of her throat and said, "No worries. We were just caught up in the moment. And don't worry, no one ever has to know."

"Thank you, Lucifer," he said. "For everything." David gave her one last crooked smile before heading inside.

Numb, Lucifer turned and started walking home.

Lucifer didn't even bother closing her apartment door behind her. She stepped over the stacks of books and piles of clothes and went straight to her mirror. There was the familiar tingle, the shift in gravity, and she was once again in the Aether.

The mirror room was still an unsightly mess, though the Harlot had at least taken the time to remove the witch-hound's severed head. Broken glass and shattered wood crunched underfoot as Lucifer made her way to the Harlot's sitting room. Lucifer found the Harlot standing next to her throne, pouring a cup of tea. When Lucifer sat on the couch, the Keeper of Secrets didn't recline on her throne as Lucifer expected. Instead, she sat down on the couch beside her and placed the steaming cup of tea on the table in front of her. But Lucifer didn't drink. She did something she hadn't done since she was a very, very young girl.

She cried.

Lucifer buried her face in her hands and wept. She collapsed, her head falling into the Harlot's lap, her wails muted in the folds of her black dress. The Keeper of Secrets stroked Lucifer's hair and said, "The first boy that ever broke my heart had the most beautiful black eyes. Oh, how I did love him so."

"You told me David loved me," Lucifer choked through her sobs.

"He did, darling," the Harlot said, her voice heavy with sympathy. "And if you remember, he also came looking for a secret. The price for that secret was his love for you."

It felt like a knife twisting in her chest. David had loved her, but the Harlot took that away. Lucifer realized that's what was missing from his smile. The Harlot had plucked out that glint of affection that had always shone through whenever David looked at her.

"You said you didn't take his emotions."

"You asked if I had taken *all* of his emotions. I did not," the Harlot said, brushing hair away from Lucifer's tear-stained cheeks. "He wished to know the way to Witchdown, thinking he could spare you the trauma of going yourself. When I told him the price, he hesitated. Truth be told, he didn't believe I had the power to take away his love for you, especially as strong as it was. Eventually he agreed, saying that if he truly loved you, he'd do anything to keep you safe."

The Harlot cupped Lucifer's chin. "He indeed loved you. His ambivalence toward you now is the proof of that love."

Lucifer clutched at the Harlot's dress, spitting through her sobs. "I hate you, Harlot."

"I know, darling." The Harlot continued to lovingly stroke Lucifer's hair. "I know."

Once Lucifer had cried herself out, the Harlot stood and waved her hand over Lucifer's cold tea. Steam started rising from the stained porcelain. "You can't spend your days wallowing in self-pity. Finish your tea and be on your way." The Harlot smoothed her dress with the back of her hands. "My time as a single parent is about to come to an end. So, if you wouldn't mind leaving," the Harlot said, reclining in her throne, "you have a phone call to make."

Lucifer sat up and rubbed her eyes. She drank her tea in one swallow. "Thanks for the tea," she said. Lucifer put the cup on the table and pointed to the mark on her shoulder. "But I'm tired of being your pawn. Don't for a second think this means I'm going to stop trying to get this hex removed."

"I am the Keeper of Secrets, darling," the Harlot cooed. "That, I *know*."

The café was crowded for a weekday afternoon. Lucifer sipped her coffee as she sat outside at one of the wrought-iron tables that lined the sidewalk. It had taken a week, but she finally got around to calling the number Buck had given her. The woman who answered sounded familiar, but Lucifer couldn't place her. She wouldn't give Lucifer her name either, only that she was willing to meet somewhere public.

Normally, Lucifer would have waited nearby to see who this woman was before making further contact, but ever since her dunk in the ice tub, she had trouble staying warm and needed some coffee to fight off the ever-present chill. But she chose to sit outside in case she needed to exit quickly.

Lucifer was letting the heat of her coffee seep into her fingers when the chair next to her slid away and a woman she recognized sat down beside her.

"Hello, Lucifer."

"Ms. Brisendine."

"Val, please." Val grinned at the barista who set down a small cappuccino in front of her. "Thanks for meeting with me."

Lucifer quickly scanned the area, looking for police, undercover or otherwise. "So Buck sold me out? And after what I did to help Gina."

Val took a small sip then said, "Don't be ridiculous. Bucky wants to build a shrine to you."

"You call him Bucky?"

In answer, Val's eyebrows arched in a rather mischievous way. Then the woman said, "As for *Night on 47th*, you don't worry about that. Insurance more than covered it. Trust me, I made out like a bandit on the deal. And I still had plenty left over after paying your medical bills."

"Oh. Well, thanks for that." Lucifer turned her coffee cup in her hands. "So why am I here?"

"I want you to come work for me."

Lucifer nodded. "I see."

"You don't sound very happy about it."

She was still heartbroken over David. Lucifer didn't think she could sound happy about anything. "Let me guess," she said. "Since I stole your painting and you paid for my hospital stay, you feel I owe you now, is that it?"

"Lucifer," Val said, gently putting her hand on her arm. "I am not that kind of person. You don't owe me anything." The woman slid her cappuccino to the side and said, "You have no family, no friends. You work alone. I know you're lost. But I can help you."

"Help how?"

"I can give you a home. A place to belong so you aren't wandering from job to job, hiding out from cops and truant officers."

Lucifer took a long sip of her coffee. "This isn't some kind of come-on, is it?"

"I'm old enough to be your grandmother. Don't be gross. I'm offering you a job."

"I do all right by myself," Lucifer said.

"Yes, you do," Val responded. "And I am honestly impressed by that. When I was your age I was too busy collecting nail polishes and hanging posters of boy bands on my wall."

Lucifer eyed Val from head to toe and back again. "Yeah, I don't believe that for a second."

"Okay, that was a bit of a stretch. But my point still stands. You're an incredibly smart, incredibly resourceful young woman who is doing all right. I can give you the resources to help you do a whole lot better."

"See, that's what I don't get. I'm a thief. I steal things."

Val leveled her gaze and locked eyes with Lucifer. "Yes, you do. You steal because you and I want the same things. To keep dangerous things out of the hands of dangerous people. And there are some very dangerous people out there, Lucifer. You were in Graeae Towers. You know what I'm talking about."

The idea of an entire office being run by people with their hands in the mystical was chilling. "The guy running the show up there, Isaac Haldis, is some bad news."

"That's the thing," Val said. "Isaac isn't the one running the show. His boss is."

"Who's his boss?"

Val moved to speak but waited until a couple walking past moved out of earshot. When they were gone, she whispered, "Madame Cymbaline."

Lucifer could feel her own eyes growing in surprise. "Madame Cymbaline is a myth."

Val shook her head. "She's real and she's CEO of Graeae Industries. Could you imagine what someone like that would do if she got her hands on a W'ektet Totem? Or the Carasinth? That's why I try to keep as many of those dangerous items locked away. But I have to get them first. You can steal those things. Unfortunately, I have to buy them. And bad people don't always want to sell."

Lucifer gave Val a sidelong glance. "What kind of dangerous things do you have?"

Val sat back with a proud grin. "I have D'valin's Spear, the Yellow Corset, three binding frames—empty, of course—a full set of Ember's *Encyclopedia Demonica*, and a various assortment of other terrible and wonderful things."

"No one has a full set of Ember's *Demonica*." Lucifer was angry with herself for letting her excitement seep into her voice. As far as Lucifer knew, she had the collection with the most volumes. But if Val had a full set, then she was a serious player.

"I do," Val said. "Complete with the Forbidden Index. It cost me a Monet *and* a Rembrandt to get it." The woman leaned close with a conspiratorial smile and said, "Take the job and I'll show it to you. You want to see it?"

Lucifer carefully placed her hands in front of her and said, "I do. But on one condition."

Val waved her hand and said, "Name it."

"You tell me how you know about me."

Val used her napkin to dab a drop of cappuccino from the edge of her cup. "When you were still in Brazil, a man named Walter found you. He took you off the streets. Walter was a colleague of mine." Val reached into her tweed coat and pulled out a faded envelope. She placed it in front of Lucifer. "He didn't trust e-mail, so he would write me letters. He talked of you often."

Lucifer pulled the folded letter from the envelope and read. It was true. Walter wrote of a little girl he had caught trying to pick his pocket. *Lucifer the little thief*, he had written. But rather than turn her in to the police, he had her translate mystical texts for him in exchange for food and shelter. That was how Lucifer learned of the world of magic.

Lucifer handed the letter back to Val. "So you've been keeping tabs on me?"

Val slipped the letter back into her pocket. "When Bucky came to me about his unique problem, I thought you could help him. Turns out I was right." She raised her tiny cup to her lips. "As I often am."

Val stood and said, "I'm finished. Let's go. I want to show you my collection."

Lucifer followed but responded, "I'm not passing up a chance to see a full set of Ember's *Demonica*, but that doesn't mean I'm taking the job."

"Yes, it does," Val smirked. "Hey, whatever happened to that boy you brought to the gallery? Are you two still a thing?" Val turned when she saw Lucifer had stopped following.

"No," Lucifer said, her voice cracking. "That . . . didn't end well."

"Good."

"Good?"

"Oh, he was cute, but Lucifer, you can do so much better than that boy. And you know what they say about there being plenty of fish in the sea." Val sauntered up to Lucifer and slid her arm through hers. "Lucky for you, I just happen to be a master fisherwoman in need of a protégé." Val pulled her along and continued, "But if you want, I suppose we could commiserate about the boys in our lives."

"Like, what," Lucifer said with a hint of skepticism, "over ice cream or something?"

"Ugh, god no," Val said. "I have a friend who owns a lumber-yard. Whenever I'm feeling down, he gives me thirty minutes and a chainsaw to do whatever I want. It's surprisingly therapeutic."

Lucifer couldn't help but admire Val's confidence and the way she held herself. She might look every bit the part of an art gallery owner, but Lucifer could easily imagine her buzzing her way through logs with a sawdust-flecked smile on her face. It was as if there was nothing in the world this woman couldn't do, and she *knew* it. Lucifer liked her.

"Val," Lucifer said. "I'll take the job, but on one condition."

"Doesn't that make two conditions now?"

"Hey, cut me some slack. I've never applied for a job before."

Val chuckled. "Fair enough," she said. "What's your condition?"

"You have to answer this next question honestly."

Val stared at Lucifer, intently focused. "Of course, Lucifer. What's your question?"

Lucifer took a breath and asked, "Do you really think my name is pretty?"

A broad, genuine smile spread across Val's face. "Yes, Lucifer," she said. "I really, really do."

EPILOGUE

T he Harlot patiently admired the collection of odds and ends displayed on her mantelpiece while her client relaxed on her couch, debating his next move.

"I think I can have you in three," he said.

"No, darling, I don't believe that you can."

The Harlot ran an elongated finger along the mantelpiece, pushing a furrow through the dust with her finger until one of the items caught her attention. She took the amber jar from its perch and held it in the firelight. Inside, two shriveled orbs glistened in the thick liquid. The Harlot couldn't help but smile at the memory of how those two spheres were once so black and beautiful.

"Your turn," her client said.

The Harlot placed the jar back on the mantelpiece and returned to her throne. Her client, an older gentleman named Daniel Westinghouse, casually cleaned his glasses with a handkerchief, completely unperturbed by the sad state of the Harlot's sitting room. Even in his fine navy suit, Mr. Westinghouse looked comfortable among the unkempt decor.

The Harlot took a sip of tea and then brought her focus to the chessboard on the table. Mr. Westinghouse's pieces were arrayed haphazardly. Though he was a keen player, he was well aware of the Harlot's innate ability to divine future events and was moving his pieces about randomly in a foolish attempt to confuse her. For some reason, she found it charming.

The Harlot slipped one of her pawns forward on the board. "Your move, darling."

"Miss Harlot—"

"Just Harlot, darling."

"Harlot," Daniel said as he began studying the board anew. "The person I represent requires anonymity. Should someone come to you inquiring about him—"

"I will be obliged to produce that information, if my price is met. There are rules, Mr. Westinghouse."

"Of course, of course," he said, sliding his bishop to take one of her two remaining pawns. "Two moves, I'm afraid."

"Oh my, but this is a conundrum." The Harlot smiled to herself and made a show of contemplating her next move.

"As for the missing effects," Mr. Westinghouse continued, "the person whom I represent is most eager to have them returned. I have come on his behalf to acquire their location so that I may retrieve them."

"*You* will retrieve them? Darling, that way lies only sorrow. If you attempt to retrieve them, you will die. And I must confess, I have grown rather fond of you in our short time together. It would sadden me greatly if you perished in such pursuits." The Harlot moved her pawn diagonally, taking one of Mr. Westinghouse's own.

"Then what would you suggest I do?"

"I will give you the name of a person who can help you. Her services won't be cheap, but they will be effective."

Mr. Westinghouse repositioned his glasses on his nose and asked, "And what price must I pay you for this name?"

"You don't need to pay me anything. The person whom you represent, however, does. Once this person returns the items to you, your client must express his gratitude to her. Personally." The Harlot leaned back and motioned to the board. "Your move, darling."

Mr. Westinghouse, committed to his strategy, quickly maneuvered his bishop into position. "I'll have you in checkmate in one move, Harlot. As for your price, it will be very difficult. But not out of the realm of possibility. You have a deal."

Mr. Westinghouse extended his hand. The Harlot grasped it

with her own, but when the man pulled his hand away, a piece of paper rested between his fingers.

"What is this?" he asked.

"The name."

Mr. Westinghouse nodded with a courteous smile and read the piece of paper. His smile sagged on his cheeks. "I don't mean any disrespect, Harlot, but is this meant to be a joke?"

The Harlot took the paper from his hand, read the name, and said, "No, that is correct. Oh!" She slapped her knee and laughed. "I understand your confusion now. No, the person you seek is Luci Jenifer Inacio Das Neves. However, she prefers to be called Lucifer," the Harlot said as she handed the paper back to Mr. Westinghouse.

"That is . . . unusual," he said.

"Ah, the great Aether itself couldn't hold all that is unusual about that girl."

Mr. Westinghouse stood and bowed. "Well, thank you very much for your time, Harlot. And I enjoyed our game."

"Sit, Mr. Westinghouse. Our game isn't finished."

Slowly, the man sat back down on the faded couch. "I don't mean to be rude, but you've lost. I'll have you in checkmate in the next move."

The Harlot examined the board. Mr. Westinghouse's pieces were scattered, while the few pieces the Harlot had in play were isolated. She couldn't help but notice how seven of his pieces seemed to form a misshapen circle, their long twisted shadows lying eerily across the board. But they were inconsequential now and no longer a part of his strategy. It was his queen that held the Harlot's attention. It was a statue of flowing elegance, a white figure of carved alabaster that sat at the edge of the board, seemingly waiting for her moment to strike.

All the Harlot had left was a rook, a pawn, and her king. The pawn was at the top of the board, small, dark, and insignificant. The piece had been worn smooth from countless years of handling, but for a single scratch toward the top.

Almost where its shoulder would be.

The Harlot touched her pawn with a delicate finger and slid it into a square at the far end of the board. "Checkmate," she said.

Mr. Westinghouse leaned forward, confused. "But I don't understand?"

The Keeper of Secrets leaned back in her throne and said, "Your king is in line with my pawn."

"Yes, yes, I see that," he said. "But how does that give you victory?"

"That is the beauty of this game, darling. If it can survive the journey," the Harlot leaned forward and whispered . . .

". . . a pawn may become a queen."

ACKNOWLEDGMENTS

B ooks do not magically appear, no matter how much we might wish them to. Were it not for the indispensable help of these wonderful people, the book you now hold would still be lost among the secrets of the Aether. . . .

First and foremost, I must thank Johanna and Ross Richie for . . . well, everything. Their constant encouragement and support over the years is the reason I'm the writer I am today. Thanks to Carey Malloy and America Young for not only sharing their creative insights and professional criticism, but also for their invaluable friendship. Many, many thanks to Lou Anders for spearheading this project and to Rene Sears for getting it across the finish line, and to Matt Gagnon, Eric Harburn, Chris Rosa, Filip Sablik, and the whole BOOM! crew for helping bring the Hexed universe to life.

Lastly, thank you to my mom and dad for filling me with a love for words. For that, my life is infinitely richer.

ABOUT THE AUTHOR

Michael Alan Nelson was born in Portage, Indiana, and grew up in a small farming community before moving to Los Angeles in 2002. He is the winner of the 2004 New Times 55 Fiction contest for his short-short "The Conspirators" and was awarded the 2011 Glyph Comics Award

Author photo by Johanna Richie

for Best Female Character for the character Selena from his series 28 Days Later. Michael is the author of the critically acclaimed comic series Hexed, Dingo, and Fall of Cthulhu. He lives in Los Angeles. Visit him at his website michaelalannelson.com, on Facebook at https://www.facebook.com/michaelalannelsonwriter?ref=hl, or on Twitter @roquesdoodle.